GW00870742

Kaleidoscope

By Ethan Spier

ISBN: 9781480132108

www.ethanspier.co.uk
info@ethanspier.co.uk
www.facebook.com/kaleidoscopenovel

Acknowledgements

Thank you to my wife and parents for working their way through the mistake-ridden early drafts of this novel and providing enough feedback to make it readable. Thank you as well to Amy Diamond at Creative Wording for editing.

For Mali and Maisy

Prologue

The Comet, 1986

Lewis Foster peered out of the tent and exhaled, pouting his lips and releasing a cloud of vapour into the chilly, February night. He could feel a light breeze gently caress his face, and watched as it carried his breath away. The sky was clear and the stars bright, although partially overwhelmed by the lights from the houses and buildings that surrounded the small back garden in which the tent had been erected. Lewis glanced to his own house, over the fence, and saw the light flick on in the kitchen. He craned his neck and saw his mother pour two cups of tea from the pot and then carry them back into the front room. His attention was suddenly drawn to the sound of his two friends scuffling with something behind him.

"Maybe we should have put the tent in my back garden," he said, pulling his head back inside and zipping the entrance up behind him. He saw Hannah defending the last sweet in her bag from her younger brother, Ben.

"No Ben, you've eaten all yours, this one's mine."

"But you've had more than me," Ben protested,

scowling at his sister.

"I'm older than you."

This seemed to antagonise Ben rather than calm the situation and he got to his feet, reaching for the bag while Hannah attempted to hold him at bay.

"Wait," Lewis shouted. "Wait a minute. Here have one of mine Ben. They're not my favourite anyway." He moved over to his own bag and handed the younger boy a single yellow sweet. Ben took the gift as he continued to scowl at his sister and placed it into his mouth.

Hannah ignored her brother and grabbed the large book entitled 'Exploring the Universe', which was sitting in the centre of the tent. She flicked through the pages until finally settling on one. Lewis watched her eyes dart across the page as they absorbed the text. She was the best reader in her class by a long way and it amazed him how she could understand the words in that book.

"It says here that after Halley's Comet passes by this time, it won't be back until the year 2061," Hannah said, looking up with huge eyes. She counted on her fingers for a moment. "We'll be eighty-three years old by then Lewis!"

"How old will I be Hannah?" Ben asked, slurping on the rapidly dissolving sweet.

"Eighty-one," Hannah said after another pause to work it out.

"That's very old," Ben whispered, contemplating the thought for a moment and staring vacantly ahead. "I bet they'll have flying cars that can go up and see it really close by then."

"Is it dark enough to see it yet Lewis?" Hannah asked, closing the book.

"I think so; I could see all the stars when I looked out

just now."

"Okay, let's go then."

The three children put on their coats, gloves and shoes, then stepped out of the tent, and into the cold air, which washed over them like a cool sheet of silk. They turned on the spot as they gazed up towards the jet black sky, which was sparkling with occasional pin pricks of starlight.

"I can't see it," Ben said, his eyes moving rapidly around the vast area of sky.

"I can't either," Lewis replied, glancing over to Hannah, who remained silent as her eyes slowly and meticulously scanned the blackness.

They stood for a few more moments, trying to locate the elusive visitor before Ben became restless. He began to race around the garden, jumping over the small wall that separated the patio and grassed areas of the garden. Lewis and Hannah continued to stare at the sky, searching for the comet. They had planned the camp-out in Hannah and Ben's back garden especially to see it and they were determined to catch at least a fleeting glimpse.

As they stood side-by-side, their breath visible as it left their mouths, Lewis suddenly felt Hannah grab his hand. She squeezed hard, her eyes moving over the dark blanket above.

"We *have* to find it Lewis," she said, then blew out a long flume of breath. "It won't be back for ages. What if we miss it?"

Lewis glanced at her - his best friend - and wondered why she wanted to see the comet so badly; they would be old next time, very old, but not so old that they wouldn't be able to see it, surely.

"I can't miss it, I *can't*... I..."

She paused and squinted for a moment, tilting her head to the side before her face became consumed by a huge smile, forcing her cold, red cheeks to swell. "There it is!" She pointed up and Lewis followed her finger towards the sky.

Ben stopped running and panted as he too, squinted and gazed in the direction of Hannah's extended finger. "I still can't see it," he said after barely a second.

Lewis tracked the invisible line from Hannah's finger towards the depths of space, but he still couldn't make anything out at first. "Me either, it's not there is it? I can't..." Suddenly his eyes focused on a tiny smudge of white, like a wisp of white oil paint on a black canvas. "Wait, it's there, is that it?" Lewis pointed.

"Yes, do you see it?" Hannah replied, beaming.

"Yes, I think so."

"I can't see anything," Ben said, frustrated. "You're making it up." He turned and began to race around the garden once again, holding his arms out and making a loud roaring sound – he was an aeroplane now.

Still hand in hand, Hannah and Lewis gazed on as Halley's Comet slipped effortlessly across the night sky. They both heard Ben eventually tire and go back into the tent, but they remained in silence for a few moments more until Lewis finally spoke.

"We'll be eighty-three when it comes back?" he asked and saw Hannah nod slowly but she said nothing. "I wonder who you'll see it with next time."

Hannah shot her head sideways and Lewis saw a confused frown furrow her brow.

"What do you mean?" she said, as if the answer was

Kaleidoscope

obvious and Lewis suddenly noticed the sparkling reflection of stars in her eyes as she spoke. "We'll see it together."

Chapter 1

Hellam

The chain that bound Travis to the steel bed frame was secured by a large padlock. He was sitting on the floor at the foot of the bed in his flat, his movement limited by the interlocking steel rings around his neck that held him in place. Sweat gathered on his forehead before falling down the bridge of his nose, mixing with the blood from his nostrils and dripping onto his shirt.

"It was stolen, for Christ sake, I'm *telling* you, *he* stole it," Travis sobbed, wiping blood from his nose with the back of his hand. He raised his eyes and stared at the man dressed in a dark black suit before him. "I swear to God Mr Hellam, I don't have the money."

Hellam was sitting in a chair on the far side of the darkened room, his legs crossed as he scrutinised Travis carefully. A half-torn blackout blind that covered the window was lowered, but daylight still penetrated the holes in the fabric. Fragments of floating dust could be seen dancing through the sparse shards of light. He glanced down at his fingernails and removed a small piece of dirt from beneath one of them before turning his attention back to Travis.

"Why did he steal it? Did you argue over something?" asked Hellam, his voice soft.

"I don't know why he stole it... he just did and now the fucker has left me in this mess! I'm not the one you want." Travis glanced up at the other man, the one standing by the door and his eyes lingered on the thick scar which ran the length of his left cheek.

"So, Callum Deacon has taken all the money and left you for dead," Hellam said, uncrossing his legs and leaning forward. "Of course, so we should let you go, correct?" The mock sincerity of Hellam's voice concealed a threat that lay just beneath the surface and Travis shuffled uncomfortably.

"I'm not the one you want..." he said hopelessly and stared at the wooden floor before him. The chain dug into the skin around his neck and he winced as he adjusted his position again.

"So where is Deacon? Where did he go with all that money?" Hellam asked. Travis shook his head but said nothing.

"Where would *you* go Travis? What would you spend a hundred thousand on?"

"I don't know."

Hellam rubbed his fingers into the palm of his hand, as if massaging oil into the skin and appeared to be thinking to himself for a moment. When he continued to speak, his voice was soft, almost tender. "When you received the goods that I provided, you made it perfectly clear that you had the money available and would make payment promptly. I trusted you Travis. Can't you see how it makes me feel when you betray that trust?" Hellam glanced down to his nails again, but seemed satisfied with their appearance this time. "You see, now I'm left with no money, no goods and no idea of where Deacon could be. My only link to this whole mess is you, Travis. It puts me in a very difficult position - it puts *you* in an incredibly difficult position." Hellam gestured around his neck, creating an illusionary chain and smiled. He glanced over to the man by the door but the scarred man's expression remained motionless and stoic. Hellam sighed and turned back to Travis. "I'm afraid he doesn't have much of a sense of humour. I'm lucky, I can find the amusing side to most situations, although this one is testing that ability I fear."

Hellam stood and slowly approached. Travis strained his neck and attempted to look up as Hellam's shiny, black shoes knocked on the wooden floor towards him. They came to rest a few feet away from where he was sitting and Hellam leaned his weight back on his heels. He suddenly looked towards the ceiling in mock surprise, as if a light bulb had illuminated above his head.

"A thought has just occurred to me Travis," he said, his voice high with excitement. "I suppose it wouldn't stretch the imagination too far to propose that Deacon and yourself had this whole thing planned from the beginning."

Travis looked up to meet Hellam's eyes and felt a piece of ice slide along his spine.

"Yes, of course," Hellam continued. "You could have agreed with Deacon that he take the money. Sure, you get a little bit knocked around for your trouble, but that's worth fifty grand isn't it? Then, you meet up with him when the dust has settled, split the cash *and* the goods... what a perfect plan!" Hellam was almost joyous as he went through the scenario, his eyes flashing and a huge smile stretching his tanned skin.

Travis shook his head and began to sob. "That's not what happened, I swear. That bastard took all the money and ran."

Hellam's face suddenly turned dark. The smile evaporated as he crouched down and spoke to Travis in a whisper, ignoring the words of the bound man.

"But the plan could have one big flaw..."

"Why won't you listen to me? That wasn't the plan!" Travis screamed.

"...What if I were to kill you Travis? Did your plan factor in that little gem?"

"Please, no," Travis sobbed, blood and tears dripping from his nose.

Hellam stood up and turned his back. His shoes knocked on the wood again as he made his way back to the chair. Before he sat down, he glanced and nodded at the man with the scar, who returned the gesture.

"No, no, please no," Travis screamed as the man walked towards him, pulling a gun from a shoulder holster beneath his jacket. He lifted a silencer from a pocket and slowly screwed it onto the barrel as he gazed vacantly at the man by his feet. Without flinching, or a moment's hesitation, he pointed the gun and pulled the trigger.

Travis screamed as the delicate bones in his foot exploded and blood sprayed his jeans and shirt. The man with the scar unscrewed the silencer with an ambivalence that came only from experience then replaced the gun in his holster before walking back to the door.

"You see what I mean?" Hellam said softly as Travis continued to scream. "No sense of humour whatsoever."

The screams slowly descended back into sobs as Travis, terrified, stared at his useless foot, holding it tight as blood ran through his clenched fingers. The room was in silence apart from Travis's sniffs and whimpers and Hellam allowed the silence to linger for a few moments as he gazed at the broken man before him.

After a while, Hellam rose to his feet again. "You've been lucky this time. You have until next week to either get me that money, or tell me where Deacon is." He walked over to the door and the gunman stood aside as he went through. He paused in the doorway and turned back to Travis. "Oh by the way, if you try to run, Kelser here will find you," Hellam said, placing a hand on the shoulder of the man with the scar. "Believe me; you do not want this man looking for you."

Hellam walked from the room and down the corridor. Kelser pulled a key from his pocket and walked over to Travis. He unlocked the padlock and threw it to the floor before leaving the room, slamming the door behind him.

***

As Hellam stepped out of the building in which Travis lived, he felt the cold air bite his cheek and he paused, gazing up at the clear blue sky. He retrieved a pair of sunglasses from his pocket and carefully placed them on.

Carl Richards was waiting on the street outside and Kelser stood beside him as they both waited for Hellam's instructions.

"I want you both to go and see what you can find out about Deacon's location. Try his usual haunts. Make enquiries. Try to dig something up. Does he have a girlfriend?"

"I'm not sure," Richards replied, "I'll ask around."

The two men walked away and Hellam looked over to see his dark grey limousine parked across the street. As he walked towards it, he saw George Langton step out of the rear door then hold it open for him, before circling the car and stepping in on the other side. Langton leaned forward and said something to the driver who started the car and pulled away.

"What did Travis have to say?" Langton asked, turning to Hellam.

"Exactly what we thought he'd say," Hellam shrugged and stared out of the window. "He claims Deacon stole the money and made a run for it."

"Do you believe him?"

"Actually, I think I do. Not that it particularly helps either of us at the moment. I need to find Deacon. Kelser and Richards are looking into it at the moment so we'll see what they can unearth."

The car turned left and made its way down a busy street in the south-west London town of Surrington. The journey would take around twenty minutes and Hellam was grateful for the time to relax himself into the role that awaited him. He turned and glanced at the man sitting beside him, who had taken a file out of his briefcase and had begun to make notes on a piece of paper with typed writing.

George Langton was tall and wore thick, wire framed glasses over sagging cheeks. A wisp of receding grey hair was neatly combed above his ears and his shirt was stretched tight over a round stomach. He had been Hellam's assistant for over twelve years, ever since Hellam started the first of his businesses in his late twenties. Langton was nearing his sixty-second birthday, but still held a sharp and professional mind and was a shrewd observer of people. Hellam suspected that Langton had already known about the more unorthodox areas of his business before he had become progressively involved in them. Now, George Langton was in the *innermost* of Hellam's inner circles and had made himself indispensable.

Hellam's first business venture had been in mobile telecommunications and was still his primary legitimate source of income. Over the years, side businesses had developed from H.K. Communications, eventually providing high speed internet solutions for multi-national corporations around the world. But this business covered other, more diverse ventures which demanded far more of his personal interest.

Slowly, over the years, Hellam had involved his assistant in the shadier areas of his world and he had been surprised by how well Langton had taken to it; treating this other side of his work with as much scrutiny and professionalism as he had with the more customary tasks. But then, as Hellam had discovered long ago, money could be an incentive that was able to distort the most moral of minds, altering them to justify their questionable decisions.

Langton was involved in various duties and was one of the few people in Hellam's organisation who knew almost as much as Hellam himself regarding the businesses.

Langton had, however, long since stated that he refused to be present when Kelser and Richards were fulfilling their primary duties - he couldn't bare violence - so Hellam had always kept the man at a safe distance from what he considered the more unpleasant aspects of the work.

"I think the speech will go down well with the crowd," Langton said, still scribbling on the piece of paper.

"Good, thank you George." Hellam said, returning his gaze to the passing buildings after a brief glance at his reflection in the tinted glass. He had noticed the appearance of several grey hairs in the mirror that morning and wondered if anyone else had. But it wasn't something he wanted to dwell on and brushed the thought away, which nevertheless, continued to linger.

Langton suddenly stopped writing and looked up, pushing his glasses higher on his nose. "How's Richards coming along?"

Richards had only joined the company three months prior and was still something of an unknown quantity. He had been working closely with Kelser who reported that he had been performing to a reasonable standard. But Hellam knew only too well that he had to tread very carefully when bringing someone new into his world; especially someone he worked so closely with on delicate matters, so he had purposely kept Richards at a distance.

"Fine, but keep your ear to the ground. He came from a reputable source, but those sources can sometimes be the ones after your blood. I know you understand."

Langton nodded and continued to make notes.

The car slowed as it pulled up outside a large building and Langton stepped out then walked around and held the door open for Hellam. They walked inside as Hellam removed his glasses, folding them carefully and handing them to his assistant while a middle aged woman, brandishing a huge smile, greeted them.

"Mr Hellam, welcome to Surrington School. My name is Elizabeth Chalker. I'm the headmistress. Thank you for joining us today." She held out her hand and Hellam shook it, smiling his most humble smile in return.

"It is my pleasure Ms Chalker, I didn't want a fuss, but it will be most interesting to see the kind of services you offer."

"Of course," Elizabeth Chalker replied. "I'll take you on a brief tour before the presentation, which is being held in our main hall in thirty minutes. Please, follow me."

The three of them walked around the school, sitting in on various classes and meeting pupils. Hellam spoke softly as he asked all the usual questions - the questions that he knew were expected of him. He played the role with rehearsed perfection which was something he was accustomed to doing.

When they entered the main hall half an hour later, most of the teachers and students were in attendance and Hellam received a warm round of applause as he took to the stage. He sat on a chair while the headmistress stood and introduced him.

As the woman spoke, Hellam looked around the hall while only half-listening to the drivel that was passing her lips. But not once did he allow his warm, humble smile to relinquish its position. He had learned how to act and *react* over the years, in spite of never truly experiencing certain emotions in his life. Not that he particularly desired to experience those things – he didn't miss them. He meandered over this for a moment before suddenly becoming aware that Elizabeth Chalker's speech was drawing to a close and he turned to face her.

"...I am pleased to introduce local businessman, entrepreneur and benefactor of our very grateful school. Please put your hands together for Mr Joseph Hellam."

The hall erupted in applause as Hellam slowly lifted himself from the chair, raising a single protesting hand to greet the welcome before walking over to the centre of the stage. The crowd slowly died down as he began to speak.

"Thank you, thank you all so much for such a warm welcome. I hadn't been expecting such a large audience, but I'm delighted to see you all here. I have a short speech to go through, but before I do, I'd like to just mention one thing." He paused as he looked out and smiled a smile that emanated sincerity and compassion but concealed much more. "I have been very lucky in my life and have had the opportunities to reward myself financially. It would not be proper if I didn't occasionally return some of that luck to the institutions and causes that provide such valuable services for this town which I love. That is why I have recently set up The Hellam Foundation, to reward these kind people. I have decided that Surrington School for Disabled Children is going to be the first to receive a donation from my new foundation and I am proud to present to you with a gift of fifty-thousand pounds for the excellent service you provide for our community."

The room erupted once more and Hellam couldn't help but notice the unreserved gratitude which illuminated Elizabeth Chalker's face. As the applause continued, Hellam wondered how it could be that he felt almost nothing but contempt for her and everyone else in the room.

Hellam had been born into wealth thirty-nine years earlier and couldn't recall a single instance in his life when he had felt anything other than indifference or contempt towards another human being. The notion baffled but didn't concern him; the truth was he didn't particularly care why that should be. After all, these traits had allowed him to become the success he now was.

He looked at Ms Chalker with superficially warm eyes then glanced down to the speech in front of him. He raised a hand until the clapping died down and then began to read, smiling with apparent sincerity in all the correct places - the places he had learned.

Chapter 2

Lewis

The sudden warmth that Lewis Foster felt as he stepped inside Maggie's café made him glad he had chosen that particular meeting point. It was a cool day, but warm inside due to the fact that Maggie hated the cold. He walked past several customers who were sitting at the tightly packed tables, careful not to knock them with his bag, and over to the counter where a short, thin woman greeted him.

"Morning, how are you today?" she asked, smiling.

"Morning Maggie, I'm fine thanks. I'll just have a coffee please," Lewis replied, handing over the correct change. The smell of cooked bacon and hot coffee filled the air as tinny music from a radio in the corner bounced off the walls.

Lewis nodded as Maggie handed him the mug then went over to a free table by the window and gazed out. The streets were busy with people wrapped up in thick coats, scarves and gloves and going about their daily business.

He sipped his coffee and waited patiently for a while then opened his bag, pulled out a small card envelope and looked at the contents inside. A smile widened across his face as he looked at the plane ticket, reading the text printed on the front again and again. He placed the ticket on the table then pulled out a notepad and pen from his bag. He began to scribble furiously on the already filled pages. He became so absorbed that he didn't notice the young woman approach his table.

"Still making your lists I see."

Lewis was torn from his thoughts and looked up, startled. "Hannah! Sorry, I was just..." He shook his head and laughed, "I'm just excited, that's all."

He looked over to Maggie, pointed to the table and she began to make another cup of coffee. Hannah sat down opposite Lewis and smiled.

"What is it with you and lists?" she asked before thanking Maggie who placed the steaming mug of coffee on the table.

"I just like to plan things. Always be prepared," Lewis replied, putting the notepad away and smiling.

Hannah laughed. "You sound like a boy scout. You can't leave anything to chance can you?" She looked down and saw the plane ticket. "So, you're finally going on your big trip around the world?" she asked as Lewis placed the ticket back in its envelope.

"Yes, this has taken quite some planning, but I fly to Paris tomorrow and then to who knows where."

"Wow, you're actually being spontaneous? That's not the Lewis I know." She smiled and reached across to touch his hand. "You deserve it though; you've worked so hard these past six years. It's time for a break I suppose."

Lewis nodded and stared at his friend. He hadn't seen her for almost three months, but they always kept in touch by e-mail, Facebook and MSN, so they had as much information on each other's lives as the other felt like sharing. Lewis knew that he had spoken about almost nothing else during that time and didn't want to dwell on his trip, but then decided on one last comment.

"It isn't too late to come with me you know," he said.

Hannah shook her head and glanced down at her coffee. "No, I don't think so. I have my job..."

Lewis was almost ready to launch into his pre-prepared speech at that point. It was the reason he had arranged to meet Hannah in the first place; he was going to persuade her to take some time off from work. He knew it would be difficult, but not impossible and then they could see the world together. But just as he was about to speak, she added a word, which cut him off before he could begin.

"...and..." She paused, releasing his hand and turning the mug of coffee on the surface of the table.

"And?"

She stopped twisting the mug and took a sip before answering. "...and I've met someone."

Lewis felt his smile drop by a fraction, although he consciously fought to keep it in its original position.

"That's great!" he said with too much enthusiasm. "Who is he? Where did you meet?"

Hannah shook her head. "It's early days yet; we've only been on a few dates but... he's nice. He's the kind of guy who doesn't like to rush things though. It's just a casual thing at the moment. I don't want to say too much; I might ruin it." She took another sip of coffee.

"Okay, well keep me updated with how it's going. You

can still reach me on Facebook while I'm away you know. Or I might even make an old fashioned phone call from time to time."

"You'd better," Hannah said with a mock-threatening stare.

They both chatted some more about news and friends as they finished their coffee and then ordered a sandwich each. The hours passed by without interruption as they shared stories and caught up on fresh news. Lewis occasionally allowed the thought of the new man in Hannah's life to surface, but quickly ignored it - he was leaving tomorrow and it was no concern of his if Hannah was seeing someone. He told himself to get over whatever he thought might happen between them; it was ridiculous to think it could ever actually occur.

They had been friends for as long as Lewis could remember. They had grown up living next door to one another. Their parents had often visited each others houses since they both had young children and sought out friends with the same. Occasionally Lewis's parents would baby-sit for Hannah's and vice-versa, so the friendship which had developed during their early years was inevitable.

When Hannah was eleven-years-old, her younger brother, Ben had been hit by a car. He had been in a coma for three days before he passed away. The event had devastated Hannah and from that day she had become a little more introverted and reserved than she once had been. Lewis had noticed the change in his friend and felt a sadness that she had lost the sparkle that used to dwell inside her, just visible beneath the surface.

As they had grown older, Lewis observed the faintest

hint of that spark slowly return - never to how it had been when she was a child - but it was there; a subtle shadow of its former brightness. Over the years their friendship had never waned. Of course, they had both had other groups of friends who they saw at school, but there always seemed to be some kind of special bond between the two of them - each one knowing that the other felt the same.

But Lewis knew the feeling had always been stronger on his part and realised that Hannah had no idea of how much he had grown to love her over the years. He had been with other girls and even had a long term relationship while at university, but none of them made him feel the way he felt when he was with her. He had come close to telling her a few times but had always shied away. They had even kissed once, a few years ago while Lewis was on the summer break from university, but Hannah had quickly laughed it off and Lewis felt inclined to do the same. They had their friendship and he didn't want to jeopardise that for anything. But he often thought about that day on the cliff and how they had spoken to each other; in a way that they never had before or since. Lewis held onto that day as the closest they had ever come to becoming something more.

While Lewis worked for a few years after college and then went to university to do an architecture degree, Hannah decided to go straight to university to study psychology. She then went on to do a year of work experience, after which she began working as a clinical psychologist, specialising in cognitive behavioural therapy. Now, both twenty-nine years old, they spoke on the internet or phone at least twice a week and although Lewis felt they had perhaps drifted a little further apart these past few years, he realised deep down that this was simply because he wished they could be closer.

After a few hours they paid for their food and then left the café, stepping back out onto the street.

"Wow, it's so cold today," Hannah said, zipping up her coat to the top. "So, when will you get back from your crazy adventure?"

"I'm planning on about three months I think. I should be pretty much broke by then."

"Well, don't forget to keep in touch."

"Of course not, I'll see you soon."

Hannah stepped forward and they hugged. He wrapped his arms around her and held her tight, wishing she would spontaneously change her mind and tell him she was going to take that time off work, dump her boyfriend and come with him after all.

"Good luck," she said as they parted, beaming the bright smile that Lewis loved so much, and began to walk away.

Lewis watched her disappear down the street then turned and began to walk in the opposite direction, completely unaware that it would be the last time he would see her alive.

***

Lewis arrived back in his flat and looked at the waiting suitcase on his bed. He needed to pack. He had been putting off the task for long enough and now felt the uncomfortable sensation of suspecting he would have to rush through it and forget something. He pulled out the notepad from his bag and glanced at the first list then sighed and went over to his wardrobe where he began to throw various assortments of clothing into the case. He was only taking the one, small suitcase with him since he wanted to travel relatively lightly.

He had worked for four years before going to university in order to fund his education. He had enjoyed his time, but the money had been depleted much more swiftly than he had anticipated, so Lewis decided to work part-time while at university. He had spent most of his evenings and weekends answering phones in a call centre. The work had numbed his brain but had provided a steady stream of income. He had even managed to begin to save money and it was these savings that he was going to use to fund his travels over the next three months. Then he planned to finally bite the bullet, grow up and begin his career as an architect.

He finished packing all the obvious items then went to the set of drawers by his bed and pulled them open one by one. He tossed the occasional semi-useful article into the case and then arrived at the bottom drawer. It contained odds and ends that didn't really belong anywhere else so he hadn't expected to find a great deal which he would be taking with him. He glanced in and was about to close it again when his eye fell upon something.

He reached in, past old mobile phone chargers and several photo albums, to a creased piece of shiny paper. He stared at it, guessing the photograph was around nine or ten years old. It showed Lewis out with a group of friends in a bar somewhere and he could vaguely remember the night out as taking place just before Hannah had left for university.

Hannah was standing in the centre, grinning at the camera with that same smile that Lewis had seen a thousand times before, and pictured in his mind a thousand more. She was surrounded by five friends, all gathered around her with their arms over each other's shoulders. Lewis was standing over to the right of the group, not staring at the camera. He was looking over at Hannah, a narrow smile on his face.

Lewis held the creased photo for a few moments and gazed at Hannah's delicate features. Finally, he folded it and placed it carefully inside his wallet.

Chapter 3

Hellam

Hellam was sitting at his desk with his ear to the phone and speaking with irritation which spilled occasionally into anger. He had dealt with the supplier for years but suddenly the prices for the cocaine shipments had almost doubled and Hellam wasn't prepared to stand such a price hike. The supplier blamed shipping costs and increased risk due to the fact that the authorities were getting a little too close for comfort.

As he spoke down the receiver, Hellam glanced up, seeing Richards and Kelser standing in the hall through the small gap in his office door. He caught Kelser's eye and gestured for them to come in. Both men sat down in the chairs opposite as he listened to the various excuses from his supplier.

Hellam rarely called his suppliers directly, but certain situations required his personal attention. It wasn't even the rise in the cost of the drugs that bothered him - he could afford it – but it was the nagging suspicion that someone was trying to take advantage of him in some way; that was a possibility that he simply would not tolerate.

In spite of his start in life, coming from a wealthy and supportive family, Hellam had always enjoyed power and control; a quality which often caused concern for his family. As a child, he had been in trouble with the police several times which confused his parents who had only ever encouraged him to follow the correct paths in life.

They had been distraught when the police had shown them photographs of their next door neighbour's Spaniel as it hung limply from a tree in a nearby park with a choke-chain pulled taut around its neck. The police had pointed an accusatory finger in the direction of their twelve-year-old son. He had denied it of course and, in-spite of the demands from the neighbour who had seen him steal the puppy from the garden, the police had simply cautioned the young boy since they hadn't got enough evidence against him for further action. His parent's were easily won over; lying was already second nature to Joseph Hellam.

During his later teenage years, he became more adept at concealing his true impulses and learned how he should act around people. He knew that he held a certain charisma; people he met often commented on how charming and affable he was. But deep down, Hellam had simply begun to mimic what he had learned from others over the years – not really feeling anything for the people he could so easily manipulate. It was all an elaborate act to get whatever he desired.

While in his twenties, Hellam had abused drugs and alcohol which once again landed him in trouble with the authorities. His family had paid for the best lawyers who managed to prevent any custodial sentences, but he had inevitably ended up with a criminal record. He once again decided that he had to reign himself in and become more intelligent in presenting the image of himself that he wanted people to see. The impulses continued and he would still use the drugs and the prostitutes, but slowly he became more proficient in hiding the darker side of his personality.

When he was twenty-seven, Hellam's father had given him some money and the names of several contacts at a new telecommunications company. His father encouraged him to buy and run the business. Hellam hated being pushed into the role, but found it difficult to refuse the offer of such a large quantity of money.

The company had been set up by two young entrepreneurs with technical backgrounds who had found a gap in the market for certain bespoke mobile phones. These could be personalised for employees at large corporations. Hellam had bought a majority share in the company, eventually becoming the sole owner of H.K. Communications. He had employed the two entrepreneurs who continued their involvement in the technical side of the business. It had eventually expanded into several smaller operations, providing specialised high-speed internet solutions for multi-national corporations around the world.

While running the business, Hellam realised how much freedom it offered him. He was no longer reliant on his family's money and was making a fortune heading the corporation. But the work ultimately bored him and he craved constant and increasing stimulus.

As the years passed by, he used his drug dealing

contacts to gradually become involved in several criminal organisations which imported large quantities of drugs to the UK, and this in turn led to him to set up several prostitution rackets around the country. H.K. Communications slowly became nothing more than the legitimate face of Hellam's growing criminal empire and he bathed in the power and control it brought him. This other, darker, world allowed him to feed his narcissistic impulses and to become his true self.

But he knew he needed to be clever. His past experiences with the police had taught him to reign in his desires and not allow the impulses to overwhelm his character. He continued to live the life of a successful owner of several large corporations and actively distanced himself from the less savoury areas in which he was involved.

There had been several occasions when the police had managed to get far too close to linking Hellam with a number of drug operations and they were immediately closed down. All ties with Hellam were severed and a number of his employees had taken the fall. They had protested of course, insisting on their limited involvement. They pointed fingers and tried to cut deals, but they had no real proof of anything. They had reported to several intermediaries before ever getting close to Hellam and, by the time the police followed this trail, the substance of their claims had become diluted and weak. The authorities suspected that Hellam was in some way involved in criminal activities; they had even started an investigation at one point, but they had never gained any hard evidence against him.

As the years progressed, Hellam's criminal interests

diversified and he gained more employees, creating contacts all over the world. His interest was no longer limited to drugs and prostitution.

He barked down the receiver as he continued to exert his will over the man on the other end of the phone, before slamming it down and looking up to Kelser and Richards.

"These people seem to thrive on their idiocy," he said, then took a long, deep breath which he slowly exhaled before placing his hands on his desk. "So, where are we with the Deacon situation?"

Kelser and Richards had been trying to track down Deacon for several weeks now and Hellam was growing impatient. Again, it wasn't the loss of the money which bothered him; it was the lack of respect that he felt Deacon was displaying.

"We managed to track down his old girlfriend, Claudia," Richards began, checking the details on a piece of paper he produced from his pocket. "But she claims to have not seen him for weeks."

Hellam nodded, "You believe her?"

"Yes. She seems to detest him as much as we do and I don't think she's that good an actress," Kelser replied.

Hellam looked at the two men sitting before him. Richards appeared to be working well with Kelser, who had been guiding him in their practices of work. Richards was a stocky man with a closely cropped hairstyle and his smooth, dark brown skin was always clean shaven. He had been recommended to Hellam just over three months earlier by Gabriel Henson, an associate to whom Hellam sold large quantities of drugs for his various dealing operations. He trusted Gabriel as much as you could ever trust people involved in that line of work, but he had told Kelser to keep an especially close eye on Richards for the first few months. There had never been any noticeable or significant slip-ups and, on the whole, everyone was pleased with the way Richards had been performing.

Hellam had hired Richards since some of the work he had taken on had been getting heavier and he felt that Kelser could do with an accomplice to aid him in his duties. The duties in question were ambiguous at best and even if they had been given a comprehensive and detailed job description, they would have been hard pushed to come up with an appropriate title. The two men were used for intimidation and persuasion whenever it was required - which turned out to be far more often than expected. However, Hellam never used them when a more *definitive* solution was required to sort out a problem. Those special contracts were given to the freelancers. Hellam kept two on semi-retainers – hired killers who demanded huge quantities of money for their professional work. There had been a third freelancer he had used, a man whose name he could no longer recall, but who had been found murdered in his house a few years earlier - the result of the risks taken in his chosen line of work Hellam had reasoned after hearing of his death.

Hellam glanced over to the other man sitting opposite him. Sebastian Kelser was in his mid-thirties, of medium height and build, and didn't appear on the surface to be particularly intimidating. But he bore an intense and unemotional demeanour. When he looked at you, he appeared to gaze through, past the eyes, as if he was only interested in what was going on inside a person's head.

This, coupled with the large scar which ran down the length of his left cheek, resulted in a man who induced uneasiness in anyone who spoke to him.

Hellam had first met Kelser five years earlier, in an event which had proven fortuitous for both men. Hellam had been in his favourite bar, Jannson's, at the time, drinking with a woman he had met at a charity event the previous day.

The evening had been going well until a man who was clearly inebriated began to bother them. The man, although drunk, still struck a formidable sight with huge muscles stretching his shirt to almost breaking point. Hellam had warned the man to leave them alone, but he had continued to bark profanity and even attempted to grope Hellam's companion. Hellam didn't have any of his usual protection around and felt reluctant to confront the hulk directly - he wasn't a man used to being in such a position.

It was at that moment that someone had suddenly appeared behind the drunken monster and pulled him away from Hellam's table. Hellam noticed the indifference in Kelser's eyes as he had placed an arm around the huge man's neck and wrenched him backwards. Kelser hadn't spoken a word, appearing unconcerned as the muscle bound drunkard spat obscenities in his direction. Kelser twisted the man's huge arm awkwardly and pushed him to the floor, turning the arm against its natural direction. Hellam could remember wincing as he watched Kelser twist and push on the limb of the screaming man, certain it would break at any moment. Kelser eventually let him up while keeping a firm grip on his arm then pushed him from the bar and out onto the street.

Amazed, Hellam watched as Kelser walked back inside and strode calmly to the bar. After a few moments, Hellam called him over and offered to buy him a drink which Kelser had accepted with a thin distortion of his lips. They had spoken into the night which culminated in Kelser disclosing that he was currently unemployed and looking for work. Hellam said that he owned several businesses and was sure he could find a place for him in one of them. The next day they had a meeting in the H.K. Communications offices and he offered Kelser a position low down in the business.

That had been almost five years ago and, as Hellam watched the man in front of him, he thought about how far he had come. Originally appearing unsure of himself, even reluctant in his early work, Kelser had slowly climbed the ladder and had begun to work much closer with Hellam, eventually becoming his personal bodyguard. He had exceeded Hellam's expectations and had now become a valuable asset. Kelser was a difficult man to talk to; rarely showing any emotion, but it was this particular attribute which also made him perfect for the job.

"So where does this leave us now?" Hellam asked, dragging himself back to the moment.

"We went to see a man who Deacon's old girlfriend told us about," Richards said. "Apparently he was an old drug dealing friend of Deacon's and would possibly know more. He was a fucking nightmare, completely out of it. But we managed to drag some information out of him." Richards glanced to Kelser then back to his boss. "He said that Deacon was hiding with some other girl who he had been having an affair with for a few months. He wasn't sure of her address but after a bit of hassle we managed to get hold of it. We'll go and check it out today."

Hellam nodded again, "Let's hope we get him. Have you heard anything from Travis? Does he have any more information about Deacon's whereabouts?"

Kelser and Richards shook their heads in unison.

"Well," Hellam continued, "If he doesn't get a little more helpful, he might have to receive another visit." He thought about this for a moment, reflecting on several possible decisions. "See what you can dig up at this slut's place. If he's there then Travis may have a brief reprieve for now."

The two men nodded then stood.

"Inform Langton of how you get on, I'll be in meetings for the remainder of the day so don't contact me."

Hellam picked up the phone again as the two men turned and left.

"Hello, how are you?" He said into the receiver when the woman on the other end picked up, his voice suddenly soft and fragile. "...That's great, listen how about dinner tonight?"

Chapter 4

Lewis

Lewis looked at the map as a frown wrinkled his forehead. He glanced up, removing his sunglasses and then looked back down. The sky was a vibrant blue and the heat from the sun baked the narrow Venetian streets by his feet. He wiped perspiration from his forehead with the back of his arm as he tried to work out exactly where he was.

He had been in Venice for two days but the maze of narrow streets, alleyways and dead ends was still as confusing as when he had first arrived. It had been an eventful few months and now, on the final leg of his journey, Lewis felt exhausted. He had visited almost everywhere he had intended to, but New York and Tokyo had proven to be a little more time consuming than he had first imagined, so he had to skip Los Angeles in the end. His money had lasted well and he had even managed to get a couple of week's cash-in-hand work at a car wash in Chicago which helped see him through. He had missed Venice on the way out, but some of the student back-packers he had run into on his travels insisted that it was a place which simply shouldn't be missed.

Lewis had checked his remaining balance and decided he had enough money to make Venice his final stop before returning home. He flew out of JFK airport and landed at Marco Polo a few hours later. After taking the water bus from the airport and wandering the city for a couple of hours, Lewis knew he had made the right choice in coming.

It was 26°C which was unusually warm for May in Venice, and it felt even warmer when spending the day walking around the maze of streets. Lewis felt a throbbing ache in his legs. He had been walking for almost five straight hours, and as he looked over to a small café bar which had tables positioned outside, he decided he needed some refreshment. He folded the map as he walked over, ordered a lemonade then sat down at one of the tables as he sipped slowly, savouring the cool drink. The bar was next to one of the smaller canals and the occasional boat hummed by with tanned, smiling faces glancing at Lewis as they passed. He stretched out his legs, closed his eyes and relaxed while the sounds of the city washed over him.

As he sat there, his mind became peaceful and his thoughts drifted. He thought of what awaited him on his return home. He was flying back home in a few days and would begin searching for a job immediately. He wasn't short of cash, but didn't want to put it off any longer. He was ready to get back into full time work. He'd had enough time off now; had gotten the travelling bug out of his system and longed to get back to some kind of normality. He could survive for a few more months on his savings and could even sell his car until the right position arose. It was time for his degree to start paying for itself.

Lewis was contemplating all of this when the image of Hannah suddenly surfaced in his mind. He smiled as he thought about her and couldn't wait to see her again. They had spoken intermittently by e-mail while Lewis had been away, but they had both been too busy to keep in regular contact. She had also seemed a little distant on the last couple of e-mails; almost as if there was something she was skirting around - something she wanted to say but couldn't quite bring herself to.

He wished she had come with him on his trip. It would have been something neither of them would ever forget and Lewis felt sad that she hadn't experienced everything he had in the past few months. It hit him especially hard here in Venice, which seemed to be a city designed for two; dining alone in one of the thousands of restaurants just didn't feel right.

Lewis sipped his drink again, glancing at the sunlight which was reflecting in the water of the canal, and it suddenly reminded him of one of his favourite memories.

It had been four years earlier and Lewis was on a summer break from university, so had returned home for a few weeks. He had caught up with all his friends and enjoyed some great times that summer, but it was one day in particular that Lewis thought about the most.

Hannah had woken him early one Saturday morning by throwing pebbles at the window of his flat. Lewis had checked his clock and saw it was 8.30am which was no time for a student to be awake, especially a student on his summer break. But he had put on his dressing gown and met Hannah downstairs.

"Wakey, wakey," she said with purposely annoying over-enthusiasm.

"What do you want? I thought we were meeting for lunch later?"

"I can do better than that," Hannah replied going over to her car which was parked by the side of the road. Lewis followed her as she opened the boot. "Ta da!" she said, waving her hand over a picnic basket half-filled with sandwiches, drinks and cakes. "We're going on a picnic. Come on, get dressed and we'll go."

"Where are we going?" Lewis asked, rubbing his eyes.

"It's a surprise, I'm driving."

After he had dressed, Hannah drove them out of town and down towards the coast. Lewis had no idea of where they were going, but Hannah seemed to know the way by heart. After over an hour of driving, she parked the car in a small car park close to the sea front, then they walked up a narrow gravel path towards the cliff face.

It had been a bright, summer's day and the wind was especially calm considering they were on the sea front. They both left the path and walked up a grassed hill to the top of the cliff. Hannah placed a blanket on the warm grass and they sat down, leaning back onto their elbows, legs stretched out before them as they gazed at the sea.

They had chatted for hours as they took in the view and watched a number of boats glide lazily across the horizon. They had eaten their sandwiches and Hannah opened a bottle of wine which she poured out into two plastic cups. The talking had slowed as they relaxed, listening to the waves gently lap against the rocks below and watching the sunlight sparkle from the bobbing water. A silence grew between them as they gazed outward - a silence which was eventually broken by Hannah.

"Do you remember that silly little kaleidoscope that

Ben used to play with?"

Lewis turned to her, his elbow touching hers as they lay side by side. "Yeah, I don't think I ever saw him without it."

"He loved that thing," she said, shaking her head slowly but not taking her eyes from the distant horizon. "He used to play with it all the time; I don't know how he didn't get bored of it. He just used to say that he loved to watch how the colours and shapes changed from one into another. I thought he was mad, but maybe I was a little bit jealous as well." Hannah sat up but still never tore her gaze from the sea.

Lewis sat up next to her, his own eyes not moving from her face as she spoke with soft melancholy.

"I wanted to have something that *I* loved as much as he loved that thing," she said slowly. "But there never was anything." She paused then turned to her friend. "We used to come here on day-trips when we were kids. Ben and I loved it - running around - and it was *always* sunny. I don't have a single memory of it ever raining here." She glanced down and chuckled to herself, "I suppose no one would go on a day-trip to the coast when it's raining though." She looked up again. "But I love this place and I don't think I'll ever get tired of it. Maybe..." She paused as her eyes scanned the scenery. "Maybe this is my kaleidoscope..." She smiled and looked down at her lap, seemingly embarrassed by what she had just said. "I think the wine is making me a bit melodramatic."

As she turned to Lewis, he moved closer and, without thinking about what he was doing, leaned forward and they kissed. It was a brief act, they parted after only a few seconds and then there was silence between them once again. Hannah looked at him and Lewis thought he could see a flicker of confusion on her face but then it was overwhelmed as a smile formed and she began to laugh. "I think the wine is making us *both* a little melodramatic!"

Lewis didn't really feel like it, but he began to laugh as well. They had mutually shrugged off what had just happened and it weighed heavy inside him.

Hannah jokingly punched him on the arm, "I think we're getting soft in our old age."

They had finished their wine, ate cakes and chatted some more but Lewis had no idea of what they spoke about as the morning drifted into the afternoon. His thoughts were snagged on the kiss; unable to really comprehend how it had even occurred.

Now, sitting at the small table by a canal in Venice, he sipped his lemonade and tried not to dwell on the memory for too long. Although he liked to think about that day, he knew it would do him no good now. He drained his glass then picked up his bag and began to work his way through the labyrinth of alleyways.

***

Hannah closed her diary and wiped the moisture away from red, sore eyes. She got up from her bed and placed the book back on its shelf. The flat was silent, only the sound of passing cars outside could be heard and she wished her flatmate, Kelly, was home; she needed someone to talk to. She thought of Lewis and wished he wasn't so far away, he was the best listener she had ever known and she had a lot to unburden. But he was probably thousands of miles away at that instant and Hannah felt a pang of envy. Why hadn't she gone with him? She knew he wanted her to join him and if the timing were different then perhaps she would have. It would have been fantastic to see the world with her best friend and would have been something she would have cherished for the rest of her life. Not to mention the fact that, had she gone, she wouldn't be in the mess she now found herself in.

The past few days had been a distorted blur of confusion and she just wanted to erase the previous three months of her life; they had only brought her pain. She thought of Joe. Who was he? She had thought she had known him, but what she had known was only the mask he wore – the mask of normality and decency. But that was what she thought he was - decent and good. It had only been a few days ago that she had discovered the truth.

The police had to be informed, she knew that, and the only thing that had stopped her from doing so before now had been the subtle shadows of doubt in her mind. Hannah knew what she had seen and knew she wasn't mistaken, but before that revelation a few days ago, she felt she had been falling in love with him. He was outwardly so kind and caring; he always said and did the right things. How could he be this other man – this monster? She had almost called the police several times in the past few days before thinking better of it. Perhaps she *had* been wrong. Joe wasn't that man was he?

But eventually the truth could no longer be ignored and Hannah felt she had no choice. She knew what she had to do, but still wished she could talk to someone about it. Kelly was around, but too busy with her own life, and Hannah didn't feel she would be able to discuss what she needed to with her anyway. She wanted Lewis; if he was here then everything would be okay.

She rubbed her eyes with the palm of her hand again and went into the kitchen where she made some tea. As she drank it, she decided that she would call the police first thing in the morning; she would put it off no longer, she had already procrastinated on the matter far too long. She knew that what she had seen had been real and was disgusted that she had spent so much time with that man without seeing him for who he truly was.

A floorboard in the hall outside creaked and she turned to the door as she finished her tea. She walked towards the door and leaned closer, hearing lowered voices on the other side. Perhaps her neighbours had visitors, she thought, but then considered this for a moment. That didn't seem right; they never had visitors. There was just the two of them in that flat and the old woman never left. Her son would go out from time to time but nobody ever came to visit them as far as Hannah knew of, certainly not at this time of night anyway.

The wood on the landing strained again and Hannah heard footsteps tap on the floor – they were right outside now. She wondered if Kelly had returned with her boyfriend and was searching for her key, but after checking the clock, Hannah dismissed this idea. Kelly would still be at work and Hannah remembered her saying that she wasn't seeing Jeremy this evening. Who was out there and why were they just standing in the hall outside the door to her flat?

She suddenly felt very cold and something stirred inside. It wasn't quite fear, but a very close relation; a strange disquiet – a trepidation. She wondered where this odd sensation had suddenly risen from and she was still contemplating this when two loud knocks pounded on the door.

***

The flight back had been delayed by an hour at Marco Polo airport, but Lewis had eaten breakfast and browsed the shops to pass the time. He arrived back in the UK at 1.30pm and took a taxi to Surrington. He told the driver to go to his parents address since they had the only key to his flat - getting a spare key cut had been one of he few things that he had forgotten to put on his list. He gave his parents the key so they could go round to his place from time to time, pick up the mail and make sure that everything was ok.

The taxi driver pulled up outside the house and Lewis paid him the fare; he would get his father to drive him home after he had accepted the compulsory cup of tea his mother would insist on making. He knocked at the door and wasn't greeted by the smiling face he had been expecting.

His mother looked like she hadn't slept for a week. Her face was drawn and Lewis thought she was going to burst into tears when she first saw him.

"What is it?" he asked, stepping inside the house.

"Lewis, come in," his mother replied and they both walked into the front room, Lewis dropping his bags in the hallway.

When they stepped in, Lewis saw his father standing by the window and watching the taxi drive away. He turned as they entered and forced an unconvincing smile in Lewis's direction then stared down to his feet.

"What is it? What's going on?"

"We have some bad news, something terrible has happened... Lewis I..." his mother began.

Lewis frowned and stared at his mother, then towards his father and back again. Weird scenarios of illness, death and tragedy in the family skipped through his mind at a hundred miles an hour. He thought about them all but dwelled on none as his mother tried to get the words out.

"It's Hannah... something's happened to her," she began to sob and grabbed Lewis's frozen hand.

"What happened?"

"I'm so sorry Lewis, I don't know how to say this..."

"What happened?" Lewis repeated firmly, his voice thin, like ice.

"She's been killed."

A void opened up beneath his feet and his legs suddenly became pieces of rubber. He released his mother's hand and slumped down on the chair closest to him.

"What do you mean killed?" he asked, a confused despair wrinkling his face. His words were quiet and thin, so much so that he wasn't even sure if he spoke them out loud or just threw them around his head. He stared at his mother. "What do you mean killed? How?" He shouted to be sure that he was actually speaking.

"Lewis... I..."

"How was she killed?"

"She was... Lewis, somebody murdered her."

Chapter 5

Hellam

Hellam looked at the clock on the wall of his office. It was 7.15pm and he knew that all his employees would have long gone by now; finished their days work and probably sitting down for dinner with their families.

He got up from his chair and walked over to the cabinet in the corner of the room, pulled out a key, unlocked the oak doors and peered inside. He removed several miscellaneous files and pulled at a small panel of apparent solid wood on the back of the cabinet. After placing the panel on the floor beside him, Hellam peered in the cavity behind the cupboard and at the pad of buttons on the digital safe. He entered an eight-digit code and the door released, springing open. He reached inside and pulled out a laptop then carried it over to his desk and turned it on.

Hellam glanced behind him, through the blinds and out of the window as the twilight of the evening bathed the street in semi-darkness, broken only by the orange glow of street lights. He reached over and pulled on the cord to the blinds, closing them a little more, then turned back as his laptop booted up.

He opened the e-mail software and logged into the secure server which resided somewhere in Sweden. The new e-mail took a few seconds to download, even on the high speed internet connection, but then it was displayed in bold text at the top of the screen. Hellam smiled; it was what he had been expecting. The message was from Alrik Olsson and the subject line simply read 'video'. Hellam clicked on the e-mail and then opened the .mpg video attachment.

The screen was filled with the image of a small, poorly lit room with a wooden chair sitting in the centre and a door dominating the rear wall. Some text was displayed momentarily over the image which showed a date then it faded away. Hellam watched anxiously as the timer in the corner of the video ran for a few uneventful seconds before the door swung open. Two men in rubber Halloween masks entered the room, dragging a third man behind them who was blindfolded and appeared to be screaming something undecipherable.

The shadow of a smile played on Hellam's lips as he turned up the volume so he could hear the cries of distress from the man. One of the men, this one wearing a vampire mask, pushed the screaming victim into the chair and began to tie his hands behind his back then proceeded to secure his ankles to the legs of the chair. The other man, who wore an old hag's face, began screaming something at the sitting man. It was in a language that Hellam couldn't understand. He then removed the blindfold and the victim, terrified, looked at his two tormentors. He spoke quickly, in the same foreign language, presumably pleading to be set free.

As the timer to the video rolled by, Hellam sat and gazed in delight at the screen. He watched as the victim was tortured for over forty-five minutes; cigarettes burned into his face, his fingers broken and his knees smashed. Even Hellam glanced away a couple of times until finally the vampire pulled out a gun and pointed it at the broken man's head. He paused as the bloodied victim whimpered and stared into the lens of the camera, then he pulled the trigger. The two men left the room and slammed the door shut behind them as the screen slowly faded to black.

Hellam smiled as he copied the video attachment into a folder on the hard drive, which was simply labelled 'Miscellaneous', and renamed the file with the day's date. He briefly scanned the list of other videos in the folder. There were forty-three altogether, each labelled with a different date. He thought about opening another one, perhaps one from a few years ago, but decided against it; not wanting to dilute the horror he had just witnessed.

He closed the folder and opened another one called 'shipments'. There were a number of spreadsheets displayed and he double clicked on 'May-June'. The spreadsheet filled the screen and he scanned the document, nodding to himself as the dates for the arrivals of various goods rolled past his eyes: cocaine, heroin and an assortment of less profitable items. After a few moments, he closed the spreadsheet and shut down his laptop then picked it up and placed it back in the hidden safe behind the cabinet.

As he closed and locked the door to the wooden cabinet, Hellam thought about the latest video and wondered what kind of price he might get for it. It had been an especially brutal film, just as Alrik had promised, and that would surely increase its value substantially. His clients knew what they liked and fortunately, so did Hellam. He wondered briefly why he took so much delight in viewing the videos - in viewing the suffering. It wasn't simply a case of knowing how much money they would fetch. Money wasn't Hellam's motivating force, and it hadn't been for a very long time, so why did he continue in these other business ventures?

Hellam called his driver to meet him outside then walked down the stairs and out of the building, locking the doors behind him. He got into his car and asked to be taken home. As the buildings reflected from the glass of the car and Hellam stared out, he thought about the question again. Why did he continue to risk everything, just to be involved in a way of life he did not need to be a part of? He suddenly and unexpectedly thought of the girl; that fucking interfering bitch.

Psychopath...

That was what she had called him after she had stumbled across his videos. Hellam had been careless and had taken his laptop home. He hadn't expected her to arrive at his front door that evening; they had arranged to meet later in the restaurant but she had said that she wanted to come over and cook him something instead. The laptop had been on his coffee table in the front room, and while he left the room to get them both a glass of wine, she had grown impatient of waiting and curiosity had presumably led her to see what was on the screen. He had been stupid and careless to leave it right there for her to find. But find it she did, and...

But that doesn't matter now, Hellam thought as the car

cruised through the streets. That situation had been taken care of and he wouldn't make the same mistake again. No one knew about the videos, and although that might be something that could change within the next few weeks, he would be very careful with whom he shared that particular portion of his business; there were very few people who could understand those videos for what Hellam knew they were - violent, macabre, *beautiful* works of art.

***

The next afternoon, Langton knocked on the door to Hellam's office, walked in and took a seat.

"I've got some good news," Langton said, smiling.

Hellam looked up from some papers he was working on and stared at him, but said nothing.

"It's about Deacon."

"Go on," Hellam said, placing his pen on the desktop, suddenly interested.

"Kelser has been in contact with me, they've found out where he's been hiding. Apparently he's been with some girl he met a few months ago. They've been staking out her flat and yesterday they saw Deacon leave to buy a packet of cigarettes."

"That's good news, tell them to proceed. That bastard has tested my patience, he's lucky I'm not sending the others round." Hellam noticed the slight frown of disapproval from Langton. "Just tell them to get on with it and get my money back."

Langton nodded then stood and left the room. Hellam

pushed the papers on his desk aside then walked over to a filing cabinet in the corner of the office. He pulled out a folder then returned with it to his desk. He opened it up and looked at the handful of papers inside, reading portions then flicking through to the photographs on the final sheet. The pictures were of an old farm house, seemingly derelict and in a poor state of maintenance. They showed interior shots of the brick farmhouse and then external and internal shots of a large barn that stood next to the building.

Hellam scrutinised the images for several moments then flicked back to the first sheet of paper where he found the number for the estate agent. He punched the number into his phone.

"Hello, Morley estates, Katie speaking, how can I help?" came a bright female voice.

"Yes, hello Katie, my name is Joseph Hellam, I spoke to you a few days ago regarding Clements Farm outside Surrington."

"Yes, Mr Hellam. I remember. Have you made a decision about the property?"

"I think so, but I'd like to take one final look if possible. Can I arrange a meeting for this afternoon?"

"Not a problem," replied Katie tapping something into a keyboard on the other end of the phone. "Let me see... can you make it at 4pm?"

"Absolutely, I'll see you there."

***

George Langton checked his watch as he pulled into

the carport. He was glad to see it was only 6pm. *Home early tonight*, he thought as he got out and walked up to his front door. He stepped inside, picked up the post from the floor and went into the lounge. He dropped the envelopes onto a coffee table by the sofa, threw his briefcase into a chair and sighed deeply as he rolled his head backwards around his shoulders and attempted to work the tension free.

His mobile phone suddenly buzzed into life as a text message came through. It was a message from Miller, a police officer who was on Hellam's unofficial payroll. Langton read the message and smiled; he would have some interesting news for Hellam on Monday.

Langton had been living alone ever since his wife had left him a few years before. He had been glad to see the back of her; at least that was what he told himself every day. She had found out about an affair he was having and had told him that their marriage was over. It wasn't the first affair Langton had had, and it certainly wouldn't have been the last. He never admitted to himself how much he missed her though she had been the only woman he had ever truly loved.

He went into the kitchen and filled a glass with water, which he gulped down and then filled with vodka and ice. He took his glass into the lounge and sat down on the sofa, sighing again and releasing the top two buttons of his shirt.

After several swigs of vodka, he leaned forward, placed the glass on the table and picked up his post. He flicked through the envelopes slowly. His eyes suddenly froze on a plain white envelope with his name and address handwritten on the front. He recognised the handwriting immediately.

"No," he said out loud as he tossed the other envelopes on the table and held the plain white one in both hands. "No, not again."

The seconds passed as Langton gazed at the writing on the front of the envelope, unable to bring himself to do anything else. Finally, he picked up the glass of vodka and downed the remaining liquid in one. It burned the back of his throat and he winced hard then slammed the glass of ice onto the table. He tore the envelope open and pulled out a single piece of paper.

Before he read it, he thought about the others he had received over the past four years. There hadn't been one for almost six months now and he had been hoping that he had been released from this torment. He had done everything the sender had asked, even though he was risking his life in doing so. He glanced down at the paper between his fingers and began to read:

Hello George,

It has been a while, I'm sorry for that. Unfortunately I've been very busy with various tasks, but I'm now going to require some further information from you. You have done very well in the past and I am extremely pleased with the documents you have provided so far.

I am going to have to ask you for more however. I require documents concerning the new bank accounts Joseph Hellam has opened in both Switzerland and the Cayman Islands. I want every piece of information you can provide on these accounts: numbers, statements and also any details on the recipients of money paid out. I'm sure you will also be able to provide me with a detailed report of where the money in these accounts has come from.

Also, provide me with an updated list of Joseph Hellam's drug and prostitution associates, including dates and shipments.
Get them to me in the usual way. I need them <u>soon</u>.

Thank you George
CC (Concerned Citizen).
P.S. Your secret is still safe with me, remember that.

Langton squeezed his hands tight and creased the paper between them then tore it in two.

"Fuck! No, no no," he yelled as he threw the paper to the floor and stood up. How the hell was he supposed to go through all this again? Langton was privy to information regarding all the bank accounts Hellam held around the world and knew he had set up several new accounts in the past month. How had this bastard found out about them? The accounts were set up in various names, some private, and some using non-existent business names. Some were legitimate; others were used to launder money from Hellam's criminal activities through to legitimate businesses. But yet again, this man wanted details of everything.

Langton asked himself, how could he know all this information? No one except himself and Hellam knew all the details of the various accounts and what they were used for. But then, this man had already found out things about Langton that he thought had been buried forever. Things that could never get out - *must* never get out.

He ran his hands through his thinning grey hair and held his head tightly for a moment. He needed to think. Picking up the glass of ice, he went back into the kitchen and poured himself another vodka which he quickly downed. There had been other requests over the past four years by the man calling himself 'Concerned Citizen'.

In the first letter he had outlined what he knew about Langton's secret and then requested that he photocopy various documents pertaining to Hellam's illegal business activities. He hadn't been specific in his request; he simply required anything that could prove Hellam's criminal activity. At first Langton had assumed the unknown man was punching above his weight and ignored the letter, despite the distinct sense of uneasiness he felt regarding the details of his secret.

The second letter had arrived two weeks later, this time it had given specific information about Langton's dark past and was much more threatening in tone. C.C. had given a definitive time limit for Langton to get the information to him or, he said, he would have no reservations in going to the police with the information he had found regarding Langton's dark past. Langton had sweated over the letter for two days before he began to photocopy documents, which he then sent to the PO Box provided by CC.

Langton knew that if Hellam ever found out about what he was doing then the best case scenario would be that he would receive a severe physical punishment before being thrown out of the business. However, he also knew that the most likely consequence of his actions would be much harsher, and as Hellam liked to say, '*definitive*'.

Langton had done everything he could to find out who owned the PO Box. It had been registered in the name of C. Citizen with a false address and was closed down the day after the documents had been received. Different PO Boxes had been set up each time Langton had been told to provide further information. Langton had even found the location of one of the PO boxes and watched it for several days off and on, until a courier collected the documents and took them to a central depot where they were unobtainable and untraceable as far as Langton could see.

He wasn't sure how the information he was providing was being used. He knew the police didn't operate like this, or did they? He guessed it could be somebody from a rival drug supplier, but if so, they weren't acting on any of the information they were receiving. It had been four years now, it was as if C.C. was simply gathering and holding onto the information for no good reason.

He sat back down on the sofa and felt the tension rise in his back as he thought about what to do. What could he do? Perhaps this would be the last time, he told himself and closed his eyes, knowing he would be unable to sleep tonight.

Chapter 6

Lewis

The half empty bottle of whiskey was on the table in front of Lewis as he sat, hunched forward, with his head resting on his arms. The kitchen in his flat was small and its table resided in the corner of the room with a single chair. Lewis raised his head. His eyes felt sore as he wiped them with the back of his hand and his head was spinning but that didn't matter. He picked up the whiskey and took another mouthful straight from the bottle then unsteadily placed it back on the wooden surface.

He had returned home from his parents in a state of numbness. He couldn't even remember the drive back to his flat in his father's car; it was a blur of passing scenery and flashing memories. His mother had explained that Hannah had been found six days earlier in her flat. Lewis had flown into a rage after hearing the news that she had been killed almost a week before and he hadn't been told. He asked his mother why she hadn't called to tell him to come home, but she had simply said that she couldn't bear for him to hear the news over the phone. Lewis had paced the room trying to make sense of the situation. How could she be dead? What had happened?

His mother had told him that Hannah's flatmate, Kelly, had found her when she returned from work. Hannah had apparently been strangled in her bedroom. Lewis shook his head frantically as he was told the information; he didn't want to know the details and yet he *needed* to be told everything.

His mother told him that the police had arrested a man who lived in the flat next to Hannah; someone called Craig Blaine, they were certain it was him. Lewis felt angry at the mention of a name that meant nothing to him; a name that he had never heard before and held no other significance. His mother told him that Hannah was being cremated the following Wednesday. Then, as Lewis felt the anger slip and distort into a sense of hopelessness and pain, he finally allowed tears to fall.

When his father dropped him off outside his flat, he had asked if he would be okay. Lewis remembered saying something, but he wasn't certain of the words, then he had taken the lift up to his flat, went inside with his bags and collapsed onto the floor - his world had just been shredded into hundreds of fragments and he couldn't think about anything except the face of the woman he loved as the life was squeezed from her.

He got up from the kitchen table, taking the bottle with him, and stumbled into the front room. He collapsed down into another chair and sipped on the whiskey.

Craig Blaine.

He kept repeating the name in his head and felt the rage inside grow with each repetition. He wished he could have met the man before the police had arrested him; he wished more than anything that he had a chance to get close to him. But then what would he have done? Would he have harmed him? Would he have killed him? Lewis thought about this in his drunken haze, telling himself he could do it, but was that because he had no chance of achieving it now? He had often heard that killing somebody, no matter how much you hate them, is something that some people just can't do. It's a myth that killing is easy. He vaguely remembered reading an article in some long forgotten magazine where a statistics expert gave various facts about how the rate of soldier's performance in war doesn't match with expected results. When they are told to kill, a majority of them, either purposely or subconsciously, aim off target. Killing is not something that comes as naturally as some people might believe.

As he thought about this diluted, half remembered fact, his mind drifted back to Craig Blaine and he became certain that he could kill that man given half a chance. But he knew he shouldn't be dwelling on these thoughts of revenge; that wouldn't help Hannah now. He had no chance of getting to the man responsible anyway.

He got up, swaying, and went into the bathroom. He gazed at the face staring back at him, eyes red, swollen and several days worth of stubble lining his chin.

"Pathetic," he said to his own reflection. "You're no killer, even if you wanted to be." Lewis sipped the whiskey as he stared into his own eyes. He had always been proud of being the kind of man he was; he didn't have a violent bone in his body - he was a pacifist. He knew he was no killer but at that moment, he wished he was.

You should have been there. You could have stopped this if you were there.

He leaned forward and rested his head on the cold glass of the mirror for a moment. He felt his grip tightening on the bottle of whiskey when he suddenly turned and yelled something as he threw it against the ceramic tiles above the bath. It shattered into a thousand pieces and amber liquid sprayed the room.

"You should have been there!" he screamed.

He stood in the centre of the room for a few moments, looking at the floor as tears fell and hit the tiles by his feet. He turned and ran the cold tap for a few seconds before splashing his face with water. He felt drained, as if some unknown force had just evaporated the last of his energy and concealed it - lost forever.

He walked back into the front room and his eyes fell on his laptop which was resting on the floor next to the sofa. He slumped down in the chair, picked up the computer and with drunken, uncoordinated movements, he booted it up for the first time in three months.

He had checked his e-mails on his mobile phone while away, but they would have remained on the server at his internet service provider after he read them. After it had finished loading, Lewis began to download all the old e-mails onto his laptop. There were over three hundred, which took a few minutes to fully download. Lewis scanned them with hazy, alcohol soaked vision, resigned to the fact that most of them were promoting offers from shopping websites or other general spam. He sorted them by sender and looked down the long list. He had received around fifteen e-mails from Hannah while he was away and, despite the certainty in the back of his mind that it would be unwise to go through them all again, he began to read them one by one.

Hannah had asked how he was getting on and mentioned how jealous she was of him for travelling the world. She had also written about her new boyfriend and how well things were going with him; something Lewis didn't particularly want to read about. She said he was a little older than her and lived a different life to the one she was used to; implying on a number of occasions that he was quite wealthy while never being direct.

As Lewis scrolled down the e-mails and absorbed her words, he became aware of a change in tone as the dates passed by. He had been vaguely aware of such a change when he originally viewed them while abroad, but here, reading them one after another in quick succession, the change seemed less subtle and to leap from the screen.

The first ten e-mails or so were the usual, upbeat writings that Lewis had grown to love. But the last few seemed to drop in tone and emit an air of melancholy; nothing specific, but a general ambience of sadness. Hannah stopped mentioning her boyfriend and Lewis thought that perhaps this change had come from the fact that they had broken up. Then, as he read the final e-mail, he became even more confused:

Dear Lewis,

I expect that you're reading this somewhere in Fiji or some other unimaginably remote location - actually I think you mentioned that you'd be in New York around now. I hope everything is still going well, I can't wait to see you when you return in a week or so. We should get everyone together and go for a night out to celebrate your return.

Things are okay here... the usual, I suppose you could say. Work is busy and it's taking up a lot of my time. Kelly is seeing someone now, so she is out quite a bit. I think she is going to be moving in with him soon so I'll be back to paying the full rent. It shouldn't be a problem though.

I wish you were home now. I have a bit of a dilemma which I'd like to share with you to be honest. It's about my boyfriend. I found something on his laptop that... well let's just say it was pretty horrible. I don't know what to do about it and I just need someone to talk to.

Listen to me going on about my silly little problems while you're trying to enjoy yourself. We can talk about it when you get back.

Can't wait to see you,
Love Hannah xxx

Lewis couldn't believe he had missed the content of this e-mail when he had first read it while still in New York. He could vaguely remember receiving it, but at the time he was in the middle of a bustling city and must only have scanned it. He usually savoured every word Hannah wrote him, but this one slipped through somehow and with the power of hindsight, the e-mail took on a new, darker tone. On the surface it still appeared to be nothing particularly remarkable, but the paragraph which described her discovery on her boyfriend's laptop, struck Lewis with unexpected force.

He thought about it for a while, going through several scenarios in his mind - what could she have found? He thought that perhaps she may have stumbled across some pornography and become upset with her boyfriend. But why would this have been the kind of thing she needed to share with someone? She may have argued about it with her boyfriend after discovering it, but it would be unlikely that she would want to share this intimate detail with Lewis. It must have been something else.

Lewis closed the laptop and placed it back on the floor, then got to his feet and began to pace the room, the alcohol in his blood suddenly seeming a little less potent. He thought about the timing of the e-mail - it had been sent two days before she was murdered. He went through the series of events, as if to feed the spark in his mind. Hannah discovered something 'horrible' on her boyfriend's laptop which was bad enough for her to mention it in an e-mail to Lewis. She called it a dilemma; what dilemma? Was it something she felt the police needed to be informed about? Was she confused as to whether she should inform the police or not? Then, two days after all of this, she was murdered.

As Lewis paced his flat, his thoughts returned to Craig Blaine. Perhaps he was her boyfriend and she had discovered something on *his* laptop. If so, did the police know about this?

He walked the room in circles for a few more minutes, his drunken mind becoming alert. He went into the kitchen and made himself a mug of strong black coffee.

***

Lewis saw Kelly sitting at a table in the corner of the bar as soon as he walked in. He managed a smile and a wave as he approached.

"Hi," he said, forcing the smile wider. "Can I get you a drink?"

"No thanks, I'm still working on this Coke."

Lewis nodded, went to the bar and returned with his own glass. He hugged Kelly and sat down on the opposite side of the table.

"How have you been?" she asked with a sympathetic tone.

Lewis nodded, "Holding up, how about you? I can't imagine what it must have been like to find her."

"It was awful, you have no idea. I can't get the image of her lying there out of my mind. I can't imagine why someone would do that to her."

Lewis sipped his Coke. Kelly had been one of Hannah's closest friends at university and their living together to save on rent had seemed like the perfect solution when Hannah had suggested it. Lewis had known Kelly for many years and they got on well, although they had little in common and their relationship was usually aided by their mutual friend.

"How was your trip?" Kelly asked, making her best attempt at changing the subject to something lighter.

"It was good thanks... I wish I had never gone on it now though."

Kelly shook her head, "There was nothing you could have done Lewis. Whoever killed her chose a time when there wasn't anybody around."

Lewis looked at her. "What do you mean 'whoever'? I thought they had the guy who did it? Craig Blaine, your next door neighbour, that's right isn't it?"

Kelly looked down into her glass for a moment before nodding.

"Yes, yes I know. I'm just being silly."

Lewis leaned forward. "What do you mean Kelly? Is

there something else?"

"No, no of course not. I'm just surprised Craig could have done something like that."

"Did you know him well?" Lewis asked.

Kelly shook her head, "Not really, no more than saying hello in the hall. He's an odd guy, no doubt about that. He's in his forties and still lives in that little flat with his mother. He would always have this odd smile on his face whenever I saw him. I know Hannah was creeped out by him now and again too."

Lewis's thoughts became caught up on the e-mail Hannah had sent him two days before she had been killed.

"So Craig wasn't her boyfriend then?"

A short burst of laughter escaped from Kelly. "No way, he wasn't boyfriend material, at least not for Hannah."

"Then why are you so surprised that it was Craig? If he was so strange and creeped you both out, then why not him?"

"I don't know, he was odd for sure. But also, he didn't seem like he would harm a fly; he spoke so softly... he just seemed like a gentle giant. He wasn't blessed with the greatest social skills, that was all."

Lewis frowned and turned to look out of the large window by the front entrance of the bar.

"You know, whenever there is something on the news about people who were the friends or family of a murderer..." he said turning back to Kelly. "...they all seem to say that they couldn't believe that person was capable of murder; they say that they just didn't seem like the type."

"I know, I know. It's just... it's difficult to get over the fact that we were living next to somebody for so long who *was* capable of that. I know he did it, the police found his blood under Hannah's nails for Christ sake. I just still can't believe it.

Lewis looked at her as she stared down into her drink. She brushed some of her blonde hair away from her face and Lewis thought he could see her eyes beginning to fill. Kelly had never seemed like the type of person to voice that kind of concern without good cause. But at the same time she didn't seem to have anything specific to say as to why it couldn't have been the man the police suspected.

"How did the police first come to suspect him?" Lewis asked, cutting through the silence.

"It was ridiculous really. They questioned our neighbours and when Craig came to the door, he had a huge cut on his neck which had obviously been made by finger nails. It was a joke how quickly they arrested him. They tested his DNA and it matched the blood under Hannah's nails. I suppose when I think about that, it seems stupid to question that it could be anyone but him really."

"What was Hannah's boyfriend like?" Lewis asked, his mind unable to release the thought of the e-mail.

"I have no idea, I never met him. She would always go over to his place or meet him for dinner and drinks. She was besotted with him at first though, I can tell you that much." She looked at Lewis, her eyes narrowing slightly. "Jealous?" she asked with an attempt at a smile.

Lewis leaned back in surprise. "No, of course not... what do you mean?"

"Come on Lewis, I know how you felt about Hannah. I'd have had to be blind not to see how you looked at her."

"I... don't know what you mean, we were friends."

"Okay," Kelly said, releasing the smile. "Hannah seemed to be a little secretive about him to be honest. I don't know what it was; she would talk about him all the time, especially at the beginning, but there would never be anything specific. It would just be comments about how nice he was to her. A few days before she died, she seemed to stop mentioning his name altogether... actually she seemed really depressed and quiet those last couple of days. I thought that perhaps it was work, I know she had a lot on and felt it was getting on top of her."

"What was her boyfriend's name?"

"Joe, I don't know his surname." Kelly eyed Lewis suspiciously again. "Why do you keep asking about him?"

Lewis took a deep breath and let it out slowly. "It's just... I don't know maybe I'm the one being silly now, but Hannah sent me an e-mail a couple of days before she was killed. I re-read it yesterday and it seemed a little strange."

"How so?" Kelly asked, leaning closer.

"She mentioned her boyfriend and said that she had found something horrible on his laptop. She said she was in a bit of a dilemma and didn't know what to do."

Kelly frowned as she thought for a few seconds, twisting her now empty glass between her fingers.

"Two days before she was killed?" she asked and Lewis nodded slowly. "She said something to me about that I think. I was only half listening. I was getting ready to go out and she came into my room and started asking me all these strange questions."

"What questions?" Lewis asked, this time it was his turn to lean closer.

"I can't really remember, like I said, I was only half listening. But it was something a little convoluted, something like, 'what would I do if I found out something bad about someone I loved?' I can't even remember what my reply was; I just sort of brushed off the question. She seemed really odd, now I think about it. I thought she was just bored and came in to see me to pass some time before I went out. I wish I'd listened properly now; from what you've just said about the e-mail, it sounds like she needed to talk to someone."

"I wish we knew who this Joe was." Lewis said. "I just can't stop thinking about that e-mail - I wish I could."

Kelly reached out and touched his hand. "I know this must be terrible for you Lewis. It's terrible for me, but you and Hannah... well you were much closer than she and I were."

Lewis looked at her and smiled weakly. "It's the worst thing that has ever happened to me."

Kelly squeezed his hand, "Sometimes it's just difficult to let it go. They have the man that did it and he's going to be punished for what he's done. That's not much of a comfort for us now, but that's what we need to think about. All our silly theories are just that; silly theories. The proof is there."

Lewis drained the Coke from his glass and nodded as he stared at Kelly.

"You're right, I know you're right. It's just so difficult." He glanced at his watch, "I have to go," he said, standing. "Thanks for the chat Kelly, I think it's helped. I'll see you at the funeral next week, okay?"

"Yes, I'll see you then."

Lewis walked out of the bar and down the street,

wishing he could be certain that the right man was going to be punished. But if he was truthful with himself, a subtle but persistent doubt nagged the back of his mind. He couldn't be sure what prevented that certainty, but knew that something didn't feel right.

Chapter 7

Hellam

The car stopped at the front of the building and Hellam and Langton walked down the steps slowly before getting into the limousine.

"Here are your notes for the meeting," Langton said, handing Hellam several sheets of paper in a small, plastic folder.

"Thank you," He flicked through the papers. "How are Kelser and Richards getting on?"

"They're going to sort out the Deacon problem today. Kelser is confident it will all be rectified by the end of the day."

"Excellent news," Hellam said with a smile, but didn't look up from his notes.

"There is one thing that does need addressing though Mr Hellam."

Hellam stopped scanning the document and closed the folder as he turned to Langton. "What is it?"

Langton glanced at the driver, before leaning in closer and whispering. "Miller has been in contact with me. He's managed to find out some information from undercover operations. He said it wasn't easy and he isn't certain of the facts yet, but it appears that Richards might be a problem."

Hellam frowned. "A cop?" he whispered, his voice low and cold.

Langton nodded, "Possibly, I'm getting Miller to double check the details, but he says that it may take a couple of days before he'll get an opportunity to do so." Langton watched his boss's eyes narrow as he became lost in thought for a moment, then spoke quietly. "Do you want me to organise something for Richards?"

"No," Hellam replied softly as he gazed out of the window. "I'll take care of it, don't worry about it."

Hellam became silent for a few moments as he turned away from Langton and watched the streets move past his window. Langton glanced down at the hand clutching the plastic folder and noticed Hellam was gripping it so tightly that his knuckles had turned white. The car remained silent for the rest of the journey, Langton not daring to utter another word, sensing the anger emanating from the man sitting beside him. Eventually they came to rest outside a building and Hellam stepped out. Before closing the door, he turned to Langton.

"Tell Kelser to meet with us tomorrow morning. I want him to deal with this Richards situation."

"Kelser? Yes sir," Langton replied and watched as Hellam slammed the door shut then went into the building for his meeting. Langton turned to the driver. "Take me to Luciano's, I'd like to get some lunch."

***

Langton asked for a table for one as he entered the restaurant and was shown to a seat by the window. He ordered a glass of water and his usual Italian vegetable salad. The restaurant was quiet, as it usually was during the week, but Langton enjoyed the peace on these occasions; it wasn't very often he managed to eat a proper lunch, but when he did, he would always come to Luciano's.

He thought about Richards for a moment and the inevitable fate that awaited the man. Langton liked Richards; he seemed to be a hard worker and didn't cause him any trouble. Now he understood why.

Richards had been recommended to them by an associate of Hellam's who had seemed trustworthy. It now appeared that the associate in question would be in almost as much danger as Richards himself. Langton felt glad that Hellam's anger wasn't directed towards him.

It was this train of thought that reminded him of the item that was in his pocket; something that had never really been forgotten since it arrived through the door that morning. The post had come early and Langton felt sure that his heart stopped for a few seconds when he saw the small, white envelope resting by the front door. The handwritten address on the front confirmed that it was another letter from Concerned Citizen.

Langton reached into his pocket as he sat in Luciano's and slowly pulled out the unopened letter. He placed it on the table in front of him and stared at it for a moment. C.C. was obviously becoming impatient; he had only received the previous letter two days earlier, how could Langton be expected to have made copies of the documents and dispatched them in such a short time? He tore open the envelope and pulled the letter out:

Hello George,

I've been watching you over the weekend and you don't seem to have made much progress in getting me the documents I require. I'm sorry to be so impatient with regards to this matter, but I require them with the utmost urgency. Get them to me within the next two days

Thank you George
CC (Concerned Citizen).
P.S. Your secret is still safe with me.

Langton bit his lip hard as he folded the letter and placed it back into his pocket. He was watching him now? It was an impossible situation and he felt panic suddenly rise inside. He sipped his water with a trembling hand and tried to calm himself.

After discovering Richards was an undercover police officer and knowing what Hellam was capable of, Langton was quite sure that Richards wouldn't be around for much longer. As he thought about the documents he had copied for his blackmailer over the years, he became more agitated. If Hellam ever found out about his betrayal, he felt sure that he would find himself in a similar position to the one that awaited Richards. But he had no choice; if his secret came out then he would be as good as dead anyway - he had long since convinced himself of that - at least this way he stood a fighting chance.

The waiter brought over his food, but Langton had lost his appetite. He picked at the salad with his fork for twenty minutes before asking for the bill and leaving. He got the car back to his office and sat at his desk in silence.

He thought about what had happened all those years

before. How could C.C. have found out about his past? No one knew, absolutely no one except... his mind suddenly rebelled against him and spontaneously conjured up the face that belonged to the small, lifeless body as it rested, motionless, in his arms. The face, the eyes especially, drawing on his attention with a gravity akin to a black hole. It was an image he had spent almost twenty years trying to erase.

"It was an accident..." he said out loud, then paused and glanced up at his open doorway. No one had heard him, but he forced himself to remove the image of the little girl from his mind; it wasn't wise to dwell on such things. He diverted his thoughts back to the letter and the documents he had already decided to copy.

***

Richards knocked loudly on the door to the flat and glanced at Kelser standing beside him. He turned back as he heard steps approaching the door from the other side. The door opened by a crack and a single eye peered through the small gap.

"Shit," Richards heard the man on the other side say as he went to slam the door shut. But Richards pushed his foot forward and blocked it from closing then pushed hard, knocking the man backwards. Both he and Kelser stepped inside and shut the door behind them.

"You're an elusive man Deacon," Richards said, moving towards him.

Deacon retreated back into the flat, his eyes wide as they darted between the two men.

"I don't know what that bastard Travis told you but I don't have that money." he said, still moving backwards until his spine finally hit the wall behind him. "He's been trying to stitch me up with that shit for a while now."

"We *know* you have that money; there really isn't any point in denying it. You know what this man is capable of." Richards nodded in Kelser's direction, who walked over to the window and slid the small, worn curtain closed. The room was bathed in semi-darkness. "Tell us where the money is and we'll leave you alone."

Deacon watched as Kelser moved slowly around the room, circling like a vulture and gazing at him with unsettling intensity. Kelser raised a hand and scratched his cheek, just below the thick scar that arched around his face.

"I don't have the money; I don't know where it is." Deacon said in a low whisper, not daring to take his eyes from Kelser.

Richards shook his head slowly and went over to the other side of the room where he picked up a small wooden stool. He placed the stool in the centre of the room and glanced at his companion. Kelser pulled out a gun and pointed it at Deacon.

"No, please God no," Deacon said, instinctively raising his hands and closing his eyes tight.

"Sit down," Kelser sneered, nodding in the direction of the chair.

Shaking, Deacon moved over to the stool and sat down, the wood creaking as it bore his weight. His eyes were fixed on Kelser as Richards walked around and grabbed his arms then used cable ties to secure them behind his back.

"Please, you don't need to do this," Deacon pleaded.

Kelser put his gun away and approached the terrified man. He stood before him for a moment, staring down without the slightest hint of emotion on his face. Deacon felt fear wash through him as he gazed up into Kelser's eyes; there was nothing behind them, just a void.

Suddenly Kelser moved behind him and Deacon felt him grab one of his fingers. Before he had time to scream, he felt Kelser grip hard and pull it backwards. He heard a crack before an intense pain radiated through his hand and up his arm.

"Aarrgh!" The guttural cry left Deacons mouth involuntarily.

"Where is the money?" Kelser asked quietly as he moved around the front again.

Richards stepped forward and leaned closer to Deacon, whose face contorted with pain. "Tell us where the money is and we leave, it's as simple as that," he said.

"I don't have the money." Deacon looked up as sweat and tears fell down his face.

Kelser stepped forward and swung a fist into Deacon's face.

***

Kelser washed his hands in the bathroom as he gazed into the mirror, his own vacant expression staring back at him. Deacon's blood was diluted with the running water and flowed down the sink. It had taken almost thirty minutes before Deacon broke. He had sustained a broken nose, three broken fingers and a heavily bruised torso before finally relenting. Kelser thought it was amazing how much pain some people could endure in the hope of wealth. Deacon had begged them to stop and eventually told them that he had placed the money in a safe-deposit box. He gave them the bank's location and the pass code for the box as blood fell from his crooked nose. Kelser had even allowed the hint of a smile creep onto his face when Deacon finally gave up his secret.

He dried his hands on a towel then went to leave the bathroom and return to Richards in the front room. As he stepped close to the door he heard the sound of low whispering from the other side and leaned forward. He could hear Richards saying something to Deacon, who was still sitting on the small wooden stool. The sound wasn't clear but Kelser managed to make out several words.

"...police... testify... Hellam... protection."

Kelser stood by the door for a few seconds as these words sunk in and he thought about their significance. Richards would have no reason to whisper in such a way when Kelser left the room unless these words were specifically not for his ears.

'Police... testify.'

The realisation hit hard and Kelser felt his jaw tighten. Richards was a cop. But how could this be? He had been recommended to Hellam by a trusted source. Kelser thought for a moment and tried to comprehend the situation but quickly shrugged it off. There was no point in asking questions of 'why', the fact was that Richards was an undercover police officer and he appeared to be trying to coerce Deacon into testifying against Hellam. That could be the only reason for this conspiratorial whispering.

He gathered himself and tried to relax. He wasn't sure how he would play this yet, but decided to not use the information straight away. He needed time to think. After moving the towel rail loudly and making several hard footsteps, he opened the door and returned to the front room. He noticed the sudden movement from both men as he entered but acted as if he wasn't paying attention.

"You ready?" Kelser asked, gesturing towards the door.

Richards nodded then went round behind Deacon and cut the cable ties from his wrists. Deacon arched his spine backwards as if to stretch through the pain in his body. He put a hand to his nose and wiped some of the blood away as the two men left.

Chapter 8

Lewis

The whiskey bottle slipped from between Lewis's fingers, into his lap and the dark liquid trickled gently over his leg. He woke with a start.

"Wha... oh shit," he said, dragging his alcohol soaked brain from its slumber. He picked up the half-empty bottle and placed it on the table by his chair with a clunk then leaned forward and clutched his head between his hands. It was throbbing and, after rubbing his eyes, he looked up at the wall clock. It was 4:17am; he had been asleep for over an hour. The whiskey soaked through his jogging bottoms and Lewis stared down at the wet patch on his leg. "Shit," he repeated.

He used the arm of the chair to steady himself as he got to his feet and staggered into the kitchen, bumping his hip into the work surface as he entered. He tore off several sheets of kitchen roll and dabbed his leg for several minutes. He cleared his throat as he dropped the sodden paper into the bin and returned to his chair.

His eyelids felt heavy, he allowed them to fall together

for a few seconds. Even with his eyes closed, he could feel the room spinning around him and a sudden nausea speared his stomach. Hitting his knee on the coffee table, Lewis lunged towards the bathroom, crashing into the door frame as he went, and threw up into the toilet. He retched for several minutes, feeling the familiar burning in the back of his throat. When he had finished, he slumped down on the floor by the toilet and began to sob.

A feeling of hopelessness had engulfed him over the past two days. He hadn't left his flat during that time and had barely eaten; the only thing passing his lips being alcohol. He was tormented by the thoughts that wouldn't leave him. The unanswered questions and the doubts about how Hannah died were eating him from the inside. But most of all, he missed her and couldn't stop thinking about every moment they had spent together.

Then there was the morning that was rapidly approaching and what that morning held. Lewis wasn't sure how he would be able to even attend Hannah's funeral, but he knew he would - he had to.

He picked himself up, wiped the tears from his cheek with the back of his hand, and shuffled over to the sink. He washed his face and drank some water then went out into the hall. He glanced at the bottle of whiskey and contemplated drinking some more before turning away and stumbling into his bedroom. The soft duvet cushioned his fall as he collapsed onto his bed and he fell asleep almost instantly.

***

Kelly shook her head as she looked over to the far corner of the hall and saw Lewis sitting on a table by himself. He had barely spoken to anyone before the funeral at the church and his appearance had dissuaded anyone from approaching him. He was sitting with a glass of water, staring into space with red eyes. Kelly was trying to determine if his eyes were red from the tears or from the obvious hangover. She had said hello to him outside the church after the service and smelt the pungent odour of alcohol that followed him. He had replied but his thoughts hadn't been in the moment, they were light-years away.

She picked up her glass of orange juice, walked over to his table and sat down next to him. He didn't look up and appeared to be unaware of her arrival.

"How are you?" she said softly.

Lewis's eyes flicked up and acknowledged Kelly, but he said nothing. He sipped his water and continued to gaze at the surface of the table. The black suit he was wearing covered an ill fitting white shirt, which had a button missing at the top and his tie hung loosely around his neck.

"You're not the only one who misses her you know," Kelly said in a sharp whisper. The words came out with a harshness that surprised her and she saw that Lewis was also surprised by them as he looked up. They locked eyes for a few moments but still Lewis said nothing. After a moment he turned away.

"I'm sorry," Kelly said. "I know how close you were to Hannah. I don't know why I said that. But Lewis, seriously, being this way isn't doing you any good. You can't go on like this; drinking yourself into oblivion."

Lewis closed his eyes for a long time before opening them again and turning back to Kelly. "I'm sorry too. I just..." He paused as he glanced around the hall at all the other people who were dressed in dark colours, talking quietly and consuming the buffet. "...I just can't stop thinking about her. Not just her, but everything. Something just doesn't *feel* right; this wasn't supposed to happen."

"Is this about what we discussed the other day? Lewis, you need to get over all this, they've got the man that killed her. There's nothing more we can do now. Obsessing over all this isn't going to bring Hannah back."

Lewis shook his head, "I know, I know."

They sat in silence for a while but it felt comfortable; the silence hanging between them like a net and allowing the captured thoughts to linger.

"Are you looking for a job now?" Kelly finally asked.

"I should be," Lewis replied, staring into space. "I can't seem to find the energy at the moment to be honest."

"I think you should start looking, it'll help to get your mind off all this."

Lewis nodded but wasn't sure Kelly was right; he didn't feel like anything would be able to take his mind away from this nightmare. He looked at all the faces in the room and his eye fell on a woman staring at him from the other side of the hall. It was Hannah's mother and he saw her work a thin smile in his direction and gestured for him to come over.

"I'm just going to speak to Hannah's mum, I'll see you later."

Kelly nodded and offered her own smile. "I hope you feel better soon."

Lewis thanked her then walked through the crowd of guests and over to the middle aged woman.

"Lewis," she said as he approached and threw her arms around him. After they separated, she took a step back and looked at him up and down. "You look terrible."

Lewis managed a smile as he looked down at his clothes. "I'll take that as a compliment." He paused, not really knowing what to say and shuffled uncomfortably on the spot. "How is everything?" he asked finally, cursing himself inside for asking such a question.

"Coping. It isn't like reality at the moment; almost as if it hasn't really sunk in... I'm dreading the moment when it does." She blinked away some tears and then appeared to consciously gather herself. "Listen, we've still got to go through some of Hannah's things and... well you knew her better than anyone. We were just wondering if you wanted to take a look... I mean if there was anything that you wanted then I'm sure Hannah would want you to have it."

Lewis shook his head, "I'm not sure I'm ready for that."

Hannah's mother touched his arm. "None of us are ready Lewis, but you were her best friend. If anyone should see to her things, it should be you, we'd really appreciate it."

He thought for a second. He had known her family for almost his entire life and the way Hannah's mother was speaking to him implied that he would be doing them a favour; almost as if they couldn't bring themselves to do the task alone.

"Okay, I'll take a look. I'll come over in a couple of days if that suits you?"

"Yes, that would be fine, thank you."

They spoke for a few more minutes about nothing in particular before Lewis walked back across the hall and returned to his table, sitting back down next to Kelly. Her boyfriend had joined her and she introduced him.

"Lewis, this is Jeremy."

Lewis smiled narrowly and shook the man's hand. He had a firm grip and nodded in return.

"Pleased to meet you Lewis," Jeremy said. He looked at his watch before leaning back in his chair and placing an arm around Kelly.

"How long have you been together?" Lewis asked half heartedly.

Jeremy looked at Kelly and smiled, "Just over four months now..."

Lewis nodded in all the correct places as Jeremy detailed the history of their relationship, but his mind wandered. He began to think about Hannah's boyfriend once again and a thought occurred to him. Why hadn't he tried to get in contact with her after she was murdered? Nobody who Hannah was close to knew who he was or how to reach him. Surely if he hadn't heard from her for a few days and she wasn't answering messages then he would have stopped by her flat; perhaps even asking her roommate where she was. But Kelly certainly hadn't been contacted by him.

Lewis began to make notes in his mind and decided there could be a number of reasons for this problem. The first could be that they had broken up before she was murdered and he no longer had any reason to contact her, which was a possibility. But the e-mail Hannah had written to Lewis two days before her death implied they were still together, albeit with some kind of problem coming between them. The second reason could be that he already knew she was dead and there was no reason for him to try to contact her. But Lewis thought it would be extremely strange if someone you were in a relationship with was murdered and you didn't at least try to contact the people they were close to in order to share sympathy of the mutual loss.

This led Lewis onto the final possible reason; what if her boyfriend knew she had been murdered and didn't attempt to get in contact afterwards because *he* was responsible for her death.

"...Lewis?"

Kelly's voice snapped him from his train of thought.

"Yes? Sorry, I was just thinking about something," Lewis said and noticed the annoyance on Jeremy's face. "Listen, I think I'm going to go now. It was a pleasure to meet you Jeremy."

Lewis got up and began to walk from the hall but noticed Kelly was following. When he reached the exit he turned towards her.

"Are you sure you're okay?" she asked with concern on her face.

"I'm not okay," Lewis replied. "But I will be. You don't need to worry about me."

They hugged and Lewis went to leave before pausing and turning back to her. She was walking away, but he tapped her arm.

"Has Hannah's boyfriend tried to get in touch with her since her death? In person or by calling her phone? Even texting?" he asked.

Kelly thought for a moment but shook her head. "Not

in person, no one has come by the flat asking me about her. The police have her mobile phone, but the detectives said they would contact me about any texts or voicemail messages for me to pass on to the relevant people. They haven't given me anything that her boyfriend might have sent."

Lewis nodded, "Okay, thanks Kelly. I'll see you soon."

As he left the hall, Lewis decided that he *had* to speak to Craig Blaine.

Chapter 9

Hellam

Kelser knocked on the door to Hellam's office and waited. After a moment, the door opened and Langton stood before him, staring for a moment before gesturing for Kelser to enter the room.

"Sit down," Hellam said from his chair behind the large, oak desk and both Kelser and Langton took their places in the chairs opposite.

Hellam scrutinised the two men. They couldn't be more different he noted internally; Langton's placid, drooping face and Kelser's intense, hollow gaze.

"We have a problem," he said finally, all business. "Carl Richards."

Kelser's expression changed by a fraction and he nodded, "I agree. I was about to raise the issue with you myself."

Hellam glanced at Langton then, interested, back to Kelser as he continued.

"I overheard something yesterday while we were sorting out the Deacon situation."

Hellam sat upright, "And what was that?"

"He's an undercover cop," Kelser replied, then paused as if to consider his last statement. "At least I think he is. He was whispering something to Deacon about testifying against you while I was out of the room."

Hellam nodded slowly. "We have the same information." He glanced at Langton, "George has a contact in the police force that helps us from time to time, and he has some information that points in that direction."

Kelser turned and stared at Langton but didn't say anything. Hellam noticed the older man shuffle uncomfortably in his seat as his eyes flicked sideways, obviously sensing the gaze from the man beside him. Kelser's eyes remained on Langton for a long time as he continued to shuffle and raise his chin, freeing his neck from the tight shirt collar.

Langton suddenly cleared his throat. "Where do we go from here?" he asked, clearly attempting to move the conversation on and Kelser slowly returned his attention to his boss.

"George, can you leave us alone for a moment, I'd like to talk to Kelser about this situation. You won't need to be involved in this problem anymore."

Langton nodded with apparent relief at being dismissed. He stood and left the room, without looking in Kelser's direction.

Hellam placed his hands on the table in front of him and locked his fingers together as the door closed.

"You've been working with us for five years now," he said, looking up to Kelser. "This will be an important job for you. I need Carl Richards to be taken care of in an efficient manner. Do you think you are capable of dealing with this or should I call in my usual... outside help?"

"I can deal with Richards," Kelser replied in a monotone. "I *want* to deal with him. He's betrayed us... he's betrayed me."

Hellam's mouth widened into a crooked grin and he nodded slowly. "I think it's good that you want to." He leaned back in his chair. "I have enemies everywhere Kelser. Some are known but some are, for the time being, unknown and these are by far the more dangerous of the two. I need someone like you around because you are my last line of defence if one of these enemies was to get too close." He paused for effect and narrowed his eyes as he dropped his voice to a whisper. "Richards got much too close. I can't... I *won't* allow that to happen again. We need to be vigilant Kelser; we need to keep our eyes open for anyone who wishes to harm our operations."

Kelser nodded, his expression stoic. "If anyone comes close to you Mr Hellam, I'll kill them."

Hellam paused for a second, taking this in. "That's good to hear. That's very good to hear. But would you really? Would you really kill them?"

Kelser looked away, lowering his gaze to contemplate the question. Hellam studied him as the silence between them condensed and congealed. The answer was inevitable before it left Kelser's lips.

"Yes I would."

Hellam nodded with a single tip of his head. "I want you to take Richards somewhere tomorrow morning – somewhere private. Find out what he knows, who he has told and what information he has passed on to his superiors. I want to know *everything*, so use whatever means you deem necessary. We've kept him at a relative distance so I doubt he has anything concrete at this stage; if he did, we'd all probably be in prison by now." Hellam paused as he wrote something down on a piece of paper then slid it across the desk. "When you've finished with him, bring him to me at this address. I'd like to have a few words with him before... well before the situation is resolved."

Kelser nodded as he slipped the paper into his jacket pocket. "Anything else?"

"No, that will be all."

Kelser got up and stepped towards the door before Hellam spoke again.

"Kelser, if you perform this task well then I'll make sure that you're rewarded."

Kelser lowered his head in a nod but said nothing as he left the room.

***

The office which was home to the more sensitive documents in Hellam's organisations was located in a building two miles from the H.K. Communications headquarters. It was rented in the name of a fictitious company and had absolutely no ties with Joseph Hellam or George Langton, apart from the fact that they both held a set of keys. The office was tiny, just eight feet square and contained only a handful of shelves; each one half-filled with files and binders.

Langton pulled up outside the building and turned off the engine to his Lexus as rain fell onto the windscreen.

He sat in the car for a few moments before pulling out the small bottle of Seroxat anti-depressants and swallowing one dry. The windows began to fog as he remained sitting in his car, waiting patiently for the tablet to take the edge off his anxiety.

He prayed that this would be the last time he would be asked to copy the documents. Whoever wanted them had never made it clear to Langton as to *why* he required them and the person in question had never acted on the incriminating evidence they provided as far as Langton could ascertain. It seemed nonsensical for someone to obtain all this information via a blackmailed employee and simply sit on it for a period of four years.

He lowered the window to clear the mist from the inside. Splashes of water found their way through the tiny gap and onto Langton's still face. He pulled out a handkerchief from his pocket and slowly wiped the moisture away. He felt an emptiness inside him that slowly became engulfed by unexplained terror. It rose from his stomach, placed two claws on his throat and began to squeeze - hard. Langton released the top button of his shirt, and gasped for breath as perspiration replaced the rain on his brow. He breathed deeply and, after a moment, the panic subsided - it always did. He slowly began to relax.

He felt something inside; knowledge of something he had no reason to possess. He knew that the reason for him being asked to copy the documents would become apparent soon; it had to. It was a feeling that couldn't be explained in any rational way. It was something that he gained very little comfort from since it was at that point that Joseph Hellam would become all too aware of his betrayal.

He closed the window, picked up the briefcase that was sitting on the passenger seat and stepped out of the car. He stared up at the sky and let the droplets of rain fall on his face, cooling his flushed skin as he thought of the only other way out of the situation he found himself in. He reached back into his pocket and once again pulled out the Seroxat. He stared at the bottle for a brief moment before shaking his head and pushing them back into his jacket.

He unlocked the main door to the office building and stepped inside to the sound of several beeps. The building was home to a dozen separate businesses, but all had finished for the day. Each business had a set of keys to the main door and the code to the alarm. Langton punched in the code and the shrill beeps stopped then he walked up two flights of stairs to the door marked 'Radian Technologies'. He unlocked the door and a second set of beeps began to sound in the small room. Langton hit the small plastic buttons on a keypad by the door and the second alarm was deactivated.

He glanced at the alarm panel on the wall. The alarm system in the office of the fictional company wasn't simply there to detect thieves but to also monitor entry. Every month a report which gave details of times and dates of each entry was automatically generated and sent to Hellam's inbox. He and Langton were the only two people who knew the office existed and it was only usually Langton who ever visited, in order to drop off new documents or shred old ones.

He looked up at the wall clock to see it was just after 8pm. He knew Hellam had grown complacent of the reports detailing visits to the office and Langton wasn't particularly concerned even if Hellam was to raise a query with him. He could explain away the incident as a simple check that all the previous month's statements had been shredded correctly; a feeble excuse but Langton didn't realistically expect his out-of-hours visit to be a problem.

He switched on the light and saw the shelves which contained files over on one side of the room. There was also a large shredding machine but very little else - certainly no photocopier. Langton walked over to the files and began to open them up.

Part of the money, illegally obtained in Hellam's drug and prostitution organisations, was filtered through one of Hellam's legitimate organisations in the form of overvalued invoices, but this method was open to scrutiny should the company be investigated for any reason. Large quantities of money were therefore deposited in various bank accounts and trusts in countries with notoriously lax anti-money-laundering laws - primarily in the Caribbean. These were then broken down into smaller amounts in order to avoid suspicion and wired to other bank accounts around the world. The funds were then split into even smaller amounts, sent on to new banks and so on. The bank accounts that the money sat in were only active for a maximum of two months before the funds were sent on and the previous account closed.

Langton kept statements for the various accounts for only one month before they were shredded and the paper trail terminated. With this system, even if the authorities were able to find this office and somehow link it to Hellam then they would only ever have a maximum of one month's worth of statements. The previous accounts no longer existed and, in any case, there would be no easy way to prove that the money had been obtained illegally since the trusts from where it was sourced were not legally obliged to disclose such information.

This system had been working for many years, although they had been forced to alter their methods several times in order to avoid detection.

Langton opened several folders, removed the statements he required and pushed them into his briefcase. He would need to photocopy them elsewhere and return them the following day. He thought about the letters from Concerned Citizen and the amount of incriminating evidence that man must have obtained over the years via Langton's own hand. He knew that the information he provided to C.C. would easily show the flow of money from the initial deposit in the trusts and on through the various bank accounts. It could all be easily traced with the correct paperwork. The same paperwork that Langton had been shredding over the years but only after copies had been forwarded to his blackmailer

He wondered what the future would bring; aware that he was providing information to some person unknown that could bring down Hellam's entire operation. *But what else am I to do?* He asked himself as he walked from the office, down the stairs and out of the building, punching in the codes and setting the alarms behind him. *There is no way out.*

He glanced up and down the street as the rain slowed and he walked back to his car. He threw his briefcase into the passenger seat as he sat down and gazed through the windscreen. He reached down and felt the bottle of pills in his pocket, massaging it slowly between his fingers as his eyes glazed over.

"You could run," he said quietly to himself, the words falling lazily from dry lips.

But where could you run? A voice in his head asked. *You're stuck George. If you run, they'll become suspicious; Hellam will wonder why you left so suddenly. He would discover your betrayal in time, and where could you go where they wouldn't be able to find you? He would follow you George and he'd send someone to get you. You know he'll find you George. He'll get you - Kelser will get you George.*

Langton felt himself tremble as the voice of his own creation sniggered and sneered in his head; taunting him for a response. But there was no response - Langton was trapped in this mess and there was nothing he could do. He glanced at the briefcase then started the engine. The rain continued to slow, eventually stopping, as he drove towards his house where he would scan and copy the documents for the waiting hands of Concerned Citizen.

***

Hellam walked nonchalantly around the room with his gloved hands clasped behind his back. The room was empty apart from a broken porcelain sink which lay in pieces by one of the walls. The plaster was falling from the brickwork and a thick layer of dust lined the bare, concrete floor. The block of flats was located on the edge of town and had been abandoned for over a year as it waited patiently for fresh funding from the owners for its refurbishment - funding that Hellam doubted would ever arrive.

The door to the room suddenly crashed open and Kelser dragged Richards in and threw him to the floor. Richards' hands were clasped behind his back and secured with duct tape. He fell hard and dust billowed up around him, his face sliding across the jagged concrete. As the dust settled around him, Richards turned over onto his side and stared up with wide eyes at the two men standing over him.

"Good morning Carl," Hellam said pleasantly.

"You don't need to do this... I..." Richards blurted out.

As the dust slowly dispersed, Hellam began to see Richards' face more clearly. His right eye was swollen, almost completely closed and the skin around it a dark shade of purple. Blood fell from the corner of his mouth and Hellam watched as Richards craned his neck sideways, down to his shoulder and wiped it away, leaving a thick, red smear across his chin.

"Do what? What is it that you think we're going to do?" Hellam asked, his voice soft.

"I... I don't know. Listen, I haven't got anything on you two. I could just walk away from this and there will be no repercussions... I swear." Richards spoke the last two words softly and they faded away, as if lethargy had overwhelmed him. Hellam saw the hope drain from Richards face as the sudden realisation hit him of just how ludicrous his plea had sounded.

Hellam turned to Kelser, "Well?"

"He denied everything at first then came clean. He's been working on a case against you for a year and then managed to secure a recommendation from Gabriel Henson to allow him closer access to you."

"How did he secure that recommendation, blackmail?" Hellam asked.

Kelser nodded, "Richards told Gabriel that he had enough of a case against him for a conviction, but said he would go easy on him if Gabriel recommended him as a potential employee to you."

Hellam glanced over to Richards, still lying on his side and spitting blood onto the floor beside him.

"You manipulative little bastard." Hellam's face twisted in disgust. "What evidence has he accumulated so far?" he asked, turning back to Kelser.

"Not much from what I can gather. He has no hard evidence as yet, just his own eye witness accounts. He said he was attempting to gather witnesses, which is probably what he was discussing with Deacon when I overheard them talking. You didn't let him close enough to you for him to accumulate any real evidence... at least that's what he said." Kelser looked past Hellam and down at Richards. They locked eyes for a moment. "If he's lying, then he's very good at it."

Hellam turned away and walked slowly over to Richards who began inching away awkwardly, his hands scraping on the concrete.

"You're very good at your job Carl... tell me, what is your real name?"

Richards said nothing; just looked up as Hellam towered above him. He shuffled away until he was up against one of the walls, the bruised skin around his eye rubbing against the soft plaster.

"I understand your reluctance to disclose that information, I really do. But we'll find out somehow. There are a lot of people out there who are untrustworthy my friend. You, for example, are an untrustworthy human being. You misled me for your own ends and this is a very disappointing outcome. I had high hopes for you Carl."

Hellam crouched down next to Richards who could do nothing but stare. He heard Richards' fast, shallow breaths and saw the terror in his eyes. "But there are many other untrustworthy people out there. How do you suppose we managed to get the information about your deceit? We have contacts within the police force that are more than willing to disclose any information at the right price. I suppose that what we should all take away from this is: *never trust anyone.*" Hellam said the words slowly and precisely so they couldn't be misheard. He smiled and leaned in closer so his face was next to Richards'. He breathed heavily through his nose and closed his eyes. "Never trust anyone," he repeated and paused for a moment as he scrutinised the bloody face before him. "I know you're scared Carl, I would be too if our positions were reversed, but this can all be over in a very short amount of time if you answer a couple more questions."

Richards remained silent and blood continued to fall from the corner of his mouth and onto his shirt.

"Do you have a family Carl?" Hellam asked.

Richards' eyes widened. For the first time, his terror was mixed with anger. "Don't go near my family. I'll kill you Hellam, I swear to God."

Hellam smiled, "I won't need to go anywhere near them if you answer my final question truthfully. I can be honest with you Richards; there is little point in bullshitting you about this. It is far too late to save yourself, but I can make it quick and if you answer truthfully I won't go near your family; you have my word."

Hellam stood up and stared down at the beaten man by his feet. "Have you handed any incriminating evidence about my business practices over to your superiors?"

Richards stared up at Hellam but said nothing for a moment.

"Remember," Hellam continued, "We will have no trouble in finding your real name Carl."

Richards paused for a moment longer and glanced over to Kelser who stood behind Hellam then shook his head and turned his attention to the floor.

Hellam smiled and nodded, "Good."

He took slow, leisurely steps over to the other side of the room, using his gloved hand to brush away some dust from his long, black coat. "Go ahead," he finally said to Kelser.

Kelser walked over and placed a foot on Richards' shoulder. He pushed hard and Richards rolled over onto his back. Richards began breathing faster and struggled to move away, but it was a useless effort. Kelser pulled out his gun and without the slightest hesitation, fired a single shot into Richards' chest. Richards grunted and rolled over to his side again, his back to the other two men. He made an odd gurgling sound as he writhed on the concrete below. Several seconds passed as he grunted agonisingly. Kelser raised the gun to finish the job but Hellam approached and placed a hand on his arm, lowering it. He smiled as Kelser turned to him.

"You told him you'd make it quick," Kelser said in his usual monotone.

Hellam tore his eyes from the writhing body and looked up to Kelser. "I think I might have lied." His lips widened slowly.

Kelser nodded and turned back to Richards who continued to gurgle and grunt with pain.

Hellam watched in silence, alternating his gaze between the dying man and the killer, noting Kelser's calm, almost ambivalent expression as the life drained away from the man by his feet.

After several long minutes, Richards' movements slowed then, after one final release of air, his muscles appeared to loosen and relax as silence filled the room.

Hellam stared at Kelser, who was replacing the gun in his shoulder holster, and a satisfied pleasure washed over him.

My own private killer, he thought.

Kelser walked away from the dead body of Carl Richards and his boss grinned. Kelser didn't return the gesture; he just stared back with his emotionless, vacant expression.

"I'm going back to the office now. Will you require help to dispose of the body?" Hellam asked.

Kelser glanced down to Richards then shook his head.

Hellam took one final look at the body of the man who betrayed him, before leaving.

As he drove back to his office, Hellam thought about all the enemies that were out there, both known and unknown and how he required a man like Kelser for his ongoing survival. As his business practices expanded, the more enemies he would accumulate. Kelser was turning into a major asset and Hellam was becoming increasingly aware that he was the kind of man who could be involved in some of his more interesting business ventures.

Psychopath.

The word had fallen from the girls lips when she had

confronted him. Her eyes had been like huge discs, staring at him - disbelieving. The word had stopped Hellam for a moment as he absorbed it, but then it was gone. Now as he thought about it, it made a kind of beautiful sense.

As he parked up outside his building, the vacant, unfeeling expression on Kelser's face as he killed Richards flashed in his mind. He realised something that he had always suspected about the man - Kelser was like him.

Chapter 10

Lewis

Lewis wanted to speak to Craig Blaine. He was certain that, in some kind of bizarre way, his mind would only be put at ease if he made contact with the person accused of killing Hannah. But he also knew that he had almost no chance of making contact with him whilst he was being remanded in custody.

It was a warm morning and he walked along the street, gazing at the pavement in front of him as his mind meandered through a series of thoughts. He had questions that demanded answers but had no way of getting them. What had Hannah found out about her boyfriend? Who was her boyfriend? What did Craig Blaine have to do with all of this - if anything?

A bus rattled past and the scent of diesel filled the air around him. He coughed and stepped away from the road as he glanced across and saw the building which contained Hannah's flat. He hadn't realised his aimless wandering had brought him this far and he stared up as cars rushed past, between him and the place where she had died.

He thought for a moment about the conversation that he had with Kelly the week before, and remembered that she had told him that Craig lived in his flat with his mother. Lewis didn't move as he contemplated something, trying to work out if the idea was absurd or just a very simple solution to his problem. He gazed up at the building as the thought lingered.

It wouldn't be completely insane would it?

Finally, he looked down and turned his head until he found what he was looking for. He walked over to the shop and went inside.

When he emerged back onto the street, he was carrying a small notepad and pen and he walked briskly across the road to the entrance of the building.

Lewis took the stairs and went through a doorway into a long corridor. Hannah and Kelly had shared the flat at the end of the hallway and, as he walked slowly towards it, his eyes became fixed on the panelled wood of the door.

Behind that door was where it had happened.

He felt a wave of nausea as images conjured by his mind began to flash before him. He didn't want to think about Hannah's final moments, but as he approached the flat, he couldn't prevent the sickening sights and sounds from entering his mind. When he reached the door, he paused for a moment and stared at the wood then turned to his left and knocked on the door to the neighbouring flat.

After enough time had passed for Lewis to begin to think that there was nobody home, the sound of slow, shuffling footsteps were heard approaching from inside. There was the sound of light clinking as a chain was attached and then the door opened a fraction, creaking loudly on its hinges. A withered, wrinkled, and pale face stared through the gap.

"Yeah?" the woman inside said.

"Mrs Blaine?" Lewis asked, smiling.

"Yes, who are you?" Her voice was low and gruff; the sound of a life-long smoker and Lewis smelt the aroma of stale cigarettes drift out from inside the flat as he thought quickly - *my name?*

"My name is… John," Lewis said, an awkward stilt in his words.

"John?" Mrs Blaine said, eyeing him suspiciously.

"Yes, John… Lennon." He cringed inside as he said the words but tried not to let it show – *this was a bad idea.*

"John Lennon?" The old woman asked, the suspicion rising as she stared him up and down through narrowing eyes. "Like the Beatle?"

"Yes, I get that a lot," Lewis said, attempting to brush off the obvious. "Listen, I'm from the Surrington Post, I'm sorry to bother you Mrs Blaine but I was wondering if you had time to answer some questions for a report I'm doing about your son."

Mrs Blaine sighed hoarsely, "No comment," she said and went to close the door.

"Please wait for a second," Lewis said, leaning towards the gap.

The woman paused, her eyes narrowing further as she scrutinised the man before her.

"I'm not here to badger you about your son," he continued. "I'm here to present *your* side of things. All we've heard from the police is how your son was responsible for the terrible crime in that flat." He pointed his pen to the door of Hannah's flat. "They don't want to even discuss Craig's side the story."

"That's right; they've already decided he did it. Well let me tell you this Mr Lennon, my son ain't no murderer. He's been stitched up by those scum... he's completely innocent!" Her voice was rising and began to echo down the hallway.

"That is why I'm here. I want to make the public aware of Craig's side of things." Lewis felt a sudden guilt wash over him; he was giving this woman false hope.

Mrs Blaine looked Lewis up and down, her eyes still thin and suspicious, and she didn't speak for a moment. He began to feel uncomfortable in his role as local reporter and wondered if it was too late to abandon this madness.

"Okay, come in." She pushed the door shut and Lewis heard her unclip the chain, then it opened again. There was another loud squeak as the hinges protested violently. She turned her back to Lewis and began to shuffle down the corridor, towards the front room. Lewis felt the guilt again, but pushed it away as he entered the flat and closed the door behind him.

Lewis followed the elderly woman into the front room as the musty smell of ancient cigarettes enveloped him. At the time of their painting, the walls in the front room were presumably not intended to be the stained yellow that they now were. Mrs Blaine slumped down in a prehistoric chair which bore stained, torn fabric, and pulled an ashtray, which was sitting on the table beside her, a little closer.

"Sit over there," she said abruptly, pointing towards an equally tired sofa.

Lewis nodded and sat down as he removed the

notepad from his pocket.

"How long have you and your son lived here?" he asked, glancing around the room.

A thick layer of dust was sitting lazily on the wooden mantelpiece which housed several small photographs. Lewis could see that the one nearest to him showed a large man standing with his arm around the woman who was sitting in the room with him now. They were on a beach somewhere. Lewis realised he was staring at a picture of the man who may have killed Hannah and his stomach tightened. He guessed the man was around 6'5" tall as he dwarfed his mother. He wasn't drastically overweight for his height but was thick set and there was a slight protrusion around his gut. His smile was broad and covered the width of his face but his mother bore a vacant expression and didn't even appear to be staring into the lens of the camera.

"Erm..." Mrs Blaine said and Lewis turned back to her. She pulled out a cigarette from a packet on the table, and lit it as her eyes moved around the room. "...Well, I suppose it must be about thirty years now. I moved here after my husband left - Craig was eleven when we moved in."

Lewis nodded and scribbled some lines in his notepad that were nothing more than indecipherable squiggles.

"What does your son do for a living?" Lewis was skirting around the reason for his visit, but he didn't want to appear too eager.

"Unemployed, he's a lazy little sod - lazy an' stupid. Not many people would employ someone like him. What is it they say about him? He's a little *slow*." Mrs Blaine emphasised the last word and then sucked on her cigarette, releasing the cloud upwards towards the ceiling, the way some people do to make them feel as if they're being considerate. She paused and glared at Lewis. "But he's no bloody murderer!"

Lewis nodded, and again scribbled something insignificant down in his notepad. It was becoming apparent that this woman didn't have a particularly high opinion of her son and Lewis glanced back to the photo. He wondered if the outward innocence and sincerity of Craig's smile in the picture could hide something more sinister.

"How do you know your son wasn't responsible for the murder Mrs Blaine?"

She took another drag on her cigarette as she shuffled in her seat.

"Because he was here with me. He hardly ever goes out an' leaves me in peace, except for the pub; he goes there now an' again. He's always around... he's been a burden on me since the day he was born, that boy."

She shuffled on her chair again, as if there was something uncomfortable underneath the cushion, and leaned forward, pushing the weight onto her legs and easing herself up with a grunt. She walked over to the mantelpiece and picked up one of the other photographs.

"Here," she said, handing the dusty frame to Lewis. "That was taken when he was twenty."

Lewis studied the photo which showed Craig standing in the room in which Lewis was now sitting. He wore a supermarket uniform and bore the same, huge smile as on the other picture.

"That was his first day at the first job he ever had," the old woman continued, moving back to her chair and stubbing the cigarette out in the ashtray. "Twenty years old an' that was his first day at work! And do you know how long it lasted? Less than three weeks before he quit. He told me he had been fired, the lazy little sod, but I found out that he had just handed in his notice." She pulled out another cigarette from the packet and lit it before repeating her earlier phrase. "He's been a burden on me since the day he was born, that boy."

"So Craig was in the flat with you all night?" Lewis said, trying to get back on track but Mrs Blaine didn't seem to hear the question.

"And you see all this mess that's going on now? Craig in custody because they think he killed someone? God knows what people in the other flats are saying about him... and *me*. He's been such a disappointment to me."

Lewis realised that Mrs Blaine probably didn't have too many people to talk to about her problems and was taking advantage of the opportunity he had given her to unload them.

"Mrs Blaine, please!" he said firmly. She stopped and turned to him with a subtle expression of shock. "I'm sorry," Lewis continued. "But if we could just get back on track."

"Well ask me some sensible questions then."

Lewis placed the photo back on the mantelpiece and returned to his seat. "What does Craig say happened that night?"

Mrs Blaine shook her head slightly, as if it was inconsequential what her son thought.

"He was in with me all night. I know that for a fact because he and I watched TV. I didn't go to bed until late an' if he had left, I would have heard him. Our front door squeaks like you wouldn't believe."

Lewis remembered the sound of the door from earlier.

"He's too lazy to oil those bloody hinges," she said, glancing over to the picture again. "Anyway, when we found out about the murder next door, he told me that he had heard someone walk down the hall outside that night. He said he got out of bed and looked through the spy hole. He said he saw two men standing outside that woman's door... you know the murdered girl."

Lewis glanced down to his notepad, trying to ignore the fact that this woman didn't even seem to know Hannah's name.

"Hannah Jacobs," he said quietly.

"That's it. Anyway Craig watched them for a moment, but they didn't knock on the door for a long time. Eventually one of them knocked, but by then Craig had lost interest and went back to bed."

"Didn't the police follow up on this?"

Mrs Blaine scrutinised Lewis again for a moment as smoke drifted from her nostrils. "You think Craig didn't ask them to? They weren't interested, they said that these men didn't even exist and Craig had made it all up."

"Did Craig say what the men looked like?" Lewis asked.

Mrs Blaine shrugged. "Yes, something like average height, average build... you know the usual. He did say that one of them had quite long hair. Blonde and straggly, he said. Oh and he mentioned that when the man went to knock on the door, he noticed that his little finger was stubby, you know, like the end of it had been cut off or something."

Lewis thought about this for a second but was

interrupted when Mrs Blaine began to speak again.

"He told me that he'd seen that man somewhere before, the one with the blonde hair and stubby finger. He mentioned something about recognising him from somewhere," she paused as she inhaled more nicotine and leaned forward. She lowered her voice, as if there were secret microphones positioned underneath her ashtray, waiting for the valuable piece of information she was about to impart. "I can't think where he would have seen him though. He only ever goes to the shop round the corner for the shopping... well there an' the pub, like I said." She paused and sucked deeply on the cigarette. "Yes... yes, now I think about it, I suppose he could have known him from the pub."

"What pub is that?" Lewis asked.

"The Golden Anchor, about a mile from here. Craig goes in there for a beer from time to time."

Lewis made a note in the pad, the first legible piece of writing he had made since arriving. He wasn't sure why he made the note; the description the old woman had given him had been based on second hand information and wasn't particularly detailed in any case. But it was something. He wrote down the name of the pub and then put a note next to it about the little finger and straggly blonde hair.

"What about the other man? Did he say anything about him to you?"

"Nothing really... something about a tattoo on his arm - it was of a bird or something I think he said. He only saw it briefly through the spy hole you see. You'd have to ask him yourself about that, I really can't remember. But all that doesn't really matter now anyway." She sighed and leaned back in her chair. "The police say that Craig made it all up. They tested his DMA and it matched some blood that was under the girl's fingernails."

Lewis frowned for a moment before realising she meant to say, *DNA*.

"Craig had a big scratch on his neck you see and the police asked him where he got it. He told them that some woman was pestering him on the street the night before when he was coming home from the shops. He didn't know who she was, but said it wasn't... the girl... you know... Hannah. He said this woman kept asking him rude things, offering him things for money, you know..." Mrs Blaine stubbed out her second cigarette as Lewis listened. He watched as her hand immediately went back to the packet, but she didn't remove another one this time. She just held the small box in her lap, as if it was some kind of security blanket, as she continued to speak. "She was some whore you see. Craig said that he kept refusing and pushed her away but then she got angry an' pulled his hair then scratched him and ran off. He said it hurt really badly and his neck was bleeding as he walked back up to the flat. That was how he got the scratches. But of course, the police didn't believe that, especially when they tested his DMA and it matched what was under that girl's nails."

Lewis scribbled more lines in his pad, outlining what he had just been told and churned it over in his mind.

"Make sure you write all this in your paper Mr Lennon," the old woman said, restlessly turning the packet of cigarettes in her hands. "My boy's slow and lazy, but he ain't no murderer."

Lewis nodded and closed the notepad. "Thank you for talking to me Mrs Blaine. I'll... I might be in touch."

He got up and went to shake her hand, but she had already turned away and had begun to light a third cigarette.

"You can let yourself out right?" she said through tight lips which held the latest cigarette in place.

"Of course."

Lewis turned and walked from the room. He opened the door which creaked loudly and shut it behind him. He glanced at Hannah's door one more time, before turning and leaving.

Chapter 11

Hannah, April 2001

The trees blurred as they rushed past the train window. Hannah Jacobs stared out, leaning her head against the glass as the sun bathed the passing fields in a beautiful yellow glow. She glanced down to her watch. The train had been delayed and she was going to be arriving later than she had hoped, but that didn't really matter; she was too excited to let something like that matter. It was a spur of the moment trip - a sudden impulse had taken her hostage and had forced her to go to the train station. This wasn't completely out of character for Hannah, but she had still felt equal degrees of apprehension and exhilaration as she purchased the ticket that morning.

She should have been studying for an exam that she had in two days, but that could wait she told herself as she pulled a small book from her bag. The book was bound in pale brown leather and had a tiny gold clasp to fasten it shut. On the cover was a picture of a single rose. She opened it and flicked through the various entries she had made in the diary since purchasing it, two years earlier. She turned to the end of the filled pages and read the letter that she had drafted earlier that morning, before deciding on her journey. She read the words she had used in the letter - words such as 'hope' and 'love', but they came across as trite and overly sentimental. Hannah wrote them on a whim after waking, but they didn't really express how she truly felt; the exception perhaps being the last sentence.

'I love you.'

She knew that the letter didn't read correctly, and wasn't written in the way she usually spoke, so she had been compelled to make the journey. She would see him in person to tell him.

Hannah already suspected that he felt the same way, but they had a close friendship, which paradoxically made expressing something like wanting to be together all the more difficult. She couldn't explain why and didn't try to over think it either.

She read the letter three times, before closing the diary and placing it back in her bag. The train slowed as it pulled into the station. Hannah got up from her seat and stepped out, onto the platform. It was busy and she jostled her way through, looking for the exit. After negotiating her way through the crowd and up the stairs, she left the platform, walked through the station and stepped out onto the street. There was a line of waiting taxis outside and Hannah gave one of the driver's the address for Lewis's halls of residence.

***

The carpet in the corridor was thin and worn down the centre. It was the same as the type of carpet that was used in most student accommodation; cheap and unfit for the huge amounts of traffic which it would inevitably have to carry. Hannah recognised it from her own accommodation, two hundred miles away.

She knocked on the door to Lewis's room and waited. She could hear loud music from a room further down the corridor and some of the other doors were open. Students were going in and out of each others rooms indifferently; it was a casual, aloof existence and privacy was something that was voluntarily handed in at the gates. This was, for most of the students, their first time of living away from home and they wallowed in the freedom it provided.

There was no reply, so Hannah knocked on the door again but was surprised when the door to the room next to Lewis's opened and a short, thin man stuck his head out.

"You looking for Lou?"

Lou?

"Lewis Foster, yes," Hannah replied.

The man was in his early twenties but his face was covered in large, red spots which, to Hannah, looked extremely painful. He raised a hand and slowly began to pick at a sore area on his forehead.

"Think he went out. He shouldn't have really; we've got a test tomorrow. I told him, but he wouldn't listen." The man pulled something from his skin, examined it and then threw it to the ground.

"Any idea where I could find him?" Hannah asked, trying to ignore his grotesque display.

The man rolled his eyes, "Hold on."

He stepped out of his room, wearing long shorts and no socks, and walked across the hall to the opposite door. He pounded hard on the wood.

"Aaron! Aaron!" he yelled as he continued to thump his fist.

The door opened suddenly and a large man with a shaved head answered.

"What the fuck is it? Jesus, I was sleeping!" Aaron rubbed his face with chubby fingers.

"She wants to know where Lou is," the first man replied, nodding his head in Hannah's direction.

"Erm..." Aaron frowned and dragged the back of his hand over his brow. "I think he said he was going down to Mindi's Bar with Abby... yeah I'm sure that was it."

"Thank you," Hannah said. "You couldn't tell me how to get there could you?"

Aaron sighed and then gave her directions to the bar. He said it was only a ten minute walk.

Hannah thanked them both again and left the building. She followed Aaron's directions and found the place easily in spite of the exterior being narrow and set back from the main line of surrounding establishments. She stepped inside and the small entrance opened out into a huge area which was filled with people talking loudly, over even louder music. From the outside, Mindi's Bar looked like an ancient, rundown pub, but inside it was fitted with shiny metal surfaces and abstract art hung on the plain brick walls. There was a small dance floor over to one side, but it was early afternoon and so was empty; waiting for the evening to arrive when the lamps would be dimmed and flashing lights would encourage people to fill it.

Hannah walked through the bar, craning her neck, searching for Lewis as she held her bag close to her side. A man, who was carrying three drinks, knocked into her and the alcohol sloshed in the glasses, splashing onto her top.

"Sorry," Hannah said, but the man just frowned as he pushed past. Hannah glared at him for a second before continuing.

She managed to make her way to the bar and leaned against it as she looked around. After a few minutes and still no sign of Lewis, she was about to give up, assuming that Aaron had been mistaken. But then she glanced further down and saw him.

He was standing, back to the bar, holding a bottle of beer. His hair was longer than the last time she had seen him and it looked as though he was cultivating the beginnings of a beard, but she recognised him immediately. She smiled and called his name, but the music was too loud and he was too far away. She moved closer, manoeuvring herself around the frustrated people who were waiting to be served, and approached him. When she was ten feet away, she saw him stand upright and a broad smile opened up his face. She watched his eyes sparkle as a pretty, blonde woman came up to him. Hannah paused and watched as they said something to each other through wide lips and then leaned in. They kissed and Lewis put his arms around the woman, pulling her closer. When they separated, Hannah felt her own smile evaporate; carried away by the gathering hollowness inside.

She moved backwards, still watching as Lewis and his girlfriend spoke to each other. He ordered her a drink then they both walked over to a table where they sat down and held each other's hand. Hannah suddenly felt hot and she turned around. She walked through the crowd, towards the exit as a twisting knot tightened in her stomach.

The air was cool as Hannah stepped outside, the loud music falling away behind her and she walked briskly down the street. She felt a tear gather and fall from her eye, down her check, but it was brushed away with the back of her hand as swiftly as it had appeared. For a reason she couldn't quite understand, she smiled and forced a chuckle. It was almost an odd validation; she was being silly. Lewis wasn't someone for her to own; he had his own life. Of course he had a girlfriend, why wouldn't he? Hannah had woken up that morning with an intention to do something, and in her own mind she had idealised it. It suddenly appeared so obvious now that it could never have happened the way she had hoped - it was a fantasy.

She wandered the city for a while; stopping for a coffee after an hour or so and watching the sky grow dark. People began to appear on the streets, ready for their night out and Hannah took this as a cue for her to leave. She caught a taxi back to the train station and, after waiting for half an hour, boarded the next train home. Her carriage was almost empty, apart from an elderly couple sitting further down.

She watched the same trees and fields pass by her window in reverse, this time silhouetted against the mellow light from a half-moon. She pulled the small, leather bound diary from her bag again and flicked to the letter she had written to Lewis that morning. She read it again, through eyes which were only a few hours older, but years wiser. Carefully pulling at the paper, she tore the letter from the book and folded it into quarters then pushed it underneath the leather that enclosed the rear cover. After placing the diary back in her bag, Hannah allowed her head to fall against the seat and she closed her eyes.

Chapter 12

Hellam

Hellam listened to the hum of the TV in the background as he read the newspaper and was sitting in the huge, leather sofa in the front room of his house. The article he was reading was positioned in the mid-section, but filled half a page.

'Local businessman and philanthropist donates over £2m to charity.'

There was a large photograph of Joseph Hellam standing outside the school to which he had recently donated £50,000. The story highlighted Hellam's charitable contributions over the years and praised him for all the good work he had done for the local community in Surrington.

He smiled quietly to himself as he read the article and absorbed every mention of his name, reading certain passages several times. He felt a warm sense of pleasure rise through his stomach, but the sense of wellbeing wasn't acquired by how much good he had done, or how generous he had been, or even that he was finally getting recognition for all his charitable donations. It was from one, simple thought that overwhelmed all others:

How easily they were fooled.

He knew that he had a higher than average intelligence, but this article had fed his self-satisfaction and perhaps, he thought idly to himself, he was a genius. The way he separated his legitimate and criminal business practices was a work of unequalled brilliance in his opinion. Here he was, being openly praised for his philanthropy and the simple fact that he had fooled them all gave him something he could treasure - the knowledge that he was *better* than them.

He finished the article quickly, ignoring the final paragraph which mentioned an investigation into his business by the police seven years ago, linking him by several degrees of separation to organised crime networks. The investigation had fallen flat when all ties had been severed and covered up months before the police had gained access to any incriminating files.

Hellam knew they were still watching him closely, as Carl Richards had proven, but he was careful and had contacts within the police who would keep him informed.

Psychopath...

That word again. The thought suddenly fizzed and crackled in Hellam's mind unexpectedly, taking him by surprise. That was what the girl had said to him. No one had called him that before and Hellam had given his own psychological profile very little thought before she uttered that word. He had always known that he thought differently from most people, but to him that was just an advantage he had over others which he could use for manipulation and control. But since that day, he had found himself dissecting his innermost thoughts more and more: why didn't he really care for anybody else?

When he was younger, he thought that everyone was the same and they were simply pretending to be upset or affected when someone close to them had suffered some serious injury, or even died. He simply couldn't comprehend how they truly felt pain when something bad happened to somebody else. It didn't affect them directly; they weren't being harmed, so why should they care? It had been only later that he had realised that these people really did *feel* things that he could not; and that realisation gave him a tremendous advantage over them.

'These people are real, they're being murdered... my god, you're a psychopath,' was what she had said.

The words buzzed around his head for a while as he thought of the girl. Her name was Hannah and they had met a few months before she had found the snuff films on his laptop. He couldn't allow her to live after seeing them; she would have eventually told the police and Hellam wouldn't allow them to start sniffing around again.

But one thing stuck in Hellam's mind from the night Hannah had found those films; her emotional outburst towards him was something that he found himself regurgitating and analysing again and again. It was such a pure reaction of horror, disbelief and incomprehension. It still amazed him that she could feel all of these things and express them with such unreserved passion. She didn't know those people and even if she did, it was *them* being murdered, not *her*.

Of course he knew the learned protocols which could guide him through how 'normal' people thought and could use these to present a false image of himself. He too could be outraged at the suffering in third-world countries when the reports were on the news, or even produce false tears as he saw the innocent victims of 9/11 fall to their deaths as they jumped from the twin towers in order to avoid the horrific fires behind. But the simple truth was he felt nothing.

It was after Hannah had said that word to him that Hellam had glanced through an article on the internet describing psychopathic and sociopathic behaviour and discovered that perhaps she had been correct in her impromptu psychoanalysis. But even this fact didn't particularly concern him; it just gave him a word for what made him different; a difference of which he was more than accepting. It was because of that difference that gave him such power over people. When push came to shove, he could turn and walk away without a single shred of remorse for his actions or empathy for those he had destroyed.

Hannah had learned that, he thought to himself quietly and his lips momentarily expanded. He took a sip from the drink that was resting on the table, before opening the newspaper again and reading the article through from the beginning.

***

The small, porcelain face of the girl stared up with open, shimmering eyes as she rested in George Langton's arms. The eyes were moist; water had gathered at the corners as her huge, dilated pupils gazed through him. A few seconds earlier, those eyes had been darting around the room as Langton tightly held a hand over her mouth. She had jerked herself violently in an attempt to break free and that had forced him to place his arm around her neck, dragging her backwards and they had both fallen onto the floor. He had held her like that for a few minutes until her struggling limbs had fallen limp. Langton had slackened his own grip and pulled her up, holding her gently in his arms, convinced that she had simply fallen unconscious. But then he had seen those eyes. They had glazed over so quickly as the life had evaporated from them.

Langton could see red blotches surrounding the irises, where tiny capillaries had burst, releasing the scarlet fluid into an ocean of white. He screamed as he stared down at her, his own terrified reflection gazing back at him from the black marble pupils.

He woke up, still screaming. He jerked upright and stared around at the darkness of his bedroom. The thin bed sheets were wet with perspiration and stuck to his clammy skin. He wrenched them away, throwing them to the floor then got up and began to pace the room, heavy gasps escaping from his lungs as he rubbed his trembling hands together. He could feel his heart pounding in his chest, but as the image of the dead girl faded, he felt it slow and breathed a deep sigh.

This wasn't the first time he had experienced the nightmare - not by a long-shot; when he wasn't haunted by the dead eyes of the girl during the day, they haunted him at night. Sometimes in his nightmares, she came back to life and spoke to him. She asked him why he had killed her, but Langton could never answer that question – it seemed to him like it was a question without an answer.

He flicked on the light and went down the hall to the kitchen. He pushed a glass under the water dispenser of his fridge and gulped the cool liquid down in one. He placed the glass on the side as he took another deep sigh.

What's done is done, he told himself, *it's in the past now George, forget about it.*

But that was part of the problem – he couldn't forget. The man who wrote him those letters, Concerned Citizen, wouldn't allow that to happen. C.C. had found out about what Langton had done, Christ knew how, but he had found out nevertheless, and had exploited that knowledge. Why C.C. wanted the documents which he had asked Langton to copy for him over the years was something Langton also didn't have an answer for. But that was a question which had seemed to grow far less significant as the years passed. Langton could only guess what the documents were being used for; evidence against Hellam was obvious. But who would require that evidence over a period of years? Like an earthquake, the revelation unexpectedly rumbled through him.

Carl Richards...

Langton hit the kitchen work surface with the palm of his hand as the pieces of the jigsaw came together. Why hadn't he thought of that before? He had found out that Richards was an undercover police officer almost a week earlier. It seemed so obvious now; it must have been Richards who had been blackmailing him all along. He had obviously been desperate to gain access to documents detailing Hellam's criminal organisations.

Langton felt a wave of relief wash over him and a spontaneous smile appeared. Richards was dead now; he was certain of that. Hellam would have had no choice but to dispatch him after discovering who he was. Did that mean that the evidence had also died? Langton thought about this for a moment and these thoughts began to disintegrate the relief he had felt just seconds earlier.

Carl Richards had only been working for Hellam for the past few months, yet Langton had received the first letter from C.C. years ago. Langton supposed that he could have been working the case for up to a year before beginning his undercover work – but for up to four years? That didn't seem right.

Then there was the blackmailing itself. If Richards really was the man responsible for the letters *and* he really was an undercover police officer, then how did he find out about the girl? Surely, as soon as a police officer found evidence that it had been Langton who had killed her; he would have been arrested immediately; not simply used as a source to get at the shady activities of his employer.

Langton shook his head and frowned. No, it simply didn't make sense for his blackmailer to have been a member of the police, and that discounted Richards altogether.

He picked up the glass and poured some more water then he carried it back to the bedroom. He placed it on the bedside table, got back into bed and flicked off the light. He leaned back on his arms and gazed up, through the blackness, and thought.

The image of the girl formed in the ripples of his mind once again, like a reflection in water regaining its clarity after a pebble had broken the surface. Langton closed his eyes as he thought about that day.

It had been almost twenty years ago. Langton and his wife had been living on the street for a couple of years, having moved there when Langton had been dismissed from the school he had been working at in Surrington. He had been a secondary school teacher in that life and the circumstances for his dismissal were such that he felt it wise to move away for a while. He had managed to convince his wife that the move was a good idea and they had made the one-hundred mile journey to the small village of Alderidge in Somerset. Langton managed to find work as a freelance accountant, finally using the degree he had gained several years before.

Working from home, George Langton and his wife settled down and enjoyed life in the small village. They got on well with the people who lived on the street and would often attend the dinner parties that were arranged by their neighbours. The street was small and quiet with only seven other families, in houses which sat on spacious plots of land.

Langton had been living in Alderidge for two years when Michelle Layne, a thirteen-year-old girl from the house next to his, had knocked at his door. It was a Thursday, just after lunch, and the street was quiet as he opened the door. He knew Michelle quite well and had been to a New Years Eve party with her parents the previous year.

"Hello Michelle, what is it?" Langton had asked, smiling pleasantly at the girl.

"Sorry Mr Langton, but I've been locked out of my house, my parents aren't home. I wondered if I could come in and call my dad's work?"

"Of course, come in." Langton had opened the door wide and closed it behind her when she stepped into the hall. "Shouldn't you be in school today?"

Michelle frowned at him, as if he had lost his mind. "No, it's the summer holidays."

Langton had nodded and smiled again, feeling idiotic for not knowing. But he didn't have any children of his own, so he often forgot about the timetable which the schools kept to. He led her into the lounge.

"I was round my friend's house today," Michelle continued. "I was going to be there all day but we had an argument and I decided to come home. Only, like an idiot, I forgot my stupid key!" She slapped her head and smiled.

Langton laughed and pointed to the sofa. Michelle walked over and sat down towards the far end, next to the small table where the telephone was sitting. He watched her carefully as she moved across and sat down. He walked over and pulled the telephone closer.

"You know his number?" Langton asked, moving in closer to the girl.

"Y...yes," Michelle said, frowning again as he leaned over her.

"Don't be nervous Michelle."

As Langton lay in his bed with his eyes closed and thought about that terrible day, he tried to convince himself that he couldn't remember what happened next. But the truth was he could remember it all too well.

There had been glancing contact with the skin on her leg, perfectly innocent, Langton had told himself - a slight brush with the back of his hand - nothing untoward. But the expression on Michelle's face had told him that she thought it had been anything but innocent. She had looked shocked and had stood up, moving away from him. She had said something, but he could only remember one word - 'inappropriate'. He remembered the word well because he hadn't expected a thirteen-year-old to say such a thing. It was a word that had forced old memories to rise inside; regurgitated from a mind that had desperately tried to forget them.

They were memories of his time at the school back in Surrington, when he had been called in for a meeting with the headmaster. The headmaster had said the same word when he told Langton that he was being dismissed. He had said that his behaviour with the students was *inappropriate* and he had no choice. He had said that such behaviour was very embarrassing for the school so he wouldn't put anything specific in the report. That time Langton had got away with it, but as he had looked at Michelle staring back at him with her eyes wide and mouth open, he had realised that this time he wouldn't be so lucky. He had got up and stepped closer to her, she had screamed so he put his hand over her mouth and squeezed tightly. He now told himself that she hadn't given him any other choice; he was only trying to keep her quiet until she calmed down and then he could have explained his actions.

But how could he have explained? He had to keep her silent... he had to stop her from telling her parents. But he had only touched her leg hadn't he? Perhaps there had been more to it than that he conceded, but buried the thoughts, desperately trying to excuse what he had done.

Langton sat up in his bed again. Sleep wouldn't visit him again tonight. He tried to stop his mind going over that day again and again. It was as if his own brain was torturing him for what he had done to that girl; victimising him for what was, after all, an accident.

Was it an accident? Langton had convinced himself over

the years that he was no murderer, he didn't want Michelle to die, but she just wouldn't stop screaming, she wouldn't... she just wouldn't stop. But he had *made* her stop.

After he realised that Michelle Layne was dead, Langton had panicked. He had paced the room, mumbling to himself about how he hadn't meant for it to happen - how he was a good man and that it was her own fault for knocking on his door.

He had glanced out of the window, up and down the street. Had anyone seen her come in? He wasn't sure, but suspected not. It was a quiet street and everyone else would have been at work. He thought about how he should handle the situation. He felt guilt flood his veins and contemplated calling the police to hand himself in. But George Langton, the man he knew only too well, was a coward and realised that confessing to such an act was something he would not be capable of. He had decided it was necessary to get rid of her.

As he fought the memories of that day from his mind, he flicked on the light switch next to his bed again and looked at the clock: 3.47am. He sighed and rubbed his eyes. He got up, went into the lounge and turned on the TV. He put on a news channel and let the reporter's words flow through him, as he absorbed nothing.

Langton had buried the body in his own garden, and in broad daylight. His garden was protected by large, thick trees and bushes and there were very few houses capable of seeing in. The single house that was visible was at the back and Langton was sure that even if there was a person staring out, they would only be able to see part of the lawn. He could avoid anyone seeing from that house by moving carefully around the perimeter, using the bushes for cover.

He had considered the potentially idiotic act of burying a body in his own garden, but stared up to the far end. He and his wife had already paid for the large area of slabs which would replace the grassy hill at the top of their garden. It was going to be the base for a large shed and the men had been booked to lay the patio the following week.

Langton had carried Michelle, carefully edging around the side of the garden and laid her tiny body underneath a bush while he went to fetch a spade. He had dug deep in the soil beside the bush, which was going to be ripped up before the patio was laid. He had made the hole as deep as he could manage, until he was certain that he had gone far enough down. He had placed her in the hole, never looking directly at her pale skin and, with sweat pouring from his brow, filled it as quickly as he could.

The disappearance of Michelle Layne had been a huge story, making it into the headlines nationwide. A large-scale search had been undertaken by the local police force, with hundreds of volunteers helping in the surrounding areas. George Langton had even been one of the volunteers, along with his wife and the rest of the residents on their street. The police had interviewed him, just as they had everyone else who lived close by. If Langton's previous history at the school in Surrington had been known, then he would have been at the top of the list of suspects, after all he lived next door to the missing girl. But the real reason for his dismissal had never been put in any official reports and his indiscretions had never been reported to the police; they had no reason to suspect the concerned man next door who was volunteering his own time to help find the missing girl.

Langton had rested more easily after the patio had been laid, and relaxed even more as the weeks slowly passed by. Langton's new shed was erected on a Saturday morning, while six-feet below, under slabs and cement, Michelle Layne rested, never to be found.

As the years passed by, the knowledge that the dead girl was buried in his garden had eaten into Langton. Both he and his wife eventually moved back to Surrington and he found employment in a new business, H.K. Communications, owned by a man called Joseph Hellam. A couple of years after that, Langton's wife found out about an affair he was having and had left him.

George Langton sat upright in his lounge and turned off the TV, using the remote control. He placed his face in his hands and rubbed the skin with his fingers, digging his nails in hard. He knew the face of Michelle Layne would never leave him now; he would be forever haunted by her glazed, dead eyes. But he knew he deserved worse than that, much worse. He got up and went back to the bedroom, where he was certain he would lie awake until his alarm buzzed at 6.30am.

***

Sarah Price pulled a sweater over her head as the door to her flat was closed. She got up from her bed, taking the money from the bedside table, and walked over to a set of drawers. She plucked a cigarette from a packet that was resting on top and lit it. She ran a hand through her tangled, brown hair as she took a long drag of tobacco and glanced in the mirror - something she hated to do. As the white smoke circled her head, she looked at the blotchy, gaunt face staring back at her. She scrutinised a red spot on her forehead and rubbed a finger over it then used a pad to rub some more foundation on her face in an attempt to conceal the blemish.

The room began to fill with smoke so she went over to the window, opened it wide and stood there, blowing white mist into the breeze. Some clients didn't like the smell of smoke and her next one would be arriving in half-an-hour. He was new and the new ones always made her nervous; she never knew what to expect. Sometimes they would be polite and gentle, occasionally nervous themselves. Other times they treated her like a piece of dirt which they had scraped from underneath their fingernails.

Sarah finished the cigarette and stubbed it out on the windowsill then walked over to the drawers again. She opened the second drawer and slid some clothes sideways, revealing a small steel moneybox. She carefully lifted it out as if it were a delicate flower and rested it silently on the wooden surface. She couldn't stop the smile from making an appearance on her face as she opened it and saw the modest bundle of cash. She placed her latest fee on top, admired it for a moment and then placed it back in the drawer, careful to conceal it underneath her clothes. She knew that anyone interested in robbing her of the money wouldn't have a tough time finding it, but she had been in the business for too long to be worried. She could read people well and was confident at assessing them before inviting them in. Anyone who, in her opinion, didn't look right wouldn't make it through the door.

She was making good money and could afford to turn away the occasional John who seemed a little too odd; at least that had been true for the past few years. Lately however, she had found herself taking silly risks, going against her better judgement just to get the cash. She had a plan and the cash was a vital part of the preparation. She went back to her bed and lay down, resting her eyes as she thought quietly to herself.

Sarah was 34-years-old and had been working the job for almost three years - a long time to be doing what she did, and she knew she wouldn't be able to last much longer. She hated her life at the moment and the only thing that kept her trying to survive to the next day was the knowledge that soon she would be back with her daughter. Cassie had been taken away from her over a year ago by Sarah's own mother after she found out about the circumstances in which her daughter had been living. Truth be told, Sarah didn't fight too hard to keep Cassie; she loved her daughter but knew that her life would be doomed if she remained with her.

Sarah had never been forced to start taking the drugs, much as she tried to convince herself that was the case, but an old boyfriend had first introduced her to the lifestyle. She followed the well worn path that so many in her situation walked. She started smoking marijuana after going out at weekends then, as the months progressed, her boyfriend slowly introduced the harder drugs. Taking pills to make the nights out more fun had been okay, but each step had led her all too easily to the next one. It had been Heroin that had dealt the knockout blow. She had tried it a few times with her friends, but after her boyfriend left her, she found herself relying on it far too much.

She used alone, knocking herself into the melancholy haze it expertly induced while she was by herself in the flat. After she made a stupid mistake one night by having a one night stand, she found out that she was pregnant. She lost her job in a supermarket and resented turning to her family for support. She couldn't bare the self congratulatory looks they would give her as they dished out the desperate variations of the usual line, 'We told you so'.

Money had been tight, but she survived for a while on the benefit payments she received. She had reduced her Heroin intake during her pregnancy, helped in part by the fact that she simply couldn't afford it, and Cassie had been born healthy. But money had been tighter than ever and the cravings didn't seem to wane. Money was so tight it had eventually reached the point where Sarah felt she simply had no choice but to take the final step.

The first time still gave her nightmares. The client had paid up, but Cassie had been screaming from the next room for the whole time. After they were finished and she had shown the customer out of the flat, Sarah began crying too as she comforted her young daughter.

And so the cycle had begun.

Sarah found that she could once again afford the drugs and her life descended into a macabre spiral of self destruction. She tried to do the best for her daughter but didn't fool herself - she wasn't just ruining her own life, she was also tearing apart her daughter's. When Sarah's mother had shown up by surprise one day and discovered what was happening, she didn't hesitate in taking her granddaughter into her own care. Even in her semi drugged-up state, Sarah couldn't bear what was happening, but at the same time welcomed the fact that her daughter would be escaping the car crash her life had become.

That had been fourteen months ago and as Sarah lay on her bed, she glanced down at the healing track marks on her arm and thought about where her life was now. She had called her mother six-months ago and had been allowed to speak to Cassie on the phone. She told her how much she missed her and couldn't wait to see her again. But Sarah's mother made it clear that that wouldn't happen unless she cleaned herself up and got off the drugs.

That had been the incentive that Sarah found she needed. It was difficult, sometimes reaching points where she felt so unbearably low that she had considered ending it all. There had been multiple scenarios running through her mind; how would each method of suicide feel and was there truly a painless death? But as the months passed by and she used less and less, the lethargy and depression had receded.

As she rubbed her arm and waited for her next client to arrive, Sarah glanced at the calendar on her wall. She had been clean for almost three months now and that was an accomplishment that at one point in her life would have seemed impossible. She had been saving money for many months, planning to move back to where she had grown up, close to where her parents still lived and close to Cassie. She had managed to claw her way out of part of the nightmare in which she had been living for the past few years, but she still had to make the final leap. When she had saved enough money to make the move and hopefully find a nice place close to her parents, then she would perhaps be allowed to get Cassie back. She would find another job. Sarah was absolutely determined to sort out her life this time and the only incentive she required was her daughter. She would do it for her.

There was a loud knock from the door - two hard bangs - and Sarah turned around. She glanced in the mirror as she walked by and ran two fingers over her ear, pushing her hair backwards. Her looks had declined over the years, thanks to the abuse she had forced on her body, but she still felt confident enough in her own skin to accept her shortcomings. This was a new customer so she wanted to impress to a certain extent; a repeat client could ensure her an income and she wouldn't have to put up with breaking in any others. She pushed her prettiest smile onto her face and opened the door.

"Hello," she said as she gestured the man into her room.

As he passed by her, she eyed him carefully and slowly closed the door. He was tall; well over six feet and muscular. He didn't make eye contact with her as he passed, but glanced around the room, pushing his cheeks upwards, as if to smile but not quite completing the expression.

"Take a seat." Sarah forced herself to look him in the eye and brush his arm gently.

The man nodded and went over to the bed. "Your name is Sarah?"

"Yes, and yours?" she replied, sitting next to him, placing her hand on his knee and crossing her legs towards him.

The man glanced down to her hand and smiled a smile that nauseated her. His yellow teeth protruded from widening lips and his breath washed over her face. It resembled a pungent mixture of coffee, cigarettes and stagnant water.

"Hal," the man replied, running the back of his hand over his nose and wiping it on his jeans.

Sarah smiled at him, feeling a familiar unease in her stomach and she turned her head away from his to get some fresh air. She thought about her daughter and forced herself to continue the act she was so well rehearsed in.

"I like that name. What do you want me to do?"

Hal's smile broadened into a sickening grin as he ran his tongue along his stained teeth. He put an arm around her and pulled her close. She felt the unease rising, but tried to prevent herself from pulling away.

"Tell me about yourself first," he said, leaning forward and kissing her neck.

Sarah winced as his lips ran along her neck and she involuntarily shuffled away. He looked up and she noticed his expression had changed, as if she had offended him by moving away.

"Okay," she said, smiling her most convincing smile yet. "I'm 26," she lied, "And I love big tall guys like you." She moved closer, but he pushed her away.

"Don't give me the bullshit. Tell me about yourself for real."

Sarah blinked, the unease inside made another lurch and she almost felt like ending it and throwing the guy out. But she knew it wouldn't be as simple as that. Sometimes, with men like him, it was easier to just see it through and avoid the confrontation. She had already decided that she wouldn't be seeing him again after tonight.

"Okay," she smiled and put her hand on his knee again. He seemed to relax. "I'm 34, I live here alone and I'm just trying to make a living."

"There," he said, putting an arm around her again. "Was that so hard?"

Sarah shook her head.

"Do you have family around here?" he asked.

This was an odd question and one that she had never been asked before. She wondered what the correct response would be to give, but in the end she couldn't really see what difference it would make so decided to tell the truth. "No, no ties," she winked and smiled again. "I'm all alone."

The man pulled her closer, his huge biceps squeezing her shoulders and Sarah glanced down, noticing the butterfly tattoo on his arm for the first time. She forced her gaze up, into his eyes. She felt sick, but disguised it expertly with yet another false smile. She knew that she wouldn't be able to maintain the act for much longer; she needed to get things moving. It soon became apparent that, that was also suddenly on her client's mind and he ran his hand up to the back of her head, grabbing her hair and pulling her closer.

"Get undressed," he whispered as his foul breath washed over her face again. Sarah didn't bother using her fake smile as she stood up and began to take off her clothes.

Chapter 13

Lewis

Lewis drove his car into the dusty car park and heard the gravel crunch beneath the tyres as he pulled up on the far side. It was a cool day and there were only a handful of other cars scattered around. As he got out, he felt a gust of wind roll in from the sea and noticed it gather up some of the dust from the floor. He walked around the back, opened the boot and pulled out a large cardboard box. He carried it out of the car park and onto a narrow gravel path.

It wasn't far, but the box weighed heavy in Lewis's arms by the time he finally reached the top of the hill. He sighed with relief as he placed it down on the grass by his feet and stared out at the calm, blue ocean below. It wasn't as sunny as it had been when he had come to the cliff with Hannah all those years ago, but the sun still broke through the clouds occasionally and he took in the view for a few moments.

The edge of the cliff was a few feet away and a new fence had been set up since the last time Lewis had been, preventing anyone from accidentally wandering too close. The fence posts were short and simply had a green wire mesh running between them, so it didn't hinder the view of the ocean. He could see a couple of boats on the horizon and watched them lumber along as he sucked in a lungful of the fresh sea air. After a while, he sat down on the grass and opened the box.

He had come straight from Hannah's parents' home. They had given him some of their daughter's possessions that they had sorted through, insisting that Lewis should be the one to have some of them to remember her by. He had taken the items, albeit with a lingering reluctance because he knew how hard it would be to go through them. But deep down he *wanted* to see these things, *her* things; possessions that she had touched and cared for.

He pulled out several books. There was a copy of To Kill a Mockingbird, her favourite novel, which bore the curled edges and broken spine of a book which had been loved too much. Lewis flicked through the pages and saw some of the handwritten notes in the margins; the book had been the copy she had studied from in her English class.

Second in the pile was a larger book with a hard cover which Lewis recognised instantly. He had seen Hannah recite endless facts from it when they were just children and, as he read the title, it brought a smile to his face: 'Exploring the Universe'. The book brought back many memories for him and he could picture Hannah's face light up as she tried to comprehend yet another amazing piece of information that the book had imparted. But there was a memory that seemed more vivid than the others.

It had been when they were just six or seven and they had both camped out in the back garden of Hannah's house. Ben had been there too. Lewis could recall the stars being especially bright that night and the cool air danced around them as they stood gazing up. The memory came with such ease and clarity as he sat on the grass, holding the book in his hands. He stared at the cover for a moment then turned back to the rest of the pile.

There were several more paperbacks but Lewis's attention was drawn to a small, padded book at the bottom of the stack. He separated it from the rest and looked at the soft, brown leather that enclosed the cover. His eyes wandered over the small gold clasp and the image of the single rose and he suddenly realised he was holding Hannah's diary. He had seen it before, but she had always been intensely private about the contents of that book. He held it for a few moments, staring in silence at the smoothness of the leather then he placed it on the grass beside him, his eyes still lingering on it for a while. He eventually forced them away and reached back inside the box.

His hand hit something hard and he picked up a small object, lifting it out but realising what it was before he caught sight of it. He turned it between his fingers before raising one end up and placing it to his eye. He pointed the object up at the bright blue sky and slowly rotated it, gazing at the semi transparent colours as they slowly realigned and seemed to absorb each other, changing from one shape into another. He lowered it slowly. Hannah must have decided to look after it when Ben no longer had any use for his favourite toy.

As he held the kaleidoscope, Lewis thought of the day

that Ben had been killed. Hannah's house had been bathed in silence as he entered and walked towards Hannah's room in little more than a daze. The news of what had happened to Ben had been told by his parents, but not properly absorbed by his young mind. He wanted to see Hannah to make sure she was okay; he could remember that feeling being overwhelming and he had been surprised by how powerful it was. He went over the back fence of the garden, as he always did, and entered her home through the rear patio doors. He walked slowly, noticing how loud his footsteps sounded on the hard kitchen floor; he had never noticed that sound before. As his feet hit the carpet of the hall, they were silenced and he glanced through the crack in the door to the front room, noticing Hannah's parents sitting in separate chairs and gazing ahead. They resembled statues; the only human part being their motionless eyes, gazing ahead, with sparkles of light reflecting vibrantly from the moisture they held. Lewis thought about entering the room, but couldn't bring himself to do so; what could he do or say that would help them now?

He stepped quietly away and climbed the stairs. Hannah's bedroom door was ajar by only a fraction of an inch. Lewis reached forward and gently pushed it open. She was sitting on the edge of her bed, her head lowered and it didn't rise as he entered, his steps loud once again as they woke the creaking floorboards. He watched her for a moment and noticed a tear fall from her cheek and onto her hands, resting in her lap. He saw that the tear was absorbed by a patch of liquid on her skin, rejoining others that had already made the same journey. Then he noticed what she was holding and walked up to sit beside her. He felt awkward and suddenly unsure if he should have come. He didn't have the right words; in fact he didn't have *any* words. But then it became clear that he didn't need any. Hannah leaned over and rested her head on his shoulder and he put a hand on hers as they both held Ben's kaleidoscope.

Lewis dragged himself back to the present and slowly replaced all the items in the cardboard box as the sound of the sea rose from below him. The last item to go back in was Hannah's diary and he contemplated it for a moment. He knew what he wanted to do, but wasn't sure if he should. He went back and forth in his mind, before guiltily unclipping the gold clasp and opening it.

He didn't read the pages but just scanned them, trying not to take in too much information. He told himself that if he didn't read it properly then it was less of a violation; not that the thought eased his rising guilt. After a couple of minutes, he decided not to read anymore and just flicked through the pages, until the book fell open at a gap. Lewis looked at the writing and then noticed that a page was missing - torn out for some reason. He looked at the dates and noticed it had been an entry from sometime in 2001. He thought little of it and continued to flick through to the end where his eye was suddenly caught by one of the final entries.

The writing was scrawled, rather than written in Hannah's usually impeccable handwriting and there were several blotches of ink where the words appeared to have been washed away. Parts of the entry didn't read in sentences but seemed to be composed of fragments of thought. As Lewis read the entry, he felt something stir inside him.

I don't know, I don't know!!! Joe isn't who I thought he was....
What am I supposed to do now?

I know he's good... but of course I don't! What were those
things? Should I go to the police? What was he doing with those
terrible films?

I can't think! I feel like screaming.
They were real people! They were really killed!
He's not.... he's not who I thought...

The entry covered a page and a half and Lewis read it
several times, piecing together the information slowly. He
noted the date and realised the entry had been written the
day before she had sent him the letter that he had found
in his flat. Hannah had seen something that belonged to
her boyfriend, Joe. It had obviously upset her, Lewis
thought as he saw where the ink had run from falling
tears. What had she found? *Terrible films...* but what kind
of terrible films?

They were real people, they were really killed!

Lewis tossed the thoughts around his head and a frown
wrinkled his forehead. A sudden realisation flooded his
mind. Whatever Hannah had found in those 'terrible
films' was what had got her killed - he was certain of it;
Joe *was* the one who killed her.

He gazed out at the sea as a cold sweat began to form
on his face, unhindered by the cool breeze. He felt his
stomach twist into a tight knot and then shrink down.
Anger began to replace the knot and Lewis felt himself
struggling to keep control. Suddenly feeling too warm, he
clenched a fist and punched the grass beside him, ignoring
the pain as it echoed through his hand.

It was him, it was him.

***

The Golden Anchor was a pub that Lewis had heard of before. There had been a number of incidents to which the police had been called several times in past few months. One man had even been seriously injured after being stabbed following a disagreement that got out of hand. He had survived, but Lewis read in the newspaper that he had spent a number of days in intensive care.

When Craig Blaine's mother had told him that her son had frequented the pub from time to time, it had surprised Lewis. Craig was a big guy but, from what he had been told, Lewis didn't think he seemed particularly street-wise and would probably have come across as easy pickings for those inclined to take advantage of someone like him. Nevertheless, that was where Craig had seen the man with straggly blonde hair that had been seen outside Hannah's flat on the night of her murder - at least according to Craig's version of events.

As he entered the pub and walked over to the bar, Lewis was still convinced that Craig Blaine was *not* the man who had killed Hannah. It was a combination of what he had read in both the letter she had sent him, and reading the strange diary entry. But even more than that, he just had a *feeling* buried inside that was fighting to be set free. It burned his stomach and writhed persistently - a nagging and elusive itch. He was sure that Hannah's boyfriend, the mysterious Joe, was the true murderer and he felt a rising determination to find out exactly who he was.

He ordered a beer and glanced around the room. It wasn't particularly busy, with only a handful of other patrons scattered around. Two men were sitting further along the bar and sipped from glasses of beer while a middle aged woman with too much make-up was drinking from a glass of vodka and staring into empty space. Three younger men stood around a dim light that was illuminating an old pool table. Lewis noticed that two of them were staring at him, but they soon lost interest and returned to their game.

Lewis didn't see anyone who remotely matched the description of the man Craig had seen. He sipped his beer while standing at the bar and pretended to check his phone. Several people entered and left as he stood there, but still no one who had the straggly blonde hair Craig had described to his mother. Lewis finished his drink and called the barman over.

"Another one please," he said, pointing to the empty glass.

The barman, a balding man in his forties, nodded and began pour another pint.

"Nice out tonight?" he asked, glancing up at Lewis.

Lewis nodded, "Not bad, at least it isn't raining."

The barman nodded and a smile flickered on his face briefly. He finished pouring, placed the glass on the bar and took Lewis's money. As he did so, he leaned in close and looked past Lewis, tipping his head forward.

"You know them?"

Lewis didn't look round but could tell he was nodding in the direction of the three men by the pool table. "No."

"They keep looking in your direction, that's all. I just

wondered."

The barman placed the money in the cash till and then returned with some change, handed it to Lewis and leaned forward as he had before. "Just keep an eye out. They come in here from time to time and can cause a bit of trouble occasionally."

Lewis nodded. "No problem. They won't find any trouble from me."

The smile flashed on the barman's face again as he stepped away, leaving Lewis to drink in peace.

Lewis took his glass and wandered over to a free table where he sat down, noticing the three men whisper between themselves as he did. Eventually they all continued their game of pool as one went to get some more drinks.

Lewis didn't look at them, and again, took out his phone and began to scroll through old messages. He paid little attention to the screen as the alcohol flowed into his system and his mind relaxed.

He sat thinking for almost two-hours, changing his drink and ordering a double whiskey, followed by several more. With each one, he tried to convince himself that it would be the one that held magical properties, and would finally numb the growing ache inside. He tried not to think of Hannah and stay focused, but his will power failed him and, as drunkenness took hold, his thoughts continued to revert to her murder.

More people entered and the bar filled up, and although Lewis tried to keep track of every new face, it became increasingly difficult as the alcohol commandeered his brain. Eventually he got up, stumbling off his chair and staggered through the growing crowd towards the door. He left the bar and went out into a shower of rain. His weather report to the barman a few hours earlier was woefully out of date and the rain soaked into his jacket as he fumbled down the street.

His mind was awash with conflicting thoughts and the convictions that forced him to go to the pub earlier in the evening were becoming confused and diluted within the haze his mind now operated.

All he wanted was to see Hannah alive again. All his theories that surrounded her death felt as if they were burrowing into his brain and twisting themselves snake-like, constricting his thoughts and preventing him from gaining any clear perspective on what was true and what was a lie.

He stumbled forward and hit his shoulder on the corner of a lamppost. He looked up at the black night sky and squinted as the rain fell into his eyes.

"What the fuck am I supposed to do?" he slurred quietly to himself as he negotiated the post and wandered into a large park which was lit by sporadic glowing lamps along a winding path. He felt his stomach spasm and threw up into a bin that stood next to a bench. He went to sit down but missed and fell to his knees as the rain came down around him.

"What do I do now?" he repeated and sobbed into his soaking hands.

After a moment, he pushed them backwards and ran them through his hair.

"Wallet."

Lewis turned suddenly at the sound of the voice and saw the three men from the bar standing a few feet away under thick shadows.

"Give me your fucking wallet," one of them repeated and stepped forward into the glow of one of the lamps.

Lewis stared at him through swaying, blurred vision. He guessed he was in his early twenties and was small and skinny. The rain fell onto a long fringe which pasted the dark hair to his forehead. Lewis grabbed the bench and managed to drag himself to his feet. The alcohol hadn't managed to numb his pain, but it had destroyed his fear.

"Fuck off," he said, stepping towards the leader, staggering slightly.

"What did you say to me?"

The man stepped forward again, pulling up his soaking white t-shirt with one hand, revealing a gun that had been pushed firmly underneath his belt. "I *will* shoot you, you piece of shit. Now, wallet!"

Lewis took a step back at the sight of the gun, but the danger posed by the object was only partially absorbed. He was shocked to see the gun, but the shock felt dull - distant somehow.

He saw the silhouettes of the two other men glance around nervously and then he stared back at the gun. Lewis realised that it wasn't just the alcohol that had suppressed the fear from fully registering; it was also the ache inside. His pain had overtaken and overwhelmed all other emotions; the pain of losing her was almost all he felt now and the threat had been vanquished by it.

"Give me your wallet, now!" The man pulled out the gun and pointed it at Lewis's head. The rain continued to fall, droplets bouncing off the barrel, a few inches from his eyes.

As he stared at the fragments of light reflecting off the shiny, metallic surface of the gun, Lewis had another moment of realisation. It was a truth that had been suddenly illuminated and it was almost comforting in its beautiful simplicity; because when it came down to it, at that particular moment, he simply didn't care. He didn't care about anything, he didn't care if he lived or died. He swallowed, still able to taste the bile as it burned the back of his throat.

"Do it then," he said quietly, staring through the rain. He felt his stomach lurch again but managed to suppress the growing need. Leaning forward slowly, he placed his forehead on the tip of the barrel. It felt colder than ice. "Do it, please. I *want* you to"

The man didn't move or say anything as their eyes became locked on each other. He adjusted his grip on the gun and pushed it forward, the barrel pushing into Lewis's forehead. Lewis could hear his trembling breath escape into the night and tried to calm himself as he fought the temptation to pull away and run.

"Give me..." the man paused, realising his bargaining position had been reduced to zero. He glanced around at his companions, who began to back away.

Lewis slowly raised his hand and placed it gently on the gun, still holding it firmly to his head.

"Please do it," he repeated in little more than a whisper for a third time.

"Don't fucking shoot him Kyle," one of the other men said nervously. "Jesus, he's crazy. He's not worth this man!"

Kyle took a moment, staring back at Lewis again but Lewis, even in his drunken haze, already knew he had won. He leaned forward again and pushed Kyle away, gripping the gun hard and wrenching it from his hand. As soon as Kyle lost contact with the gun, all three men suddenly turned and began to run away, down the narrow path and out of the park.

Lewis stood in silence, staring in the direction the three men had fled and suddenly realised he had been holding his breath. He exhaled slowly before feeling his stomach twist again and he lunged towards the bin. His legs were unsteady and he sat down on the wet bench when he had finished. He stared down at the gun in his hands, noticing they were shaking; he may not have felt his fear, but it had still been present, lingering beneath the surface.

Studying the gun, Lewis realised he had never even been in the presence of one before and the steel grip felt alien between his fingers.

The rain began to slow and eventually stop as he sat on the bench for what seemed like hours, staring solemnly at the object in his hands.

"What do I do?" he repeated to himself slowly. He focused on the trigger and gently placed a finger over it. He stopped repeating the sentence and one final, barely audible word, slipped his lips as he gazed down. "Joe."

Eventually he blinked for the first time in decades and pushed the gun into his jacket pocket. He stood up, feeling a little steadier now and looked around the darkness that swallowed up most of the park. He turned and began to walk home.

Chapter 14

Hellam

The wheels of Hellam's car spun on the soft mud as he sped down the slight incline towards the farm. The sun was just setting beyond the horizon and for a fleeting moment, Hellam wondered why he felt nothing for the sight of the dark pink glow which spread like ink on blotting paper through the pale, blue sky. He had often heard people refer to the setting sun as 'beautiful', but continually failed to understand any meaning behind such a comment. He dismissed the thought and brought the car to a standstill beside the huge, wooden barn which stood next to a derelict, brick building. He turned off the ignition and rolled his shoulders backwards, tilting his head up in an attempt to relax the muscles. It had been a long day and he wanted to go home but also had to check on the preparations. He stepped out of the car and walked towards the barn.

He pulled a cigarette from his pocket and lit it as he approached the doorway, exhaling a white cloud of smoke as he caught sight of two men standing inside. As he entered the barn, he saw that there were three floodlights on large upright stands, pointing towards a central area and illuminating the rapidly darkening space.

"It's looking nice," Hellam said, nodding as he approached the two men and they turned towards him. "Are those working off the generator?" He pointed towards the three floodlights.

One of the men - tall and muscular - nodded. "Yeah, we finally got it going. The fucking thing had seized up, but it should be fine now."

Hellam turned towards the other man who was fiddling with some wires which were trailing along the dusty, concrete floor. "Tyler, have you got the camera sorted out?"

The man glanced round, "Yeah, hold on."

He got up and walked away to a small sectioned off area on the far side of the barn. Tyler was much shorter than the first man, due partly to his hunched, crooked posture which sliced a good half-foot from his extended height. He had a sharp, ratty face and sported a wispy, goatee beard which clung to his pale skin like a man clinging to the edge of a cliff. He walked with a slight limp across the barn and disappeared behind a partition on the opposite end. He returned seconds later, carrying a stand and small box which he placed in the centre of the three floodlights. Hellam watched as he set up the stand and then pulled a small, digital camcorder out of the box, screwing it carefully on top.

Hellam smiled as he surveyed the scene, "Perfect."

The two men glanced at each other as Hellam took a long drag on his cigarette.

"Where are we on the other matter? Have you found a

candidate?" he asked, speaking through the smoke.

Tyler nodded towards the muscular man standing beside him, "Hal has found her - sounds like she'll do the job." Tyler smiled through cracked lips and ran his hand under his nose, then across his shirt.

Hellam looked at Hal, "Who is she?"

"Some whore," he replied, stretching sideways. "I went to see her last night. She doesn't have any family around here; no one will miss her."

Hellam stepped closer to him and dropped his cigarette on the floor, pressing his shiny black shoes on the butt and twisting. "You're sure?"

Hal scratched his arm and Hellam noticed the familiar butterfly which decorated the bicep, its dark green form motionless. "Of course," he replied confidently.

Hellam stepped closer still, and leaned into the huge man. "You're sure?" he repeated in a whisper.

Hal frowned, "I just said didn't I?"

Hellam scrutinised him for a moment and then nodded before turning and stepping away.

"What else is there to take care of?" he asked.

Hal walked over to one of the lights and adjusted it downward so the light was cast towards one end of the triangle that the three lamps formed. "Nothing much, it's just..." He stepped back, looked at the light and then adjusted it a little further before continuing. "It's just we've never had one like this before. I mean, how do these things work?"

"I've shown you the fucking films, you know what's expected. Just mess her up for a while before you end it. That's what the clients want; that's what these people pay for."

Hal glanced at Tyler and nodded slowly, "Sure."

Hellam frowned and looked at Tyler, then at Hal and back again. "If you want some support, just ask."

Hal looked up to the roof of the barn and wandered over to the camera, twisting it on the stand carefully and lining up with point where he had just positioned the light. When he was satisfied, he turned back to Hellam.

"I didn't say that did I? We can handle it. It's just I've never had a job like this before."

Hellam had been using the services of Hal and Tyler for years and was on the whole pleased with the work that they had performed for him. They killed with professionalism and efficiency and he had never had the need to doubt their expertise in this area. That was what made them so perfect for this latest business venture.

Hellam had been purchasing the snuff films from his contacts abroad for many years and selling them on with enormous profits, but now he needed to begin making his own - he *craved* to make his own. It was no longer enough for him to view the victims being tortured and murdered in far off countries. He wanted to witness the task first hand; he wanted to be there and to relish the pain in person and, perhaps one day, he would even perform the task himself. But not the first, certainly not the first. He had to be sure that there was an efficient system in place for him to be anywhere close when a victim was being processed. There were so many factors to analyse: choosing the correct person, someone who wouldn't be missed or even noticed to *be* missing for at least a few weeks; the correct and efficient disposal of bodies; the absolute and clinical methodology of completing the task from start to finish.

Hellam had originally assumed that Hal and Tyler would be perfect for the task. He would pay them far more than they would get for any traditional kill, but for that price they would be expected to perform a little extra; something special for the camera. At first he thought this wouldn't be a problem, after all they had both killed for him in the past.

But the more imminent the task became, the less convinced Hellam was that they would perform it adequately. To Hal and Tyler, there appeared to be a radical difference between simply dispatching a debt ridden drug dealer, and torturing an innocent victim to death; a difference which Hellam couldn't fully comprehend.

He thought about the girl who had seen the films on his laptop and how Hal had been almost reluctant to carry through the job that had been asked of him. It had been a reluctance that Hellam had never seen from the man before. Hal had even questioned Hellam, *why does she need to be killed? What has she done?* But in spite of these questions, the job had been carried through and Hal had done it with as much efficiency as he had all the others. Hellam felt the subtle reluctance from Hal even though he couldn't fully understand it; he was paying him enough money after all, what was the problem?

He stared at the two men standing beneath the floodlights and thought about all of this. Then he thought about Kelser and remembered how he had taken care of Richards - no hesitation, no questions.

"I think I'm going to bring someone else in regardless," he said finally, ignoring Hal's protesting snorts. "I know someone who can take the pressure off you." He pulled out a packet of mints from his pocket and threw one into his mouth. "Just get the victim here and I'll sort out the rest."

***

Sarah Price was shivering as she waited in the queue at the supermarket. Friday nights were always the busiest and she mentally reprimanded herself for leaving the shopping so late in the week again. She had left without her cardigan and the walk from her flat had been much colder than she expected. She placed the basket of groceries on the 'ten items or less' counter and rubbed the goose pimples on her arm into submission.

"Cold dear?" the woman behind the counter asked as she dragged a loaf of bread over the bar code scanner.

Sarah looked up and saw the woman smiling at her sympathetically. "Yes, I forgot my cardigan. It's okay though, I only live round the corner."

The woman continued to smile as she nodded and pushed the groceries in front of her to a monotonous beeping melody.

Sarah began to pack her shopping into plastic bags and noticed the smile on the woman's face disappear suddenly when she glanced over Sarah's shoulder at the next customer waiting in line. Sarah turned her head and saw a huge grin smeared over the face of a large man behind her. She involuntarily took in a sharp breath as she saw the butterfly tattoo on the huge man's arm. Their eyes locked on one another as mutual recognition flowed between them. He continued to grin as Sarah turned away and finished packing with increased speed.

After she had paid and began to walk away, she glanced back and saw her client from the previous day pay for a single packet of chewing gum and then begin to follow her out. She could hear his huge boots thump on the floor behind her and she focused on the sound; so much so that his footsteps seemed to drown out the multitude of other noises in the shop.

Thump, thump.

His steps mimicked Sarah's own precisely and, in perfect unison, they stepped out of the supermarket onto cold, wet pavement. The thumping seemed even louder out there, in spite of the noise from passing cars and distant music as they were carried and distorted by a gathering wind.

Just keep walking and get home, she told herself, increasing pace and feeling the plastic bags scrunch on the sides of her legs. *It's busy; there is nothing he can do here.*

Sarah thought she heard a snigger from behind her but refused to turn her head and acknowledge it. Although she had previously cursed the noise from living on such a busy road many times before, she now felt a deep gratitude for the passing cars and pedestrians.

The day before with the client had been horrendous. When they had finished, Sarah had dressed, but the man who was now following her, Hal - she wouldn't forget that name - had remained in her bed and kept asking her questions. He wouldn't leave and the questions had become more and more personal which had gradually begun to unnerve her. She had had a bad feeling about Hal since he first entered the room and all she wanted was for him to leave her alone.

It was rare for clients to want to stay for longer than absolutely necessary after they had finished - quite the opposite in fact, most couldn't wait to get out of the door – but Hal just wouldn't leave. Eventually, Sarah had managed to persuade him to get dressed, but even then he continued to ask questions about her life as he lethargically dragged his jeans over his legs. She began to refuse to answer the questions but that didn't seem to stop him from asking and, after forty-five minutes, she allowed her frustrations to show and screamed at him to leave. He had just grinned at her; the same grin that she was sure was still on his face now as they stepped in perfect harmony along the soaking pavement.

As the questions continued, Sarah had eventually opened the door and managed to push him out as he sniggered and half-heartedly pushed back, as if he were playing some kind of game. She slammed the door shut and stood, leaning against it for a few moments as she caught her breath, knowing she would never be seeing the lunatic again. That was until he had appeared behind her in the queue.

There had been clients in the past that had pestered her, but this man was different - Sarah sensed something that she didn't like from this man; he unnerved her and she wanted to get as far away from him as possible.

It could have been a coincidence that he had been behind her in the supermarket and was now following her home - perhaps they lived in the same direction - but she suspected otherwise. In fact it was more than that; she *knew* he was following her because he had more questions to ask and more answers to hear. He was insane, she was sure of it.

Glancing along the road behind her, but careful not to meet the eyes of her follower, Sarah stepped off the curb and noted that the thumping steps behind her splashed in a puddle as they too left the pavement. She trotted the last few steps to avoid an approaching car and she turned back around. She saw the huge, tattooed man standing in the centre of the road waiting patiently as the car passed in front of him. He still wore the grin: wide and menacing.

She increased her pace again. The two plastic bags knocked against her legs as she half-ran towards her building. She was only a hundred feet from the front entrance and as she ran, she noticed the footsteps behind her weren't quite so loud.

She continued, spurred on by the *thump, thump* as Hal's feet slowly died away. When she reached the entrance, she glanced back, half expecting him to be almost upon her in spite of what her ears had told her, but she was wrong. She gasped for air, her chest rising and falling as her heart pounded violently through her skinny frame. He was gone. She stared along the street but there was no sign of him on either side of the road.

Relief fell like a blanket as she entered the foyer of the building and began to climb the stairs. She sighed deeply, finally catching her breath again and began to feel her heart slow, no longer mimicking the thumping footsteps that had followed her home. When she reached the door, she placed the two bags on the floor by her feet and pulled out a set of keys. She suddenly heard a sound from behind her.

Her head shot around to the sound of footsteps thumping up the stairs behind her. Her face contorted with terror and she began to fumble with her keys as the footsteps slowly got louder. She could hear sniggering as they approached, but the source of the sound was out of view; hidden behind a bend in the corridor. Adrenaline began to surge through her veins yet again and her hands began to tremble; she couldn't get the key to her door separated from the rest and a small whimper left her mouth as her panic increased. The footsteps reached the top of the stairs and began to turn the bend. Sarah glanced back with huge eyes and she saw a young couple stumble into view.

They were arm in arm and drunk. They sniggered to themselves as they fell from one side of the hallway to another, occasionally laughing out loud as their heavy feet scuffed across the carpet. Sarah watched as they approached. They almost knocked into her as they went past, seemingly oblivious to the fact that she was there at all. She saw the man laugh again and fumble keys into a door further down then they shuffled into the room together.

She sighed, the air calming her again as it slowly entered and left her lungs. She smiled to herself, a physical manifestation of the relief she suddenly felt. The keys went into the door easier this time, but she noticed a small scratch on the lock plate which she quickly disregarded - determined to not allow the unwelcome bout of paranoia to continue. She picked up the bags and walked inside, pushing the light switch with her elbow.

After she had put her groceries away, Sarah went over to the radiator and felt it with the back of her hand. It was stone cold. She contemplated turning it on for a moment before deciding that she would just put on the cardigan she had forgotten to take out with her. She hummed quietly to herself as she went through the open door to the bedroom and didn't bother to turn on the light since the lamp in the front room penetrated the gloom enough for her to see the wardrobe. She opened the cupboard door and pulled out a cardigan which she threw over her shoulders, relishing the sensation as the soft wool moved over her skin.

She paused for a moment, *what was that?* She heard something behind her, a sound that was so slight, she wasn't even sure if it had been there at all. Then it came again, a low shuffling sound of something moving slowly over the carpet. She frowned and turned as her eyes adjusted to the semi-lit room. Then they began to expand.

In the corner of her bedroom was the outline of a short, hunched figure which slowly began to move. The figure was obscured by the light but appeared male and as he approached, he dropped something beside him – something small, a plastic container or bottle, but Sarah was too shocked to dwell on it. She took in a deep breath, ready to exhale in a violent scream but the figure lunged towards her, his features becoming apparent in a split second as they reflected in the light from the front room.

"Shut your mouth," he sneered, spittle falling from his mouth and onto the wispy beard which clung to his chin. He pushed her backwards and she fell onto the bed, hitting the sheets hard before being flung to the opposite side and falling to the floor. She tried to scream again but only a shrill croak left her mouth as she hit the floor and pain resonated through her elbow. She turned round quickly and saw the man hobbling towards her from the other side of the bed with surprising speed.

"What..." Sarah said as he approached and tried to

move away from him, but her back hit the wall. "What do you want?"

The man grabbed her arm with spidery fingers and pulled her closer. In his other hand, Sarah noticed he was holding something which looked like an old, flannel. She pulled away and kicked out hard with her leg. He grunted with pain as her foot collided with his knee and he released her momentarily. She tried to get to her feet, pulling on the sheets of the bed to help her up, but they fell away and she collapsed back to the floor. She felt her attacker come round behind her and throw an arm over her shoulder then he pulled hard, towards his chest and she let out a scream. It was louder this time. *Surely somebody heard that,* she thought as she gasped, ready to call out again, but then her mouth was covered with something. She felt fabric and a vaguely sweet aroma drifted up.

She breathed hard and suddenly felt dizzy so she pushed off the floor with as much strength as she could muster. The man fell back and the cloth was released from Sarah's mouth. She heard him mutter something as she lunged up and climbed over the bed. A hand clamped around her ankle and dragged her back. She kicked out again, but this time he was prepared. He grabbed her other foot and swung it out sideways. She turned and looked up at the pale skin and dark eyes of her attacker as he leaned over. He picked up a lamp by her bed and swung it down. As the lamp struck her head, Sarah thought she heard the porcelain base shatter, but then there was only darkness.

Chapter 15

Lewis

Lewis stared at the gun resting in his open palm and scanned the coarse metallic grip as his hand slowly closed, fingers whitening as they tightened. The memory of the previous night had penetrated through the drunken fog from which it had been formed and Lewis could remember almost every detail. He could barely believe how he had reacted and was even more astonished that he had gotten away with it. Every cell in his body was telling him that he should be dead now; one more casualty of one more gang. But somehow it had worked. He had called Kyle's bluff and came away, not only with his brains intact, but also carrying the very weapon that had been used against him.

He had thought about taking the gun to the police and handing it in since he knew the gun laws were uncompromisingly rigid, especially regarding handguns. If he was caught in possession of it and had no reasonable explanation as to why, then he was sure he would face a severe punishment, perhaps even custodial.

Lewis also considered handing it in because he had absolutely no idea of how it worked or even how to check if the thing was loaded. He didn't trust himself to not accidentally shoot a bullet into his foot or shoulder as he tried to fathom how to check.

But deep down he knew that he wouldn't hand it in to the police because of a reason that was beginning to push the limits of his own rationality. It was the same reason he wasn't taking Hannah's diary to the authorities and requesting they immediately divert their investigation away from Craig Blaine and towards her mystery boyfriend, Joe. The reason was absurd and lurked in parts of his mind that thrived on such things. The reason was *he* wanted to find out what happened to Hannah himself. Involuntary laughter escaped him as he thought about this, still staring down at the gun.

Who do I think I am? He thought, and twisted the heavy metal object in his hand.

He was certain that, were he to go to the police with any evidence he *thought* he had, they probably wouldn't even act on such information. What he had found in Hannah's diary and the letter she had sent him, spoke to him in secret subtexts that only he could truly decipher. They hadn't *known* her. In fact almost nobody knew her the way Lewis did and he realised that perhaps this could both help and hinder him in different ways.

He knew that what Hannah had written in her diary had come from her heart and she had been genuinely confused, upset and even scared. It was plain for him to see, but would everyone else see it that way? Had his closeness to Hannah obscured the facts that were presented on the opposite side of the table?

The police seemed confident that they had their man in Craig Blaine and the DNA evidence against him was perfectly clear - linking him directly to the crime. That was something that still bothered Lewis; how *had* Craig Blaine's DNA found its way under Hannah's fingernails? There was the far-fetched story told by his mother about some unknown woman scratching his face. But how had Craig's torn skin found its way to Hannah? The more Lewis thought about everything he had learned regarding her death, the more it began to feel like reading a book with chapters out of order or even missing completely.

Some things made sense, and he was absolutely certain in his own mind that Joe was in some way responsible for her murder. Yet he couldn't piece everything together with any coherence in order for it to make complete sense. He needed to find Joe to get to the answers, but he had precious little to go on. Nobody seemed to know who he was; Hannah had even kept him a secret from Kelly, why would she do that? Would Joe have requested that from her for some reason?

Lewis crossed the carpet of his flat and placed the gun down delicately in a drawer by his bed, wondering again why he insisted on keeping it. Could he ever really bring himself to use it? Even if he was absolutely certain that the elusive Joe had really murdered the woman he loved, and was standing before him, just waiting for the bullet. Could he do it?

Lewis dismissed the thoughts with rising unease. He was no murderer. There was something inside him that he was sure was innate in all good people; something that prevented him from killing another human being.

But was he sure?

Perhaps there was no *innate goodness* and everyone is capable of murder given the right circumstances.

Soldiers in a war are told that they're fighting for truth and freedom to justify the inevitable death that comes with their job. They are able to rationalise their actions based on this belief, even if that means that people on the opposite side, who believe just as strongly that they are the ones fighting for the greater good, have to die.

But even soldiers hesitate, or miss shots deliberately. Lewis remembered the article he had read that had discussed this statistic. Did that prove that there was something inside us that stops us from killing, even if we believe it is for the good of our king or our country?

When Lewis thought of someone forcing their way into Hannah's flat, beating her and then placing their hands around her throat as she begged for her life, his muscles contracted with rage.

As he closed the drawer, obscuring the gun from his sight, he tried to stop a fabricated image of her lifeless body from forming in his mind. He had never seen such an image; would never want to see one, but it was conjured like some cruel, sadistic trick by his mind nevertheless. He felt his jaw tighten and his teeth clamp down hard.

Could he kill whoever did that to her?

"Yes," he said in a low whisper, his teeth remaining tight.

But as quickly as the word left his mouth, doubt once again splintered this fleeting clarity.

He turned around and walked towards the door, picked up his jacket from the arm of the chair and swung it onto his shoulders before leaving.

***

The first thing Lewis noticed after stepping inside The Golden Anchor for the second time was how much busier it was compared to the previous evening. The bar was three people deep, all waiting to be served and he noticed that all the tables had been taken; even the pool table had been commandeered for the purpose of resting drinks. The worn, green fabric bore several wet rings from the bottom of glasses and even a purple stain where, presumably, a glass of wine had spilt. People were gathered around, chatting and leaning or perching on the edge of the wood.

The music, released from several old speakers in each corner, was loud, but overwhelmed by the bustle and chatter inside the room. It was only after Lewis had worked through the crowd and was waiting at the bar, that he realised it was a Friday night. He had no particular need to keep track of the days and they had all blended into one monotonous span of time, broken only by light and dark as he tried to bury his grief in a tsunami of alcohol.

He realised that he had willingly fallen onto a path which would eventually lead to nothing but self destruction; his constant drinking and self-pity were taking their toll on his health. He felt as though he was ninety-years-old and struggling to make it through each passing day. The only reason he continued to get out of bed in the morning was due to the vitriol he felt as he pictured someone placing their hands around Hannah's throat. Each morning he would try to convince himself that it would be the final time; no more drinking, no more self pity. He needed to focus. But as the hours passed and the reality of the day eroded his conviction, he began to allow his melancholy to sneak through unnoticed and overwhelm him.

What would Hannah think of him if she could see him now? He wasn't looking after himself properly; hadn't washed for several days and was drinking himself to oblivion. She wouldn't have wanted this for him.

He glanced around as he waited, but saw no sign of the three men who had attacked him the previous night. He wasn't too sure how he would handle the situation if they approached him while he was sober and demanded their weapon back - he was sure illegal firearms carried a hefty price tag - but decided not to concern himself with that for the time being. He pulled out a five pound note from his pocket and held it in his hand as he waited to be served. He looked up and down the bar at the eager faces either side of him, checking for any men who had straggly blonde hair, but saw no one fitting the description. After a few more moments a barmaid approached him.

"Yes love, what can I get you?"

"A scotch..." Lewis paused, looking at the inverted bottles behind the bar and then looked down and through the fridges behind the woman. "Actually, I'll just have a Coke."

The barmaid nodded, brought over a bottle and glass filled with ice and took his cash. Lewis poured the contents of the bottle into the glass and then manoeuvred his way back through the crowd. There still weren't any tables free so he walked over to the corner of the room and stood next to a lifeless fruit machine, beside the pool table.

He sipped his Coke as he glanced around the room. The noise of chatter was almost deafening but he didn't try to focus in on any one particular conversation, although he could hear a couple arguing on a table close by. He allowed the noise to wash over him and took nothing in.

As he stood there, trying not to appear as if he was observing every person who entered and left the bar, Lewis noticed someone he thought he recognised. But when he looked again he saw that the blonde haired girl only resembled the person he thought she was. Abby Whitehead had been his girlfriend for almost two-years while they attended the same course at university. They had started out as friends and Lewis had always been convinced she was out of his league; she was extremely pretty and drew attention from most of the male population in any room. But they gradually grew closer and after one drunken night out with the rest of their group, they kissed and one thing led to another. They became inseparable for a while and spent almost all their free time together. Eventually, perhaps in part due to the initial intensity of their relationship, the flames had died down and they had slowly eased out of love with each other. It was a sad time for both of them, but also one which Lewis rationalised as simply a chapter that had ended.

He finished his drink as he thought of Abby and that period of his life, unaware of how thirsty he had been. But the drink hadn't quenched the real thirst; the one that could only be satisfied with alcohol. He tried to resist, telling himself that wasn't the reason he was there. But it was a battle he knew he was always destined to lose.

After making his way back to the bar and waiting for another five minutes, he ordered a double scotch and then stood, leaning on the wood as he drank. He turned occasionally as people entered or left, but his concentration quickly became overwhelmed as his mind relaxed. He stared into the amber liquid and then knocked it back, wincing before ordering another.

As the evening progressed, the crowd slowly thinned and more space appeared at the bar next to Lewis. A stool became free and he dragged it over and sat hunched over his glass as he tried to think of nothing; a task which became easier as his intoxication increased.

He turned his wrist and looked at his watch: 11:38pm. The music was still thumping and, although less busy, there were still around twenty people gathered in groups in various parts of the room. Lewis knew he hadn't reached the levels of drunkenness he had attained the previous night and, in a summoning of will power that surprised him, resisted ordering another drink. He sat on his stool and twisted the empty glass between his fingers.

Someone brushed past behind him and stopped a little further along the bar. Lewis heard the man strike up a conversation with the barman, they seemed to know each other, but Lewis didn't look up. He continued to turn the glass, tipping it onto one edge and watching the light reflect from the transparent contours as the last residue of liquid rolled around inside. It reminded him of something, but he didn't have the energy to drag the memory through his whiskey addled mind to be fully recognised. He just let it rest there, a little beyond reach. But the sparkles of light on the glass pleased him for some reason and he imagined them turning and twisting into one another.

He looked over the bar and saw someone staring back at him; someone he barely recognised. His reflection in the stained back-plate, below the optics of liquor, was obscured by numerous smudges, but his features were still discernable, albeit alien to him now. The skin beneath his eyes was discoloured and seemed to droop down to his cheeks. His hair was long, unkempt and greasy as it fell over his forehead and ears. The stubble on his chin had grown into a thin beard and extended around his jaw. Unlike the glass in his hand, his eyes were now devoid of the brightness they once had; they appeared tired and hollow - lifeless. He drew his gaze away from his reflection and across the smudged mirror to the man standing further along the bar.

Lewis felt his jaw loosen and fall open as he caught sight of the man's skinny features. He was taller than Lewis - probably a few inches over six feet - and had long, gangly arms. He wore a tight fitting t-shirt over a lean torso and smart, skinny jeans which looked new and expensive and held a brown jacket in his hand. He was still chatting with the barman and smirking occasionally as he reached up and dragged clumps of his thick, blonde hair away from his forehead.

Lewis stopped twisting the glass and froze perfectly still, as if paralysed by the sight of him. He barely took a breath as he stared at the reflection of the man who stood less than five feet from where he was sitting. He watched as the man reached up again and dragged his left hand back through his hair, removing the several strands which had fallen down over his face as he spoke enthusiastically with the barman. Lewis focused in on the hand and saw that half of his little finger was missing; as if surgically removed just after the second joint.

It was him. Craig Blaine *had* seen him – he *did* exist.

Lewis ripped the bindings of his gaze away and stared straight ahead, feeling the ice cold tip of a blade shoot down the length of his spine. He focused himself and began to listen to the conversation the man was having with the barman.

"...and when the bitch left, she took the cat," the man said, still smirking. "As if I'd care about that little shit; it just pissed and shat everywhere, never used the litter tray at all."

The barman smiled and nodded as he changed one of the empty bottles behind the bar. "How long were you together?"

The man glanced over in Lewis's direction but paid him no mind then ran his hand through his hair yet again before turning back to the barman. "I dunno, over a year. I never really liked her anyway. I knew she was sleeping around and I had a few girls on the go at the same time. She was just someone to help pay the fucking rent!" He snorted with laughter as if he had just made the funniest joke anyone was likely to hear for several decades.

"You had other girls? Yeah right, you're no Casanova, Jonah," the barman said, chuckling to himself. "In spite of what you think about your mane."

"You don't know shit. I have plenty of women after me pal." Jonah picked up the glass of liquor in front of him and gulped down the last drop. "Get me another drink will you. Do your job and stop insulting your customers."

The barman took the glass and turned to fill it. Jonah turned to Lewis and leaned in closer.

"You believe the shit this bloke is giving me?" he said jovially, prodding Lewis on the shoulder.

Lewis turned and looked at him. He guessed Jonah was in his mid-to-late thirties, although his skin was heavily wrinkled around the eyes and forehead. His long, thin face stretched out and he had a pointed chin which appeared to be freshly shaved. His cheek bones were sharp, like small razors just beneath the surface of the skin. Lewis could smell the faint aroma of expensive aftershave drifting over from the man as he looked at him, unable to move.

"You believe it?" Jonah repeated after Lewis denied him a response.

Lewis stared at him for a moment longer before raising one corner of his mouth in acknowledgement then turned back to the mirror. Jonah leaned back up with a confused frown and when the barman returned with his drink, Lewis glanced over and saw him make a face to his friend and nod over as if to say, *what's his problem?*

Lewis sat in his chair and barely moved. He could actually feel the sensation of blood being pushed through his veins and arteries as his heart pounded inside his chest. His hands felt as if they were throbbing from the force of the racing blood. But he didn't dwell on these sensations and turned his attention back to the conversation that was taking place a few feet away.

"So what are you going to do about the rent now she's gone?" the barman asked, leaning on the opposite side of the bar.

Jonah shrugged, "I'll manage. I'm still getting quite a bit of work."

"What is it you do again?"

Jonah smirked again and slurped on his drink. "This and that, I'm freelance you see."

"Freelance what?" the barman asked, placing a hand behind his neck and leaning back as if to stretch out a knot in his muscle.

Jonah snorted. "Whatever comes my way, you know. I'm not too fussy as long as the pay is right... and it usually is."

The barman shook his head dismissively; he had obviously had this conversation with Jonah before and didn't look as though he wanted to pursue it any further.

Lewis glanced across occasionally and absorbed the features of the man sitting just feet away. As the time passed, he began to memorise the minute details of his face and could feel himself beginning to hate them all. Finally, he pushed his empty glass away, stood up and walked out of the bar.

When he stepped outside, Lewis walked briskly along the street, turned the corner and leaned with his back to the cool bricks of a terrace house. He took several long, deep breaths as he tilted his head back against the wall and gazed up at the sky. He wanted to stare up and see the stars but they were hidden. Thick, black clouds hung overhead and concealed the vista.

He began to feel his heart slow and the pounding sensation subsided as he continued to breathe long and deep. After a few moments, he heard the door to The Golden Anchor slam shut and raised voices. He hesitated before moving to edge of the corner and peering round.

It was the couple who had been arguing earlier in the evening. They walked down the street and the woman began shouting something as she pushed the man away, who kept trying to block her path. Lewis watched as they walked away from him and their voices became faint.

He was about to turn away when the door to the bar opened again and Jonah stepped outside. Lewis moved back so only a single eye was observing and watched as Jonah pulled some chewing gum from his pocket, threw it into his mouth and began to walk in his direction. Lewis ducked back away from the corner and ran across the deserted road, making his footsteps as quiet as possible. He saw a small gap between an off-license and a row of houses and stepped into the narrow alleyway. He was in almost total darkness and craned his neck to look back to the corner.

Jonah chewed his gum with large movements of his jaw as he turned the corner and continued to walk along the street. He took brisk strides and moved quickly as he continually brushed his long blonde hair away from his face with his incomplete left hand - it was obviously a persistent habit of his. When he had got far enough away, Lewis stepped out from the alley, pushed his hands into his jacket pockets and began to follow.

It started to rain and Lewis saw Jonah, fifty feet ahead of him, begin to increase his pace to a slow jog. Lewis did the same, not taking his eyes off the brown jacket. Jonah took another couple of turns before stopping outside a house, half way down a narrow road lined with dying trees. Lewis walked by the road, glancing at Jonah as he spat the gum out onto the pavement.

Lewis slowed his pace when he reached the other side of the street and paused behind one of the trees, certain that Jonah hadn't seen him. He peered round and watched as the gangly man went through a broken wooden gate and made the three steps up to the front door of the house. Lewis wiped the rain from his forehead with the back of his sleeve as he saw Jonah disappear inside and a light flick on in the window.

Lewis stood motionless behind the tree, his eyes focused on the house for a few moments as the rain fell harder. The dead branches above his head did nothing to shelter him from the drops as they fell, soaking into his jacket. But he didn't notice how wet he was getting; his mind was roaming somewhere else completely. It was a place that was unlike the one he had inhabited recently; it was a place where things were beginning to make sense - or at least broken fragments of something which closely resembled coherence.

Eventually Lewis turned away from the house and began to walk home. He strode on automatic pilot, not thinking of the route he was taking, but focused on something else. He gazed at the pavement before him and kept repeating a set of words in his head.

Jonah.
Jonah.
Jonah.
Joe.

***

The skin around Craig Blaine's eye was tender. He winced involuntarily as he touched the dark purple patch of skin that surrounded it while staring into the mirror. He turned around and hobbled over to the bottom bunk, limping on his bruised right leg. He sat down slowly on the steel frame which creaked from the burden of his weight.

He had been moved to the cell only the day before in an attempt to prevent any further 'accidents'. He had the entirety of the ten by six feet room to himself, but the walls continued to close in. When he had left the cell that morning, he had felt just as vulnerable as when he shared; threats being constantly whispered in his ears as he walked through the corridors. One of the guards had told him that the other inmates can spot an easy target from a mile away and that Craig needed to toughen up.

But Craig didn't know how; he could barely understand why he was there in the first place - he hadn't hurt that girl next door, why had they picked on him? His situation hadn't been helped when the other inmates had found out that he was suspected of murdering a young woman in cold blood. In the unspoken echelons of command in the prison, such a crime placed him towards the bottom, with only paedophiles and child murderers residing below.

Craig knew he wasn't a clever man - his mother told him so often enough - and he realised that this was why he was such an easy target for the others. They wanted anyone they could dominate and have power over. Now that he had his own cell, they seemed to be after him even more.

He felt a sting in his eyes as he sat on the bottom bunk and began to mutter to himself in a voice that was barely audible.

"I didn't do it, I didn't do it..."

He repeated the words in one continual stream as tears fell. He raised his hands to wipe them away and his face contorted with pain when he accidentally brushed against the bruised eye, but he continued to mumble the words with increasing volume.

He looked down at the light grey prison uniform he was wearing. He was on remand and had the option to wear his own clothes if he wished, but Craig just wanted to fit in with the others. He stood up slowly and turned to the bunk bed behind him. He pulled the frame but it didn't move; it had been bolted to the wall. He wiped the tears away again, ignoring the pain and took off his shoes. He lowered his trousers and began to tie one of the fabric legs around the angled steel frame of the top bunk as he continued his ominous chant.

"I didn't do it, I didn't do it, I didn't…"

Chapter 16

Hellam

The ambient lighting in Jannson's cast long shadows along the walls from the ornate decorative sculptures which were located around the room. It had been a favourite location of Hellam's for many years and he had come to know Henrik Jannson, the owner of the bar, very well. Henrik even allowed Hellam to use the small function room at the back of the building for occasional business meetings free of charge.

Hellam took off his suit jacket and brushed it down before placing it beside him on the cushioned seat of the booth. He saw a member of staff spot him and disappear through a doorway behind the bar. Henrik came out a few seconds later, smiling, and Hellam gestured a drinking motion. Henrik nodded and said something to the staff member and she immediately began to prepare Hellam's drink.

Hellam looked at his watch. He had arrived a little early but that didn't matter; waiting in Jannson's wasn't a chore, even on a relatively busy night like tonight.

"There you go sir."

Hellam looked up and saw Henrik's wrinkled, smiling face staring down at him. He was holding a tray containing a single glass.

"Thank you Henrik." Hellam took the glass and sipped.

"Are you here alone tonight?"

Hellam shook his head. "No, I'm meeting Kelser; just a discussion about business."

He noticed Henrik's expression change by the most subtle degree. His eyes had darkened and the smile faded by a fraction. Hellam thought about how just the mention of Kelser's name appeared to send a wave of fear through the man and this pleased him immensely.

"Would you like the function room?" Henrik asked, restoring his smile.

"No, that won't be necessary tonight thank you."

Henrik nodded. "Well, if there is anything you require then don't hesitate to ask for me."

He turned and walked away and Hellam pulled out his mobile phone from his pocket. He flicked through his calendar on the screen and made a mental note of the various meetings he had to attend the following day. There was a meeting listed that Langton had not briefed him on that afternoon and he felt a slight annoyance at this. Langton had not been performing up to his usual standard and Hellam thought quietly to himself about this slip in quality for a moment.

He replaced his phone and looked up to see Kelser walk through the door. He raised his hand and Kelser approached him, removing a wet jacket.

"Take a seat," Hellam said, turning to the bar.

The barmaid walked over. "What can I get you?"

Kelser looked up at the woman and Hellam noticed that she was trying not to focus in on the scar.

Hellam had never asked his employee about the injury or how it had happened; their relationship didn't seem to permit such a question which felt a little strange to Hellam who would never stop himself from asking a question if he was curious about something.

"Just water, no ice," Kelser replied, resting his elbows on the table and the woman walked away.

Hellam had never seen Kelser drink anything other than water in the five years he had known him.

"Thank you for coming tonight," Hellam said. "I just wanted to have a word with you about a couple of things."

The barmaid returned with a tray and placed the glass of water on the table in front of Kelser who said nothing. Hellam turned and watched her walk away and then glanced around. The booth was set against the wall and had high backed seats; no one in the adjacent areas would be able to hear their conversation easily.

Kelser drank half of the glass in one go and stared back at his boss.

Hellam continued, "I have been extremely impressed with the work you have performed for me over the past few months." He paused, waiting for a reaction from his employee, but there was none. "Especially the way you handled the Richards situation. That, I believe, was your finest hour. You dealt with it in a professional manner that I was very pleased with. There have been no further developments or repercussions so far and I think we can safely say that the matter is closed for the time being."

Kelser nodded slowly, his expression devoid of any

emotion.

"There will always be interest from the authorities in my various businesses. They have suspected me of certain dealings for years, but as long as I'm... as long as *we're* vigilant then I don't see them becoming a serious threat in the near future. The Richards situation was unfortunate and I don't want the same thing to happen again. I am going to scrutinise future employees with a much finer comb and I expect you to help me with regards to that side of things."

Kelser nodded again but still remained silent.

Hellam glanced around again. "But there are a number of people in my employment that I do trust completely. That is why I want to offer you a position in a new section of the business. If you're interested that is?"

"Of course," Kelser said, draining the last of the water.

Hellam smiled, "Good. I want to show you something. Come with me to the office and I'll explain there."

***

The light from the corridor penetrated Hellam's office and provided enough illumination for him not to turn on the lamp. Kelser was leaning back in a chair while Hellam walked over to the cabinet in the corner of the room and unlocked the door. He glanced round before tapping in the code to the electronic safe and saw Kelser staring absently out of the window into the dark night. When the safe door opened, he lifted out the laptop and returned to his desk where he turned it on.

"Tell me, what did it feel like to kill Richards?" he asked

casually as they waited for the laptop to boot up.

Kelser turned his attention from the window, as if awoken from some dream, and stared at Hellam in silence for a few moments. "What do you mean?" he asked finally, his voice quiet - almost menacing.

Hellam was taken aback by the tone Kelser was using and suddenly felt a shiver roll through his muscles. This subtle atmosphere of threat that appeared to emanate from Kelser was unnerving, but it wasn't the first time Hellam had felt it. He had witnessed Kelser use a similar technique when intimidating someone on Hellam's own instructions.

"Did you enjoy it? Did you enjoy killing him?" Hellam asked, leaning forward.

Kelser stared through him for a moment and appeared to consider the question; dissecting it in his mind as if the answer was deeply elusive. Finally he answered in a barely audible whisper.

"Yes."

Hellam smiled and leaned back in his chair as a sense of immense satisfaction flowed through him. "I thought so, because..." He paused and flicked his hand between the two of them. "...Because you and I are the same Kelser. I can see it in you and that is why you are the perfect person for the task I have in mind."

He turned to the laptop and clicked on a folder, typed in a password and a number of video files were displayed, each one named with a date. "I've never killed anyone with my own hands; a situation for that to happen has never arisen and I have people who take care of those less dignified aspects of my business." He leaned towards Kelser again and dropped his voice low. "But that doesn't mean I haven't thought about it; what it would be like to take someone's life, in the same way you took Richards'. But more, much more than that, I want to see the agony in their eyes when they know they're going to die. I want to see them lose all hope and finally give in to the inevitability of their own demise." He paused, wondering if he had already gone too far. "Do you understand?"

He could feel the excitement rising inside him. He was finally sharing his darkest secret with someone who he suspected would understand, but he knew he was taking a big risk in spite of this suspicion. He waited for Kelser's reply for what felt like aeons, but when it finally came, he felt only relief.

"Yes," Kelser said in the same, low whisper.

Hellam broadened his smile and turned back to his laptop as he spoke.

"There are people who share our passions Kelser - lots of people, and some of them need this passion... this craving, to be satisfied. Not that they want to actually get their hands dirty and perform the task themselves you understand - that would be far too risky. But they do want to witness it even through second hand methods."

Hellam rotated the laptop so Kelser could see and clicked on one of the video files. As it began to play, he moved his eyes between the screen and Kelser, monitoring his response, and continued to do so as they both watched the entire 45-minute film in silence.

When the victim had finally been killed, Hellam closed the lid of the laptop and pushed it to one side. "I have a contact in Sweden who has been making these films for a number of years. He sends them to me and I sell them on to my clients. My clients are *very* wealthy men Kelser, and these films can make huge amounts of money."

Hellam stopped for a moment and tried to analyse the man sitting before him. What he had just shown Kelser would have shocked almost anyone else into outrage - he was absolutely certain of that - yet Kelser seemed to have no reaction whatsoever. It was as if he had seen this kind of brutal torture and murder thousands of times before – as if it was old news.

Kelser scratched his cheek, rubbing a finger slowly along his scar. "These are snuff films," he said quietly. "Who buys these?"

"There are hundreds of people around the world who are willing to pay thousands for these films. There are numerous underground internet forums filled with potential customers. It's simply a matter of being intelligent and careful when making the transactions. You don't need to concern yourself with that side of things, I have that part organised and there are systems in place. But my contact charges me thousands for each of these films, and because of this, profits are not what they have the potential to be."

Kelser gazed at Hellam. "Who is your contact?"

"That doesn't concern you either. Everything is set up." He tapped the top of laptop gently. "Everything I need to run this business is stored in here; supplier and customer contact details are all heavily encrypted of course and only I will ever have access. But the important part of all this is that I want to cut the middle-man out of this operation." His eyes became wide with excitement. "That is why I want to start making my own films and that is where you come in. You have the qualities that I require in order to make these videos; I saw it in your eyes as you killed Richards. You are someone who can do this for me and I will make you a very rich man. Do you think you could do what we have just seen?"

"Of course." Kelser's answer came without hesitation.

Hellam looked at him, a little surprised at how readily he accepted. He had expected to have to convince him, but he already seemed accustomed to the idea.

"Are you certain?"

"Absolutely. But, I need assurances from you regarding certain things."

"Go ahead."

Kelser slowly twisted a silver ring on his right hand as his eyes narrowed. "Who are the victims and where will you source them from?"

"I have two trustworthy men who are responsible for that side of the operations. They have been told to find people who won't be missed - they have already acquired the first victim, a prostitute with no ties, nobody will even know she has gone for at least a few days... perhaps weeks."

Kelser considered this for a few moments. "What about the filming location?"

Hellam smirked. "I've been working on that for some time. Come, I'll show you."

**

As they drove, Hellam phoned Hal and told him to call Tyler then for them both to meet him at the farm in twenty minutes. Silence filled the space between Hellam and Kelser on the drive, but it felt natural and comfortable. There had been doubts in Hellam's mind about including Kelser in his latest project - he had doubts about including anyone new in that side of his life - but they were very minor compared to some others. He had far more confidence in including Kelser than he had been in the initial meetings with Hal and Tyler.

Hal and Tyler were professional killers but they had never been involved in anything of this nature and Hellam had wondered how they might react. What he did know, however, was that they were greedy and could be easily paid off. Not only that, but he also had far more on them than they could prove against him if they were to get cold feet on the deal for some reason. Hellam hadn't been so sure that Kelser could be bought off quite so easily, but he *had* been far more confident that Kelser would be willing to be included. After all, Hellam had said it to him earlier that evening; *you and I are the same Kelser.*

As Hellam drove the car down the dirt road towards the farm, he could see that Hal and Tyler had already arrived. Hal's car was parked at the rear of the building and a sliver of light could be seen through the barn door. Hellam parked then he and Kelser walked towards the large wooden building.

"I have used the two men you are about to meet for private contracts over the past few years," Hellam said. "They are more-or-less trustworthy, but more than that, they are greedy. They're used to getting the job done in a quick and efficient manner, which isn't necessarily the correct approach when making the kind of films we have in mind. I need someone like you to put on a show for the camera."

Kelser remained silent but Hellam almost thought he

saw the smallest hint of a smile, toying around the edges of his mouth. But then it was gone. Hellam opened the door to the barn and they both stepped inside.

Two of the floodlights were illuminated and bathing the concrete floor in a yellow glow. Tyler was leaning against one of the heavy duty stands that held the lights and Hal was sitting in a chair which was positioned in front of the camera. He turned and stood as he heard the door open.

"Hal, Tyler, this is Sebastian Kelser," Hellam said, waving a hand in Kelser's direction as an introduction.

Hal and Tyler nodded suspiciously and eyed Kelser up and down as he approached the floodlit area. His hands were pushed into his jacket pocket and he was glancing past the two men, looking around the barn.

"What's he doing here?" Hal asked, staring at Hellam, annoyance wrinkling the contours of his face.

"This is the man who will be running things here," Hellam replied, smiling and ignoring the disgruntled expression on Hal's face. "He has the relevant qualifications to see that the task is performed to an acceptable quality."

"Is this a joke? I thought this was our gig," Tyler chipped in as he shuffled forward.

"It was, but Kelser here can..." Hellam began but was interrupted.

"I'll do the job right, that's why I'm here," Kelser said, gazing intensely at Hal.

Hal slowly approached him and stared. Kelser stood perfectly still and absorbed Hal's gaze with indifference as the two remained inches apart. Hal sneered then circled around him and over to Hellam.

"I told you last time, we don't need help, we know how to do our fucking jobs," Hal said, ignoring Kelser now and speaking directly to Hellam.

"Your duties won't change. You are still in charge of acquiring the subjects and setting up the operations here. Kelser will be the one who performs the kill," Hellam reasoned. "Your pay will remain the same and you will still report directly to me, not to Kelser."

Hal glanced back to the scarred man, who was wandering around the rear of the floodlights and scrutinising a dented steel table beside the camera, then he turned back to Hellam.

"I'm not happy about this. Tyler and I work alone, you know that. This wasn't the deal we discussed."

"I know and for that I apologise, but this is the way it is now and you and Tyler need to live with it if you want your money," Hellam relaxed slightly as he sensed that the mention of money had quelled the anger in the two men. He stared at Hal and Tyler for a few moments until finally they looked at each other and shrugged with reluctant acceptance.

"As long as the money don't change okay?" Hal forced the words out with a low guttural tone as if to highlight his displeasure.

Hellam nodded and smiled again. "Now that we have the awkwardness out of the way, where are we on filming times? How soon can we begin?"

Tyler shuffled his hunched frame forward. "I think we're all set. The subject has been acquired." He motioned towards the rear of the barn in the direction of the sectioned off partition.

"I want to see the victim," said Kelser suddenly and

began to walk towards the partition.

Hal and Tyler glanced over to Hellam who shrugged and they all followed him to the far side of the building.

***

Sarah Price could barely see through her swollen red eyes. They had been tormented by tears for almost twenty-four hours. She had awoken with an agonising pressure in her skull, remembering the attack in her home immediately. The terrifying images of the hunched man who had been waiting for her in the bedroom sparked a fresh wave of panic and she flinched herself out of the grogginess. She moved back, but hit something behind her.

It was dark, but her pupils had already been dilated from unknown hours of unconsciousness so she could make out several shapes in the gloom. There was a doorway to her right with a small amount of light creeping through, but directly in front of her were several thin vertical shapes. She squinted and reached forward slowly and...

"No," she said quietly to herself, panic forcing a crack in her voice.

She placed her hands around the steel bars before her and followed them round, rotating her body in a complete circle. She moved her hands over the bars which were each separated by about three inches and she began to make a high pitched whimper - not quite a scream - as she realised they surrounded her. The floor was hard and she tilted her head back to see more silhouetted bars above her. She was in a cage!

"No," she screamed and pulled at the bars in desperation.

Then the tears had arrived and hadn't left her as she spent hours screaming for help and hysterically clawing at her tiny prison. But no one had come to her rescue and she heard no sounds except her own trembling breath and pounding heart.

As the hours passed, they beat down her attempts to break out of the cage and she curled herself up into one corner where she began to sob quietly.

She may have slept, she wasn't sure, but after several more hours, she heard voices beyond the doorway. A light came on and shone onto the floor, illuminating the cage as she heard mumbling and cursing. She thought about screaming for help, but considered this for a moment and remained silent; halting her breathing for as long as possible so she could hear. She couldn't make out any words, just the subtle sound of distant voices before they eventually died down. After a few more minutes, she heard a door slam open and more voices, raised this time as if arguing.

Sarah shuffled closer to the bars and leaned forward to see if she could make out any words but it was no use. Then she heard footsteps approach the doorway and she retreated away from edge of the cage again.

A man entered the room and stared at her. He gazed at her with dark, unmoving eyes. Free of the restraints of emotional shackles, they burned her skin and she felt prickles on the back of her neck. He had a thick scar running the full length of his left cheek, beginning just below his eye and ending before reaching the bottom of his jaw.

"Please... I, please," Sarah said in a trembling panic, fresh tears stinging her sore eyes.

Three other men entered the room behind the first and all stared at her in a similar way; as if she were some kind of newly discovered species that they had captured and were now studying. But the first man was the one who escalated the fear inside her. His eyes never left hers as he approached the cage.

"Please," Sarah repeated, but wasn't sure which words should follow.

The man with the scar remained silent, continuing his macabre study of her.

Sarah tore her eyes from his and looked at the other three men. One was dressed in a pristine, black suit and smirked as he watched her. Then she saw the other two men and screamed involuntarily as she recognised the huge man who had followed her home; the tattooed butterfly clearly visible on his upper arm. The final man shuffled forward and she realised that he was the one who had attacked her in her flat. He was the one who had brought her here.

"What... what do you want from me?" she asked, wiping moisture from her cheek. "Please, let me go. I won't go to the police, I swear."

The man in the suit appeared to enjoy this but the one with the scar remained still, his expression stoic as he stared at her. He was next to the cage now, the other men behind him as he crouched down so his face was level with hers. The others began to whisper among themselves about something, but Sarah's wide eyes became fixated on the man before her. He placed his hands on the bars and she pushed her back up against the opposite side of the cage, barely three feet away. He remained there, motionless, for a few seconds before he suddenly whipped out his hand and grabbed her arm. He tried to pull her close, but Sarah resisted and pulled away, pleading softly. His hand remained on her arm and he continued to pull until their eyes met. Sarah wanted to see something as she stared into his face; some kind of humanity or empathy, but she saw nothing. It was as if any emotion he was once capable of feeling had long-since been evaporated.

He squeezed her arm and held it still then, very slowly, ran his thumb gently over her wrist. Sarah frowned, confused by this gesture but wanted nothing more than to remove herself from his presence. Finally he released her and stood up before returning to the others.

The four men continued to whisper, casting occasional glances in her direction until they finally left the room. She heard them shuffle around beyond the door for a while before the lights went out and the sound of car engines outside roared into life. They grew quiet before disappearing completely and she knew that, once again, she was alone.

Thousands of unanswered questions hurtled through her mind as she curled herself up and softly mumbled indecipherable words. The questions faded as her thoughts were overcome by the reappearance of the pounding in her head. She remembered her daughter, a million miles away, and focused on the image of her smiling face in a photo which she kept in a frame by her bed. But it was now only available from deep inside her mind, in a place where this nightmare could never reach. Hours passed in silence until the pain in her head faded and she slowly, and unexpectedly, drifted into sleep.

Chapter 17

Lewis

Lewis finished the last of his fried egg with stale toast and pushed the plate across the table. Sitting in his flat, he leaned back on his chair. His stomach felt bloated; it had been the first proper meal he had finished in what felt like weeks and he sighed with satisfaction. He had been surviving on only bread, butter and alcohol so it felt good to have something to fill him up.

The face of Jonah had barely left his thoughts since waking and he had to constantly persuade himself that he hadn't imagined or dreamed the events of the previous night. He had been drinking and his mind had been foggy, but the moment he first laid eyes on the straggly haired man to the moment he disappeared behind the front door to the house, was clear in Lewis's mind. Craig Blaine had been telling the truth all along - at least that was the way it appeared.

The thought had occurred to Lewis that Craig could have just decided to pin the murder on someone he had seen frequent The Golden Anchor from time to time, but he didn't think so. Something hadn't felt *right* about Craig being the culprit; something unseen and something Lewis couldn't put his finger on. But when he saw Jonah, *that* made sense - he was certain that it was him, along with some unknown accomplice, who murdered Hannah.

The revelation that Jonah existed had brought with it a sensation of excitement; one that Lewis wasn't completely comfortable in feeling. He felt a tinge of guilt as the thrill of finding the man registered inside, because the thrill had been born from tragedy, and one that made him nauseous when he allowed it into his thoughts. But deep down, he knew better than that; the excitement he felt was one born from justice. He knew that Jonah was responsible and he wanted him to pay.

Lewis had decided almost as soon as he had awoken that he would inform the police of Jonah and his whereabouts. He had to do it for the sake of the innocent man currently waiting behind bars for the inevitable conclusion to his trial. He didn't expect the police to immediately see the truth as it appeared to Lewis and automatically release Craig, but surely they would have to consider that line of enquiry, and that at least would be a start. Once they began to follow that path, they would have to follow it to its conclusion.

Lewis felt positive for the first time since returning from his travels and was optimistic that he could prevent an injustice from occurring. He didn't want an innocent man to be punished whilst the real killer continued his life; living with disregard for the devastation he had created.

Lewis got up from his chair, took his plate into the kitchen and rinsed it in the sink then walked back into the front room and picked up his phone. He double checked the number from the online directory on his laptop screen and then dialled. After five rings a gruff, female voice answered.

"Yeah?"

"Mrs Blaine? It's... John from the newspaper, do you remember me?"

There was a long pause on the other end and Lewis could hear the breath of the old woman moving slowly over the receiver. It was long and drawn and the gap lasted so long that, for a moment, Lewis thought she was going to hang up.

"I remember," came her flat reply finally, followed by a hoarse cough. "What do you want?"

"I'm calling with some good news Mrs Blaine... at least I hope so. The man who Craig said was outside Hannah's door that night, you know, the one with the missing finger? Well I think..."

"Save it," Mrs Blaine cut in, her voice plain and matter-of-fact. "He's dead."

This time it was Lewis who initiated the gap of silence. After a few seconds he blurted out a half-question.

"What? Who..."

"They called this morning. Craig killed himself last night an' they found him in his cell." She spoke in a monotone as if she felt nothing, but Lewis heard her voice falter on the final few words; a bitter resentment riding in their wake. "Put that in your paper. Tell them an innocent man is dead!"

Lewis heard a click and then silence as she hung up. He stood with the phone to his ear, staring vacantly ahead as the world continued around him. Finally he lowered the receiver and held it by his side as he slowly walked over to the window and looked out at the street below. His vision blurred momentarily as moisture gathered which surprised him for a brief moment, before it was blinked away.

An innocent man, he thought to himself with repetition, *he was an innocent man.* But doubt grew and the words changed inside - *was he an innocent man?* The conviction Lewis felt had become a question without him even trying. The existence of Jonah proved nothing and Lewis couldn't deny this simple fact. But no matter how much he tried, he simply couldn't quash the notion that Craig didn't *feel* like the killer and Jonah did. It was true, he couldn't be sure of this fact but he suddenly became overwhelmed by the need to find an answer - to find the truth. All thoughts of informing the police about Jonah had suddenly been blown away by a hurricane of conviction.

He could go to the police and they *may* investigate Jonah, but there was no guarantee and even if they did then there was no guarantee they would find anything. It's easy to deny, deny, deny, especially when there is little hard evidence to the contrary. If he went to the police and they couldn't get anything on Jonah, then it would be too late; he would have played his hand too early and missed his chance. Lewis suddenly confessed something to himself that he was trying to keep buried somewhere - somewhere where all the ludicrous and insane ideas lived. The truth was, he didn't *want* to go to the police.

He turned away from the window and walked into his bedroom to the set of drawers. He opened the top one and saw the gun lying on top of several old bills; so out of place it almost appeared to be a toy. He reached down, placed his hand around the grip and picked it up, squeezing the handle tightly between his fingers. It felt more comfortable than it had before, as if it had moulded itself to Lewis's most outlandish ideas. He needed an answer to his question and the gun presented the only way that Lewis could realistically see himself getting one.

***

Later that day, Lewis drove to the street where he had seen Jonah enter the house. He parked a hundred yards away and waited. The minutes dragged by with frustrating lethargy and morphed into hours as Lewis sat patiently while the mid-day sun warmed the car. He took off his jacket and threw it on the back seat as he stared at a patch of shade, cast by a tree further along the road. He wished he had parked under that tree but he knew that he would have been too close to the house.

At half past two, Lewis saw a short, dumpy man in baggy jeans walk down the street and stop outside Jonah's house. He paused for a moment before walking up the short path and knocking on the door as he looked around nervously. Lewis leaned forward in his seat and rested his arms on the steering wheel as watched. Jonah eventually answered the door, spoke briefly to the man then they both disappeared inside.

A few minutes later - ten at the most - the dumpy man emerged from the door, pushing something into his pocket, and walked back down the street in the direction he had arrived.

Lewis sat back in his seat again and continued to watch and wait. His stomach groaned as hunger pangs came and went, but he refused to leave. He wanted to see what kind of man Jonah was, although he already had a reasonable idea. He couldn't be sure, but he suspected the short man who had visited earlier had bought something from Jonah and Lewis didn't consider himself jumping to conclusions when he decided it was probably drugs; the shifty demeanour of the short man as he arrived and left gave the impression that he was relatively unaccustomed to that kind of purchase.

Lewis had decided to follow Jonah for a few days in order to see if that could provide any information which would help him come to a conclusion about the man. He had already decided that he would confront him and get the answers he wanted anyway, but he thought it prudent to get to know a little more about him first.

As the hours passed and the car continued to warm, Lewis's eyelids began to feel heavy. He leaned back onto the head rest and allowed them to close.

Sleep came quickly and he dreamed of being back in his flat. Hannah was still alive in his dreams and he could pick up the phone and call her if he so chose. He was reading something but didn't know what it was. The words were familiar to him, but he couldn't quite place them, so he flicked the book over and looked at the cover but it had faded. The text and picture on the front were almost completely white, as if washed away; bleached into an indecipherable smudge of white and grey. Lewis turned back and continued to read until he finally came across a passage that he recognised. He had read this book before and this particular passage was well known; it was a famous. It was spoken by a character called Atticus to his daughter:

'I wanted you to see what real courage is, instead of getting the idea that courage is a man with a gun in his hand. It's when you know you're licked before you begin, but you begin anyway and see it through no matter what.'

In his dream, Lewis read and re-read the passage several times before slowly placing the book down, realising now that it was *To Kill a Mockingbird*. He looked again at the cover and this time could make out a small pattern in the picture. It looked like it was a picture of a face, smiling and staring at him. He narrowed his eyes as if this would clarify the picture somehow and saw that it was a photo of a woman he knew very well.

He got up and walked over to the drawers by his bed and opened the top one. He couldn't remember where he had found the gun originally, but picked it up anyway and stared at it with curiosity.

"Courage isn't a man with a gun in his hand..." he said quietly to himself as he gazed on.

Suddenly there was a loud bang at the door; a single thump and Lewis stared at it with wide eyes, suddenly feeling a sense of overwhelming dread. He stood, staring at the dark, wooden panels until a second knock shook the frame. He walked over, still carrying the gun, and slowly turned the handle. As he pulled the door open, he grimaced as the face of Jonah came into view. Lewis took a step back and squeezed the gun in his hand then noticed a second man standing behind Jonah. The second man's face was unclear, but on one of his arms Lewis saw the tattoo of something... a bird? He wasn't sure and didn't particularly care. He raised the gun and saw a crooked, snake-like grin overwhelm Jonah's features. The gun shook in Lewis's hand as he aimed at his forehead, between two strands of straggly blonde hair, and then gently squeezed the trigger.

Lewis woke with sweat falling down his face. The car was hot and he wiped a sleeve over his head and then lowered the window. His heart was beating rapidly and he took in a deep lungful of air as he rubbed his eyes. He glanced down at his watch and saw it was almost 5pm now. He had been in the car for close to five hours and he suddenly realised he was desperate to relieve himself.

He got out of the car, glancing briefly at the house, and walked down the street in the opposite direction. The owner of the corner shop was reluctant, but allowed Lewis to use the lavatory if he purchased enough, so Lewis returned to his car carrying a bagful of groceries he didn't need. He threw them on the back seat and settled back into his chair.

Just before 5:20pm, Lewis saw the door to the house open and Jonah stepped out. He was wearing the same clothes as the previous night and made the now familiar gesture of running a hand through his thick hair, before walking down the road and away from the car.

Lewis hurried out and began to follow him on foot, trying to keep a distance that he felt comfortable with. The sun was lower in the sky now but still powerful and long shadows covered the pavement while a rolling breeze curled the fine branches of the trees.

Jonah walked quickly, but adrenaline aided Lewis and he had no trouble in keeping pace. Jonah turned the bend and Lewis saw him stop at an ATM further along. People wandered by and Lewis crossed to road to look in the window of a book shop while he waited for Jonah to finish. Lewis was no spy, but he was confident that Jonah hadn't noticed he was being followed.

Jonah stuffed a wad of cash into his back pocket before turning and continuing along the street. Still on the opposite side of the road, Lewis followed, barely taking his eyes off the man as they strode down several more streets, each lined with shops and places of business. More people filled the streets as they finished work, and Lewis almost lost sight of Jonah a couple of times, before noticing his incessant habit of continually combing back his hair as he walked along.

Around a mile away from where they had started their journey, Jonah walked into a bar called Jannson's. Lewis considered following him in but wasn't sure if he would be pushing his luck and decided not to risk being noticed before he had enough time to get more of an idea of who this man was.

He noticed a small café on the opposite side of the road and bought a coffee before returning to the street and sitting at one of the metallic tables provided outside. He sipped as he waited and watched the door. He was surprised when Jonah returned a few moments later carrying a bottle of beer and sitting at one of the small tables outside Jannson's. Jonah gulped his beer as he thumbed his phone and continually checked his watch.

Suddenly a black limousine pulled up outside Jannson's and two men got out then it pulled away and parked in a bay further along. One of the men was dressed in a pristine black suit that looked very expensive and took off an equally expensive looking pair of sunglasses. The two men walked over to the table where Jonah waited. The second man was taller than the first, but older, and his face sagged around his cheeks.

Lewis sipped his coffee and stared at them as Jonah placed the phone in his pocket and stood up to shake hands with the man in the black suit, ignoring his older companion. Lewis frowned as a gradual sense of recognition dawned on him. He had seen the man in the suit before; perhaps in a newspaper article or on local TV - he wasn't sure. He couldn't remember his name but was certain he had been reported on due to some kind of charity donation and was relatively well known in the area. But why would he be meeting with someone like Jonah?

A man came out of Jannson's and spoke to all three men then disappeared back inside before returning seconds later with three drinks on a tray. As he watched the three men have their conversation and drink their drinks, Lewis withdrew his own mobile phone from his pocket and switched on the camera. As casually as possible, he raised it and took several photos of the three men, zooming in as much as the five mega-pixel camera would allow without distortion.

The three men chatted for around twenty minutes before the smart suited one stood abruptly. The older man joined him and they walked briskly towards the limousine where the man with the sagging cheeks opened the door, allowing the black suit to enter. Then, as they drove off, Lewis's attention was drawn back to Jonah who had returned to thumbing his phone. He contemplated getting another coffee, unsure of how long he would be waiting, but then Jonah stood and began to walk back along the street towards his house. Like before, Lewis allowed him to get a distance away and then followed him along the same route which they had taken earlier. He paused at the corner of Jonah's street and watched him disappear into his house. Lewis then returned to his car.

On the drive back to his flat, Lewis's thoughts continually returned to the black suited man. Where had he seen him before? It wasn't too long ago, he was certain of that, and the fragmented images in his mind regarding the man were fuzzy and indistinct, but were there nevertheless.

The traffic thinned as rush hour passed and the roads became clear. When he arrived home, he parked up and took the stairs. As he opened the door and stepped inside, he pulled out his phone and studied the photo he had taken of Jonah and his two companions, questioning again why these two smart, apparently respectable men, would be meeting with him. It made little sense to Lewis and he felt his mind swirl as the new information clogged inside.

He grabbed a notepad from his bedroom and began to write fragments of a list which contained anyone who had been in some way linked to Jonah and Craig. Naming the people he knew, and describing of the ones he didn't. The list was short and made even shorter when Lewis crossed out Craig's own name - disregarding him for the moment.

He stared at the page and rested the pen between his lips while his eyes slowly narrowed then he booted up his laptop. He transferred the photo he had taken on his phone to the computer then printed a copy out on letter-sized paper and placed it on the table in front of him.

He stared at it for a moment, focusing on the man with the black suit. The familiarity with the features of the man had only grown stronger on the drive back and Lewis couldn't stop wondering about him. He felt a subtle yet nagging sensation in his head and he found it impossible to ignore. Where had he seen that black suit before? The half-remembered article or news report about charity donations surfaced again and he thought for a few minutes before turning back to the laptop.

He double clicked on the internet icon and did a search for 'charity work, philanthropy, Surrington' then hit the return key. Thousands of results popped up in seconds but nothing of particular interest registered with Lewis. He clicked on the 'images' section and the screen was filled with small, thumbnail pictures associated with the search.

He scrolled slowly until he saw a picture about a quarter of the way down the page. The thumbnail showed a number of people, but Lewis centred in on the tiny pixels that interested him. He clicked on the image and a website for the local newspaper was displayed.

'Local businessman donates £30,000 to Surrington Hospital.'

Lewis looked at the picture, which was larger and had greater clarity now. It showed a representative from the hospital and several nurses standing in one of the wards and shaking hands with a man in a dark suit. Lewis glanced down to the print out on the table beside him and saw immediately that it was the same man. He read the caption underneath.

'Francesca Williamson shakes hands with Joseph Hellam after receiving £30,000 for six new dialysis machines for the renal centre at Surrington Hospital.'

"Joseph Hellam," Lewis said under his breath, suddenly recognising the name. He had heard it many times and couldn't believe he had forgotten so easily. Joseph Hellam was well respected in Surrington for his philanthropy and due to the fact his businesses had helped restore certain, dilapidated areas of the town.

"Why would you meet with someone like Jonah?" The words left his mouth slowly, almost as if, by saying them out loud, they would provide some kind of revelation. But the answer didn't come and simply hung there as he gazed at the laptop screen.

He turned away, forgetting about Joseph Hellam for the time being and picked up the print out. He became absorbed in the blocky pixels which formed the three faces. Jonah's thin smirk drew him in and Lewis focused in on the man he was gradually becoming obsessed with. Had Hannah seen that smirk moments before she had died? Had that incomplete hand been one of the ones which had squeezed the life from the woman he loved?

The room around Lewis faded away until all that existed was himself and the photo. His mind conjured pictures and scenarios of death and revenge; a fantasy that lived only inside his head. Then he remembered the gun and tore himself away from the photo, wrenching his thoughts back to reality. He slowly turned back to the computer screen and began to type several more searches into Google and YouTube.

Chapter 18

Hellam

Hellam threw the silk sheets to one side and sat on the edge of his bed, rubbing the sleep from his eyes. The master bedroom in his house was large but sparsely furnished: king size bed, bedside table, huge mirror covering one wall and a large television hanging on another. The morning sun penetrated the curtains and the scent of freshly cut grass flowed in through the open window; Eugene, his gardener, had obviously been busy. He walked into the en-suite bathroom, had a shower, a shave, and dressed in one of his usual dark suits before going into the kitchen. He flicked on another large TV and half-listened to the morning news as he made coffee.

He enjoyed the peace during the mornings, before his two housekeepers arrived, and he had the place to himself. He felt tranquil and relaxed during that time more than any other, and he had a chance to consider what the coming day would bring. His thoughts drifted to Hal and Tyler and the barn and the task that they would be completing for him that evening. He closed his eyes and pictured the scene as the smell of coffee filled the room.

He picked up his phone and dialled Kelser's number. It was answered after a couple of rings.

"Yes Mr Hellam?" Kelser said.

"Kelser, could you meet me for breakfast? I want to discuss the details regarding this evening with you."

"Yes, of course."

"Meet me at Darcy's in an hour, it'll be quiet there."

Hellam pushed the 'end call' button and turned his attention to the news.

***

Darcy's Café *was* quiet, just as Hellam had predicted. It was a small place and set back from the main street in a narrow alleyway, but it was reassuringly expensive and both the coffee and food were exceptional in Hellam's opinion.

Kelser was already waiting for him at a table in the far corner, away from the single other patron, when Hellam arrived and they both ordered their food immediately.

"The food here is excellent, have you been before?" Hellam asked after they ordered.

Kelser shook his head and poured himself a glass of water from the jug on the table. Hellam knew that Kelser wasn't a man who enjoyed or participated in small talk, neither was Hellam for that matter and he decided to move straight on to business.

"Filming will take place at 10pm tonight. I want you to meet Hal and Tyler at the farm."

Kelser nodded slowly and gazed through his boss as

Hellam continued with the instructions.

"You won't need to worry about the filming technicalities; Hal and Tyler will deal with all that. I just want you to... put on a good show, you know what I mean."

A single further tilt of Kelser's head reassured Hellam and he leaned in, dropping his voice to a whisper.

"Make it last," he said slowly, his voice thin and lined with sheets of ice. "Make her suffer. I want to see her pain."

Hellam thought he saw the vacancy of Kelser's facial expression falter for a second; almost as if he was trying to suppress a gnawing emotion that was forcing him to do something. Was it a repressed smile? Could it be true that Kelser was excited by the prospect of torturing that innocent woman to death?

Of course you are, thought Hellam, *because you and I, we're the same.*

Their food arrived and they both ate in silence for a few minutes while Hellam studied his new prodigy between mouthfuls. He suddenly decided to share something that had been lingering in his mind a lot lately.

"You know..." he said, washing some bacon down with a sip of coffee, "...A former girlfriend of mine found some of those films on my laptop."

Kelser looked up and Hellam immediately noticed his shock – at least an expression as close to shock as Kelser ever approached.

"She was snooping around and stumbled across them while at my home one evening and do you know what she called me?" He paused and again, leaned in close. "A *psychopath*, she called me a psychopath." His voice was incredulous at this and he glanced around the café. "She became hysterical and started shouting, as if she had been given impromptu permission to psychoanalyse me. She knew immediately that the films were real and couldn't believe what she had found."

"What did you do?" Kelser asked in a whisper.

"She left, I let her go. What else could I do? She was shouting like a mad woman and I'm not going to tolerate that in my own home."

"You let her go? Did she not go to the police?"

Hellam smiled and pushed the last fried mushroom into his mouth. "I called her an hour or so later, after she had calmed down a little. I tried to reason with her and convince her that the films contained actors and that it wasn't real. She didn't believe me of course, but I think that bought me some time."

"Time for what?"

Hellam gazed at him, "The only solution that presented itself."

"Who did the job?"

"Hal, together with another man. They paid her a visit when she was alone and performed the job extremely well. They even pinned it on her simple minded neighbour. I wish I could have been there to see her face as they did it. That prying bitch deserved everything she got from those two. In fact, she deserved far more."

Kelser raised one corner of his mouth into a smirk and continued to eat his food.

"She couldn't understand those films like you and I can," Hellam continued, enthusiasm growing. "She couldn't understand how people could pay thousands for each one, or how they could enjoy witnessing such suffering. But she was missing the point completely, don't you agree? These films are about being human and about the lengths of human suffering. They are *not* just films of death - they are works of *art*."

Hellam suddenly became aware of a subtle change of atmosphere between them – a levelling of like minds. He felt a certain satisfaction at finally finding someone with whom he could confide his darkest secrets – someone who could understand. At that moment he became convinced that they were two lost souls colliding, finally able to share their obsessions.

"This one will certainly be a work of art," Kelser quipped, wiping his mouth with a napkin.

Hellam grinned and called the waiter over to ask for the bill.

***

George Langton stared at the empty bottle of Seroxat pills that was resting in his hand. His vision blurred momentarily, and then returned. He wasn't sure how many pills had been in there, but was certain there had been enough; it was a relatively new bottle and some days he forgot to take them at all. He tried to screw the plastic cap back on, but he couldn't line it up correctly so threw the bottle and cap across the table of his lounge. They rattled across the wood and fell to the carpet on the opposite side, not making a sound. Langton leaned forward, swaying, and finished the glass of vodka in front of him then grabbed the bottle of clear liquor and leaned back in his chair.

"I'm sorry," he said for the hundredth time that morning to the ghost that lived inside his mind. "I'm sorry, I didn't mean to... to..."

Tears began to fall from his already swollen eyes and he wiped them away with an unsteady palm. He lifted the bottle, which inexplicably seemed heavier each time he drained some of the liquid away, and took several long gulps. He felt nauseous but knew he could keep it down; he *had* to keep it down. He tried to focus through the tears but saw several versions of the room around him and each one began to spin slowly.

"I didn't mean to... I'm sor..."

His head fell back and his hand relaxed, releasing the bottle which fell to the floor by his feet and bled the rest of its contents onto the soft carpet.

Langton's eyes closed. The final tears were liberated and inched their way down.

***

Burning.

Langton gagged. He felt fire in the back of his throat and vomit lurched from inside him. He felt something in his mouth and pulled away but something else on the back of his neck prevented him from doing so. He gagged again and tried to open his eyes but it was too bright.

More vomit.

He realised someone was pushing fingers down his throat and tried to pull away again but felt that it was a hand on the back of his head that was stopping him.

"Ak...no, urgh..." he forced out, but the fingers

remained.

The third gag was harder and he coughed, spluttering around the gloved fingers in his mouth then finally he was released. He rolled over to one side and continued to splutter his throat clear.

His head throbbed and there was a voice coming from miles away, carried by a wind of distortion, but Langton didn't care about that. He tried to roll again in an attempt to get away, but it was impossible now; he had been drained of the last ebbs of any remaining energy and he lay on the carpet as confusion and pain engulfed him.

He tried to open his eyes again and fought against the intensity of the light around him. The room was circling him like a waiting vulture as he lay motionless. The walls were awash with blurred shapes and colours. He heard the voice again and it sounded louder this time; closer, more urgent. There was a sudden sensation of air on his right cheek and he felt someone's breath brush against him.

"Welcome back," the voice said.

"Wha... who are you?" Langton managed to force out as he turned to look at whoever was beside him. He felt movement and saw a blurred silhouette beside him elongate; whoever they were, they were now standing over him. There was silence for several years and Langton felt himself slipping away into unconsciousness again. A sharp pain burned his cheek as the gloved hand slapped.

"I'm just a concerned citizen," the voice said slowly.

Langton widened his eyes, "You... you basta..."

The shape moved away as Langton tried to focus on him, but it was no use anyway. It was so damn bright and the room wouldn't stop moving. He felt so tired - he just wanted to sleep this nightmare away.

"It looks like I got here just in time," the man said. His voice was calm and displayed neither kindness nor hostility. "Why would you go and do something like this?"

Langton managed to raise a hand to his face and rubbed his eyes but his vision remained obscured. "You know why... you know better than anyone..."

The shape moved slowly around him and sharpened slightly so Langton could see a vague outline of the man, but the details were still obscured. The blinding light curved around him, distorting him into some kind of monster.

"But why George? You were home free; I no longer required your services. You had already given me everything I wanted." The voice was low and sincere, at least to Langton's swaying consciousness.

"I don't give a shit about what you wanted, you..." Langton felt his stomach tighten and thought he was going to throw up again but the sensation subsided. He suddenly felt the pain in his head throb violently and raised a hand to his forehead, but then, like the nausea, it slowly evaporated.

"Why then?" the voice asked.

"You brought it all back. Perhaps... maybe I hadn't forgotten about what I did but I had pushed it away. I had found a way to convince myself it wasn't true." His voice cracked while his throat continued to burn. "Then you sent me those letters and it all came back. She won't leave me now... this is the only way."

The silhouetted figure before him crouched down and leaned in close. "Where is she George? Where did you put her body?"

"F... fuck you," Langton spat.

"If you truly feel remorse for what you did to Michelle Layne then you should tell me the truth." Again, Concerned Citizen's voice was calm and showed no signs of hostility.

"I can't," he spluttered. "People can't know. My family, they think I'm a good man, I *am* a good man for Christ sake."

The figure swayed in the rotating room before him and lowered his voice. "You are *not* a good man George, we both know that."

Langton felt fresh tears fall and he sobbed pathetically, turning his head away and burying it deep into the carpet.

"And what family? You have no family."

The words carried blades and they sliced into Langton's flesh. "Please, don't make me..."

"You are, and always will be alone. But Michelle Layne had a family; Michelle Layne *still* has a family. I should have told them what I know years ago, but I'm like you George - selfish. I had things to do before I could let them know about how you murdered their daughter. But now those things are almost complete and the time has come for you to tell me where you buried the girl."

"No, no, please," Langton sobbed, wishing he could burrow through the floor and fall into infinity.

"Tell me where you put her."

"I can't, I'm a good man... I'm good."

"You're a child abuser and a murderer," the man said, using an almost soothing tone which contradicted his words.

"It was an accident... an accident. I'm so sorry, I didn't mean to..."

Langton suddenly felt a pressure on his right leg and

turned away from the carpet. The blurred figure was holding something and pushing it against him.

"Tell me where," the figure said.

Langton shook his head then there was a loud bang. He screamed as pain rippled through his calf and he reached down to where the bullet had entered.

"Please, no..." Langton screamed.

"Tell me where you put her after you killed her."

Langton saw the figure raise the gun and push it into his other leg, the dark metal suddenly clear in a world of distorted shapes. The pain in his leg reverberated up his body and came in agonising waves. He wanted to die, he wanted to kill himself and wished it would all be over but he knew that whoever this man was, he would not stop until he got his answer. He stared at Concerned Citizen's outline as he gazed back, motionless.

"Tell me."

"Please stop."

"Tell me!" The voice louder, aggression seeping through now.

"She's..." Langton sobbed again as pain surrounded him. "She's in the garden... my house in Alderidge; she's buried underneath the shed. She's there. I'm sorry, I'm so sorry, please... stop."

The figure retracted the gun and pushed it into his jacket then stood and gazed down at Langton. As his eyes began to clear, Langton almost thought he saw something that he recognised about the man's demeanour but it was quickly forgotten as fresh waves of agony reached up his leg.

"If you're lying, I'll come back and next time I'll make sure you tell me the truth," the man said nonchalantly.

Langton wanted to say something but didn't know which words he could use. He watched the man walk across the room and pull something from his pocket. Langton almost screamed again, thinking it was the gun, then he realised Concerned Citizen was making a phone call. His voice sounded distant again, but Langton managed to make out that he was requesting an ambulance. When he had finished, he walked back to Langton, placed two hands beneath his shoulders and began to drag him across the floor towards the hall.

"It's over for you now. You should count yourself lucky George," he said dropping him to the floor of the hallway. He stood over Langton for a brief moment as if to study him then suddenly turned and left through the door, leaving it ajar behind him.

Langton watched as the hallway turned and stretched around him and his head began to pound, almost matching the blinding pain in his leg. He felt something akin to relief which surprised him as he tried to contemplate what would happen now. His emotions morphed several times as he waited; relief was overwhelmed by horror and dread at the thought of prison. But that, in turn, changed into a strange and reluctant acceptance.

His mind lulled and he felt unconsciousness rise again. By the time the paramedics arrived, his eyelids felt like lead and confusion dominated his thoughts. As one of the female paramedics leaned over him, he whispered softly in her ear.

"Tell Michelle I'm sorry."

Chapter 19

Lewis

Lewis raised the gun in his right hand and supported it with his left, the way he had seen on the YouTube videos which he had studied the day before. The sun hung in a clear, blue sky and penetrated the branches of the trees that surrounded him. The forest was an hour's drive from his home, but he knew it was large enough and empty enough to not be heard - at least he hoped that would be case.

He raised the gun, holding it as steady as possible, and closed one eye as he aimed for a tree about twenty feet away. He glanced around, but thought that he probably wouldn't have seen anybody even if they were there since the thickness of the trees prevented a clear view. He took aim and squeezed the trigger. The gun fired and a loud thunder clap exploded around him. Lewis instinctively shrunk at the sound.

"Jesus," he said, the flicker of a smile widening around his mouth; he hadn't realised how loud it would be.

It was only after he had begun to search the internet

the previous evening that he had discovered he had acquired a .22 calibre Smith and Wesson semi-automatic handgun. It wasn't particularly powerful, but the kick he had felt as it fired seemed powerful enough and it sounded like a bomb had gone off in the quiet stillness of the forest.

He had found videos on YouTube showing how to operate a similar gun and he simply applied what he had learned with great care. He didn't entirely trust himself not to shoot a bullet in his foot before the day was out, and checked everything several times. He found that the gun was capable of holding ten rounds but it only had eight remaining; Kyle had obviously fired a couple when he owned it. Lewis decided he would make only four practice shots in the forest, since he was unsure of how to obtain more bullets and didn't want to show up at Jonah's with no ammunition.

He looked up and saw that a fragment of bark had been displaced from the trunk of the tree he had aimed at, and he felt an unexpected pride wash over him. He raised the gun again and fired a second shot. Knowing what to expect this time, he didn't shrink away and absorbed the kick from the gun through his arms and shoulders with much more success than the first attempt. He watched as the bullet created a second hole in the tree and bark exploded from the trunk.

He lowered the gun and thought about what he was doing - something he tried not to focus on too much. Was he really going to go through with it? Lewis Foster wasn't someone who fired guns or someone who obsessed over revenge. But then again, Lewis Foster wasn't someone who'd had the woman he loved brutally murdered before.

She had been taken away from him in the worst possible way. No, Lewis Foster *wasn't* someone who fired guns.

But everyone can change, he thought quietly as he stared at the bullet holes in the tree and slowly raised the gun for a third shot.

***

When he returned to his flat, Lewis made himself several slices of toast and ate them slowly as he stared once again at the photo of Jonah. It was resting on the coffee table before him and he found it difficult to focus on anything else; his attention continually drawn to the thin, blurred features of a man he didn't know, but was nonetheless growing to detest.

Suddenly there was a knock at the door and Lewis brushed crumbs off his shirt as he walked over.

He saw Kelly's smiling face staring back at him as he opened the door.

"Kelly... hi, what are you doing here?"

"Sorry to just turn up like this, but I was in the area and thought I'd pop in to see how you were feeling." she said as he gestured for her to come in.

He sighed, "A little better, but still not great, you?" He went into the kitchen to make them both a coffee.

"The same."

He waved a hand towards the sofa and she sat down, placing her bag beside her.

"Did you hear about Craig Blaine?" she asked as he brought the coffee over and then sat down in the chair opposite.

He had seen a short section in the newspaper about Craig's death so he didn't have to tell her about the meeting with Craig's mother - he didn't want her to know about how far he was going to get to the truth.

"Yes, I'm not sure how to feel about it to be honest," he replied.

Kelly shook her head, "No, I know what you mean. I sort of feel relieved that there won't be a trial now. I'm not sure how I would have handled that. But at the same time, I wanted him to answer for what he did to her; how could anyone do that to another human being?" She shook her head again and stared down at the coffee between her hands as steam swirled from the mug.

"I don't know."

Lewis thought briefly of the gun which was now resting silently in the drawer and then of Jonah.

They sat in silence for a moment and a strange unease gathered between them for a reason that Lewis couldn't quite fathom. Kelly rotated the mug of coffee in her hands idly as she looked around the room uncomfortably. Lewis noticed her eye fall on the photograph of Jonah and his two companions between them and a frown appeared on her face. Lewis went to pick up the photo, annoyed at himself for leaving it out but Kelly suddenly leaned forward and rotated the image towards her then picked it up.

"What's this?" she asked, studying the three men.

"Er…" Lewis hesitated as he tried to think. "It's just a picture I took. I saw the one on the left acting suspiciously around the car park in my building so decided to take a photo on my phone in case anybody's car went missing." He felt himself tense inside, it was a ridiculous excuse but he didn't have time to think. He looked at Kelly, but she didn't seem to be listening to him anyway. Her gaze was on the picture and she didn't say anything for a long time.

Lewis shuffled uncomfortably in his seat, wishing she would put the picture down and forget about it, but he became aware that something was wrong.

"What is it?" he asked.

Kelly glanced up. "I think I know this man."

Lewis felt his mouth fall open by the smallest fraction as her words sunk in and he looked at the photo in her hand. "Which one?"

"Him." She pointed towards the oldest of the three men, the one with the sagging cheeks and thick glasses.

Lewis couldn't say anything for a moment. He looked at Kelly then down to the photo and back again. "You know him?"

"Yes, I'm sure it's him. I mean he's a lot older than the last time I saw him. But it's definitely him." She stared closer at the print out.

"Who is it?"

Kelly lowered the picture and looked up to Lewis. "He was a teacher in my school – Mr Langton."

"He's a teacher?"

"Well, he *was*, I mean that was a long time ago and…" Kelly's voice trailed off and her eyes began to glaze over.

"What is it?" asked Lewis.

The frown on Kelly's face distorted slightly and she began to mumble something to herself. "Mr Langton, Mr Langton… George Langton…"

"What is it?" repeated Lewis, barely able to stop himself from shouting.

She looked at him. "Nothing… it's just I was speaking

to a friend a few years ago and her mother was Mrs Benedict, the art teacher from my school." She placed the picture on the table and drew her attention back towards Lewis as her voice lowered conspiratorially. "Anyway, we got talking about old teachers and she mentioned Mr Langton, his first name is George... I don't know how we got onto him. Well she told me that her mother found something out about him. I remembered that he left our school quite suddenly while I was there, although I didn't know why at the time – no one did."

Lewis nodded, squeezing his hands together as he listened intently.

"Well my friend's mum said that he was sacked because he was touching the younger girls. It was enough for a few of them to feel uncomfortable and some of them told their parents. Apparently he was forced to resign, but the school never reported it officially since they didn't want the embarrassment. My friend's mum was appalled when she found out and quit her job shortly afterwards." Kelly sipped her coffee, her eyes wide and enthusiastic as she spoke. Occasionally she glanced back down to the print out of George Langton. "The school covered it up and convinced the parents not to take it any further if Mr Langton was dismissed. The police were never involved."

"What happened to Langton?" Lewis asked.

"He moved away, my friend told me that her mum said it was to a village in Somerset somewhere, I don't know where though."

"I guess he must have come back," Lewis said.

Kelly nodded, "I wonder if he's still working as a teacher? God, I hope not."

Lewis shrugged and drank his coffee then placed the

empty mug back down.

"Did he ever touch you?" he asked, not really thinking and regretted the question immediately.

"No! No way, I wouldn't have let him. I didn't have him in any classes anyway. What a sicko."

She regarded Langton's slightly blurred features in the photo then said, "That's really strange how I walk in here and you have a photo of him."

Lewis forced an uncomfortable smile. "Yeah, I was just taking a photo of the other guy, the long haired one… just a coincidence I guess."

Kelly nodded slowly, unconvinced, but she appeared to brush it off. They chatted some more about work and about Hannah before the conversation slowed and trickled to an eventual stop. Finally, Kelly stood up and they hugged then she thanked him for the coffee.

"Anyway, you seem a little brighter than last time we spoke. I hope things will get better for you… for both of us," she said as Lewis showed her out.

"Thanks Kelly, me too. Speak again soon."

Lewis washed the empty mugs in the sink as his mind churned. As the days had passed and he had discovered more and more information about Jonah and the people he had met with, it only raised further questions: why would Joseph Hellam be meeting with someone like Jonah and why would an old school teacher somehow be associating with either of them? Lewis was getting tired of all these questions; he needed some answers.

He went back over to his chair and turned the laptop on. He started internet explorer and typed 'people directory uk' into Google. A website called 192.com was displayed as one of the sponsored links and Lewis clicked on it. He did a search for George Langton in the UK and a list of around thirty names was displayed on the screen. He scrolled down the list slowly and saw that one of the addresses was in Surrington, although the full address could only be found by paying a fee, which didn't interest Lewis for the moment. The Surrington entry was for a Mr George R. Langton who had been registered on the electoral role from 2002. The listing also showed previous owners for that address but this also didn't particularly hold much interest.

He cleared the search box and typed in 'George R Langton' then hit the enter key. This time three items came up - the first being the one in Surrington, but below this there was a listing for George R Langton in a village called Alderidge in Somerset. The column next to the listing showed that he had been on the electoral role in Alderidge between 1993 and 1998.

Lewis stared at the screen, trying to absorb the information and make sense out of it. He got up and fetched his notepad and pen then returned. He wrote George Langton at the top of the page and then began writing down all the information about his current and previous addresses. He turned the page and wrote 'Jonah' on the top. He jotted down Jonah's address and turned the page again. This time he wrote 'Joseph Hellam??' then left the page blank.

Lewis remembered that Craig's mother had told him how Craig had seen two men on the night of the murder; Jonah *and* another man, one with a tattoo of a bird, or something similar, on his arm. He considered this for a moment but this man still hadn't made an appearance and Lewis decided to focus his attention on Jonah and the other two for the time being.

He looked back at the laptop screen and was drawn to the listing of George R Langton in Alderidge – it was in Somerset.

"Alderidge... Alderidge..." he whispered to himself and rubbed the smooth plastic of the pen with his thumb. Yet again there was a nagging itch in Lewis's mind; a familiarity with the name of the village.

He opened a new tab in internet explorer and typed 'Alderidge, Somerset' into Google. The second result was a Wikipedia page for the village and Lewis clicked on it. The page was short and highlighted the location and population of the village, together with a small photo of a church - the central feature.

He scrolled down and then saw a section near the bottom of the page called 'Disappearance of Michelle Layne' and he immediately knew why he recognised the name 'Alderidge'. He read the short section several times:

'In July 1995, Michelle Layne, a thirteen-year-old girl went missing while walking from a friend's house to her home on Forest Road in Alderidge. Media interest around the country focused in on the disappearance but, despite thousands of man hours trying to find the girl, she is still missing. The Superintendent in charge of the enquiry at the time said, in a 2001 TV interview, that he strongly suspects she was murdered by persons unknown and that it would be very unlikely her body would ever be found.

In 1997 her parents founded the Michelle Layne Charity in order to help locate missing children around the UK.'

The Michelle Layne disappearance had dominated the news in 1995 and although Lewis himself was only seventeen at the time, he could remember it well.

He wrote some more details down on his pad and then went into the kitchen. He ran the cold tap for a moment before pouring some water into a glass and downing it in one. He walked back to the laptop and closed all the searches relating to George Langton; he had spent enough time on that little diversion. He needed to focus on Jonah; he was the one who was involved in Hannah's death and he was the one who would give him the answers he required. He glanced over to his bedroom where the gun was sitting patiently.

'Courage isn't a man with a gun in his hand...'

Lewis didn't feel particularly courageous when he thought about what he needed to do to get the answers. Perhaps Atticus Finch was right; Lewis didn't have courage, but he certainly had a gun.

***

As the sky outside Lewis's window inched from navy blue towards black, he filled a glass tumbler with water then drank it down in one. He ignored how his hand shook as he tipped the glass back and, after finishing, slammed the glass on the kitchen table as if to banish the doubts that were ever present.

He checked his watch: 8.05pm. Then went into the bathroom and splashed cold water on his face. He hadn't eaten anything since just before Kelly's surprise visit and his stomach rumbled as he ran a towel over his skin. He thought he should probably eat something but wasn't convinced he would be able to keep it down so disregarded the thought.

He walked into the front room, put on his jacket and went back to the drawers by his bed. He pulled open the top one and lifted out the gun then, very carefully, pushed it into his pocket. It felt heavier than it had a few hours earlier, even though the gun contained just four remaining bullets. Lewis wondered if it would be empty when he returned home. Self doubt wandered around him again, sniggering at his every move and undermining his will. He took several long, deep breaths before walking out of the door and locking it behind him.

The calmness of the evening outside represented a stark contrast to Lewis's mental state as he walked down the street; he was a mass of anxiety and could feel gathering perspiration on his forehead that had nothing to do with any physical exertion. His hand was clamped around the gun in his pocket, as if he was clinging to some kind of macabre security blanket.

He tried to focus his thoughts on the job at hand and why he was doing what he was doing. He thought about Jonah and Craig Blaine, but most of all he thought about Hannah.

He reached the corner of the street where Jonah lived but he hesitated as he rounded the bend. The gun still felt heavy in his pocket and weighed down his steps as he approached the front door. He felt his breath quicken uncontrollably as he walked up the path to the door, noticing the light in the window at the front of the house. He fought a final moment of doubt as it attempted to smother his conviction, but he knew it would never be able to stop him now; he knew what he had to do. As he pushed away all the uncertainty, he took a huge lungful of air and knocked on the door.

He heard footsteps approach from the other side and noticed they stopped suddenly. Lewis felt hot as he looked at the door, seeing the spy-hole for the first time - Jonah was staring at him.

"What do you want pal?" came an irritated voice from behind the door.

"I..." Lewis stumbled, "I was sent round here for some stuff?"

"Stuff? What stuff you talking about pal?"

He had barely begun and already he was losing it; Jonah was bound to know he didn't have a clue what he was talking about.

"I don't know, they sent me. They said you'd have some stuff," Lewis replied, almost ready to cut his losses and turn away.

Suddenly he heard a lock click from the other side and the door swung open. Jonah stood with a white vest hanging loosely over his skinny frame, his blonde hair smeared across his forehead.

"Who the fuck are *they*?" Jonah asked, scowling.

Lewis stared at him for a moment, startled to be face-to-face with him so suddenly. He fumbled with the gun in his pocket and noticed Jonah glance down, a crease dividing his forehead. Lewis wrenched the gun from his pocket, almost dropping it to the floor as he pulled it free but then adjusting his grip just in time. He raised it and pointed it at Jonah's transforming face.

"Hey man, what the hell is this?" Jonah asked, his mouth wide and hands instinctively drawing up from his side in surrender.

"Get inside!" Lewis rasped through tight, thin lips and

pushed forward, forcing Jonah back into his house.

"What the hell is this? What do you want?" Jonah stepped backwards allowing Lewis to enter, who pushed the door shut behind him but not daring to take his eyes off the man whose house he had just invaded.

"Go in there," Lewis said, nodding to a door on the right which he presumed led into the front room.

Jonah backed up and went through the doorway, his hands still out by his side. "You want some smack? I can sort you out, no worries pal, you only need to ask. Free of charge, you know what I mean?"

Lewis followed him in and gestured to an old sofa which was covered in magazines and discarded crisp packets. "Sit down."

"What's this all about friend?" asked Jonah, his eyes huge with attempted sincerity.

Lewis stared at him for a moment as anger seethed inside. This *was* the man, he knew it. He pulled out a small photograph from his pocket and threw it onto the sofa next to Jonah.

"What's this?" Jonah asked, picking up the picture.

"You recognise her?"

Jonah looked at the photograph, but said nothing for a moment.

"I said, do you recognise her?" Lewis repeated and gripped the gun tightly between his sweating fingers.

Jonah looked up slowly and gazed at Lewis in silence before hesitantly shaking his head. "No man, no I don't recognise her."

"You're lying," Lewis said, trying not to yell. "You were seeing her and then she found something she shouldn't, so you murdered her. Am I right?" The words came out too quickly and Lewis wanted to make them clearer, highlighting their significance. "You murdered her!"

"You don't know what the fuck you're talking about pal."

"Am I right?" Lewis stepped forward and pushed the gun so it was just a few feet from Jonah's face.

Jonah leaned back, away from the gun and turned his head sideways as he squeezed his eyes shut. "I've seen her before but she wasn't *my* girlfriend."

A frown filled Lewis's brow with tight knots. "Y... yes she was, you killed her."

Jonah opened his eyes again and looked up. "I didn't do anything. She wasn't my bitch!"

Lewis tried to think of something to say but nothing came out. He felt a droplet of sweat fall from the end of his nose and his grip on the gun relaxed. "If that's true then where had you seen her?"

"Listen pal, she was just someone who got on the wrong side of someone else. A friend of mine asked me to come along for the ride. I didn't have a clue what he was going to do. I tried to stop him for Christ sake. I was there but I didn't do shit."

Lewis suddenly noticed his own breathing had become rapid and shallow. "What do you mean you were there? Who killed her?"

Jonah seemed to relax slightly and lowered his hands to the sofa beside him as a smirk began to spread across his face. "I don't know who you are, but you really need to get your facts straight before barging in someone's house with a gun."

"Who killed her?" Lewis repeated, his voice cracking.

"What's it to you? Who the hell are you anyway?"

"I want to know who killed her!" Lewis wiped sweat from his face with his free hand as he fought to keep his desperation in-check. The gun felt heavy, but he extended his arm straight, as if to highlight the threat.

"Okay, okay, just calm down," Jonah sighed, his eyes flicking from Lewis's face to the gun and back again. "Listen, a guy called Hal did the job. I was there, sure, but I didn't do shit. Anyway that don't matter, we were both puppets man; Hal was told to do that job like all the others. He didn't know her, it was just a payday."

"What do you mean; you were told to do the job?" Lewis asked, trying to comprehend what he was being told - he had been so certain. "Who told you to kill her?"

The smirk spread wider across Jonah's face and he leaned forward slowly. "Look man, I know I shouldn't say anything but I ain't gonna die for that lunatic." Jonah stared at the gun in Lewis's hand for a moment before meeting his eyes again. "He's the one who tells us to do all our jobs - Joseph Hellam."

Joseph Hellam? The words almost physically knocked Lewis to the floor. *Why would Joseph Hellam want Hannah dead?*

"You see," Jonah continued, seeming to relish the obvious revelation. "She was Joseph Hellam's bitch, not mine you stupid fuck."

Joseph Hellam, Lewis said the words in his own mind a thousand times, *Joseph Hellam, Joe Hellam... Joe.*

Suddenly Jonah shot up from the sofa and lunged at Lewis, almost knocking the gun from his hand but Lewis tightened his grip as he fell backwards. Their bodies fell to the floor and Lewis noticed Jonah was holding something. He looked down as they hit the carpet and saw a knife, gripped in Jonah's tight fist - pulled from some hidden place.

Lewis swung the gun sideways and hit Jonah's hand, knocking the knife loose and altering its trajectory. Lewis rolled and pushed Jonah sideways so he could lift himself to his elbows. Jonah flicked the blade round and swung it at Lewis's throat but Lewis saw the threat with enough time and grabbed his arm with his free hand then pushed it back to his stomach. The knife lay flat on Jonah's stomach as Lewis raised up and pushed his weight down so he was almost lying on top of his enemy then he swung the gun up and pointed it at Jonah's head. Jonah stopped struggling and looked at the barrel which was only inches away from his temple. One of his arms was pinned behind him and the other was positioned between himself and Lewis, still holding the knife but held in place by the weight above.

Heavy breaths fell from Lewis's mouth as they gazed at each other. He moved the barrel of the gun down so it was touching Jonah's head and saw the terror rise in the man's eyes. He could hear Jonah's breath quicken into small, shallow gasps as his eyes darted around for a second before focusing back on Lewis.

"So what now man?" Jonah asked, a nervous smile flashing on his face. "You gonna shoot me?"

Lewis stared at him. He now knew for sure that this man was one of the people who took the life of the woman he loved. His earlier suspicions, strong as they were, had still held lingering doubts. But those doubts had now been vanquished. He gripped the gun so tight he felt the tendons in his wrist begin the throb with exertion as moisture ran between skin and metal.

"So what now?" Jonah repeated.

Lewis *wanted* to pull the trigger, *wanted* this man to pay for what he had done. He felt pressure on his finger tip and the trigger moved a fraction but then he released. Images of Hannah flashed in his mind as he stared at the face of one of her murderers; images of their day by the cliff and images of her pale skinned face moving closer as they finally kissed. This man claimed he hadn't actually killed her, but he had been present. He had been part of her death. Lewis tried to squeeze the trigger, but again, something inside stopped the act and he suddenly realised something that terrified and comforted in equal measure.

He felt all energy leave him as the realisation struck. How did he ever expect it to be any different? He was no killer and everything suddenly became clear. He knew he wouldn't be able to do it. The thought of killing Jonah in cold blood was something he had fantasised about, but now the moment was here, his resolve faltered and an instinct, he never knew he had, took over.

This thought seemed to be spontaneously and imperceptibly transmitted to Jonah lying beneath, almost as if he had some kind of insight into Lewis's mind. A slowly developing grin expanded the muscles around Jonah's mouth.

"You can't do it can you?" Jonah sniggered, staring at Lewis's motionless eyes. "You can't can you? You *want* to, I can see that you *really* want to, but you just can't."

He kicked out and rolled over, pushing Lewis down and grabbing the gun from his hand. He smiled and threw the gun across the room then lunged forward, this time pinning Lewis to the floor and holding the knife in front.

Lewis felt the last of his energy sap away, as if he had

depleted any final reserves of adrenaline. Jonah leaned in close so he was just a few inches away from Lewis's face and dropped his voice, whispering gently as he slowly raised the blade so it was resting next to Lewis's left eye.

"What a pathetic fuck you really are," Jonah taunted, gently touching the skin around Lewis's eye with the tip of the steel.

Lewis struggled, but his body felt like lead. His right arm was held down by Jonah and his left outstretched by his side. Jonah moved up and placed his knee on Lewis's left arm, preventing any movement and then stared in silence at his prey. Lewis gazed back, the light glistening from the steel blade which was millimetres from his eye.

"Did you love this girl? Is that what all this is about?" Jonah whispered softly.

Lewis didn't reply.

"I bet you did, I bet you loved her so much, you thought you'd be some kind of superhero and come over here and teach me a lesson didn't you?" He paused and moved the blade slowly around Lewis's eye. "Well you're not a hero my friend. You're a stupid cunt." Jonah's face changed and he smiled with pride as he raised his voice. "It was a pretty tidy job as I remember, killing her I mean. We hired some slapper to get some hair from her next door neighbour. We did our homework first you see; we knew that bloke wasn't the sharpest knife in the drawer, know what I mean? Anyway, this slapper, she ended up scratching the shit out of his neck and we put some of his blood under your tart's fingernails," Jonah sniggered to himself and used the knife to move some hair away from his brow. "Worked like a charm from what I hear. Didn't the police arrest him?"

Lewis still said nothing and attempted to move his arms, but it was useless.

"Yeah I heard they did," Jonah continued as he tilted his head sideways and moved some more of his blonde hair away from his face with his shoulder.

He moved the knife to the corner of Lewis's eye again and gently pushed. Lewis felt a sting and a tear of blood rolled down his face. He winced and saw Jonah chuckle above him.

"This bitch you loved, she was terrified when we got into her flat; you know that pal?" Once again Jonah lowered his voice to a whisper as he leaned in close, his breath rolling along Lewis's skin as he spoke. "She put up one hell of a fight, I can tell you that. She *really* wanted to live. I can remember thinking that Hellam didn't need to pay me for this one. It was fun."

"You sick bastard," Lewis said, his teeth clenched and he felt anger begin to writhe in his stomach.

Jonah laughed, "You don't know the half of it. But hey, I was just following orders. Hellam is the one who told us to do it; he's the one you should be pissed off with." Jonah glanced away as if a memory had just returned. "I can remember Hal laughing as I did what I did."

Lewis's eyes widened and he struggled hard but his arms remained clamped to the floor as he twisted sideways.

"Yeah, that's right," Jonah continued, holding him down. "I killed your whore, Hal was watching as I did it; Hal likes watching. But like I said, she *really* wanted to live. She struggled like you're struggling now; fought like a dog. You can't know what it's like to have that power over someone; you don't know what it's like to watch someone die - to take their life away. But let me tell you this…" He moved his mouth close to Lewis's ear, still holding the knife in place and, with agonising sloth, whispered gently. "…It was an absolute pleasure to put my hands around that whore's throat and watch her die."

Lewis yelled something indecipherable and knocked his head sideways then raised his knee to impact with Jonah's back. The knife dug into Lewis's face and slid down as blood spurted from the wound. But he felt almost no pain as he twisted sideways and pushed himself free. The impact of Lewis's knee sent Jonah hurtling forward and he fell to the ground. Lewis turned, ignoring the blood which was falling from his own face and lunged, grabbing Jonah's hand which still clutched the knife. He forced it round in the opposite direction, and pushed Jonah's arm against him then leaned forward and slid the blade into Jonah's chest.

An odd gurgling scream fell from Jonah's lips as half the blade entered between his ribs. They both stopped moving, Lewis back on top and staring into Jonah's dilating eyes.

"Now I know what it's like," Lewis said softly, his voice shaking as the eyes focused on him. They locked gazes and he slowly leaned forward, using all his weight to push the rest of the long blade into Jonah's chest.

Jonah gurgled as his muscles relaxed and blood fell from the wound. Lewis remained motionless until Jonah's eyes rolled back, the lids falling half closed before they flickered and relaxed.

Lewis felt his heart pound and was suddenly aware of the pain in his face. He raised a hand to his cheek and then pulled away. Blood covered his fingers. He stood up and looked down at the dead body below, the knife protruding from the left side of Jonah's chest. He stepped away; his legs felt like rubber and he stumbled across the room to pick up the gun.

He saw a t-shirt lying on the floor and picked it up then pushed it onto his bleeding cheek. He looked around the room, noticed the photo of Hannah and picked it up then forced the gun into his pocket and staggered towards the doorway. The room was a scene from hell as blood soaked the floor around Jonah's body. A rising panic swelled inside Lewis and he fell out of the room, stumbling down the hall and through the front door then began to stride down the dark street, pushing the t-shirt against his sliced face.

He walked quickly and avoided the street lights as he rushed home. His mind began racing at a thousand miles per second. He began a half-jog, trying not to think about the image of Jonah lying with the knife buried in his chest. He thought about the pain in his left cheek, sliced open and still bleeding heavily. He thought about how he was now a killer. But most of all, he thought about Joseph Hellam.

Chapter 20

Hellam

Hal glanced at his watch as he paced the barn. Everything was set and Tyler was doing last minute checks on the lighting cables to make sure nothing would interrupt filming; once they began, they wouldn't be able to stop.

"What time is it?" Tyler asked, looking up from his task of securing the cables to the base of one of the floodlights.

"Five to ten, he should be here by now... what's his name? Keller?" Hal replied.

"Kelser, Sebastian Kelser." Tyler stood up, and walked over to Hal. "Hellam seems to think he knows what he's doing."

Hal snorted, "Hellam's been making some bad calls lately. Did you hear that he hired an undercover cop? A fucking cop!"

"He told me, but he also said that Kelser sorted that problem out. I don't know Hal, don't underestimate this guy. He makes me nervous."

Hal grimaced, "Makes you nervous? He's a little punk

who thinks he's the shit. I should put him in his place when he arrives and hasn't got Hellam around to hold his hand."

Hal paced across the barn floor, scuffing up the dirt with his shoes as he passed by the chair which was positioned in front of the camera. "Hellam thinks he's got some kind of natural talent for this stuff or something. We've been doing this for years, we're professionals and if that little shit... Keller... Kelser, can't even be bothered to turn up on time then we should sort this job out ourselves."

Hal looked over to Tyler who responded with a non-committal shrug then glanced at his watch again. "Come on that's it. It's ten now, let's get things started." He began to stride towards the back of the barn and Tyler followed.

***

The noises and lights beyond the bars and the doorway had woken Sarah earlier and she shuffled and fidgeted around in the tiny cage as she tried to hold herself together. This nightmare had been going on for days and felt never-ending. She had been fed like a dog; with bowls of water and cold, stale food. Her stomach was knotted with cramps and she had a constant headache which pounded her skull day and night. Not that she really knew which was day and which was night anymore; time blended together into an elongated mass of horror while she was surrounded by the darkness of the room.

Occasionally she would hear cars approach then footsteps, as one of the men arrived with some more food and water then led her to a filthy toilet on the other side of the room. The large one, the one with the tattoo on his arm was the worst. He never spoke to her, just stared and smiled in a way that made her stomach lurch.

Sarah wasn't religious but she had caught herself praying several times while locked inside the cage during the past few days. Her prayers all revolved around her daughter as she wondered if she would ever see her again. She had made a mess of her life; she knew that. The drug addiction and her profession were never going to lead her along a path of happiness. But she was changing, she told herself, everyone deserves a second chance don't they? Everyone can change.

She heard steps approaching and she backed away from the bars. The larger of the two men entered first and pulled out a key from his pocket which he slid into the large padlock that secured the door to the cage. Sarah didn't know if she should consider this good news or not; were they letting her go? The large man opened the door but said nothing as he reached inside, grabbed her by the arm and began to drag her out.

"No, no, please," she said hysterically. "Are you letting me go? What's happening?"

She writhed in an attempt to free herself but his grip was too strong and the second man shuffled in with his hunched form reaching out to help restrain her. The two men carried her through the doorway and the light in the wide space was almost blinding. Sarah assumed she was being taken outside, but as her eyes adjusted to the light, she realised she was in a huge barn which had been illuminated by several large lamps.

"What are you doing with me?" she asked desperately

but neither of the two men responded.

She gazed around the huge space as they carried her over to a central section where there was a chair and something else she couldn't quite see. The large man threw her down and she landed on the thick wood of the chair with a thump. The other man went behind her and grabbed both of her arms, pulling them back and sending a shooting pain through both her shoulders.

"What is this? What are you going to do?" she pleaded but still didn't get any response.

She felt the hunched man pull her hands together, tie them behind her back and attach them to the chair with something that felt like plastic. The tattooed man moved away from her and revealed a digital video camera attached to a stand that was pointing directly at her. Her eyes expanded as she saw something that was positioned on the floor beside the camera.

Something in her heart yelled out the truth before she could fully comprehend what she was seeing. A small metallic table was standing over to the right, just within view of the camera. The table was old, beaten and dented but that didn't hold her interest for long; she was focused on the implements that were lined up neatly on the distorted, steel surface. Sarah suddenly knew what was going to happen to her and at that moment all hope evaporated. They were going to kill her. She could think of nothing else to do, so she began to scream.

***

The building felt cool as Hellam stepped out of the lift

and began to walk down the darkened hall towards his office. It was overcast outside and a few sprinkles of rain dotted his suit. He wished he had taken an umbrella during the short walk from Jannson's but he hadn't known he would be making the journey on foot. His driver had been called away unexpectedly to deal with a family emergency; something to do with his wife, not that Hellam paid much attention. He just grudgingly let him take the car home. Hellam's own vehicle was in the car park at the offices so he decided to make the walk rather than take a taxi - he didn't like making small talk with the drivers.

The walk had given him a chance to contemplate what was happening on the farm. He glanced at his watch and saw it was a few minutes past ten; they would have begun by now. He felt electricity in his veins as excitement rose and he thought about what Kelser was going to do. Hellam couldn't wait to see the results, knowing that his employee wouldn't disappoint. He wondered if he himself would be there during the filming of the next one, but he would wait and see. He couldn't afford to take any chances if he was going to be present, and wanted to be sure the correct systems would be in place. But he *wanted* to be there and he felt a pang of envy at Kelser's opportunity.

He pushed the door open to his office and turned on the light. The keys to his car were in his office desk so he walked around and pulled the desk drawer open. The keys were there but Hellam paused as he picked them up. They were lying on something and he looked puzzled, moving them aside to see. It was a small, creased photograph.

He picked it up and gazed at the various people in the

image then he realised that he recognised someone in the centre. But he couldn't fully understand why a photo of this person would be in his desk drawer.

It's her, he thought silently as he stared into the eyes of Hannah Jacobs who was beaming back at him through the image. *'You're a psychopath'*, the words echoed through his head as he looked at her pale-skinned face. She was surrounded by a few others, obviously a group of friends on a night out and they were all grinning with wide, unforced expressions as they posed for the picture.

Why was this photograph here? How had it found its way into the desk? Hellam tried to process the set of circumstances that could have brought such a photo to him but he was lost. He had never seen it before and was certain he hadn't been given it by Hannah. Even if he had, why would he keep such an item?

He wanted to put it down but for some reason couldn't take his eyes away. He studied it slowly for a few moments. His eyes moved meticulously over all the other people that surrounded Hannah then, as they fell onto a man standing over to the right side of the picture, his lips parted and his mouth fell open.

The man wasn't looking at the camera like all the others, he was staring over to the girl at the centre and smiling quietly, not for the camera, but for himself. Hellam swallowed as he studied the man's features. He was a few years younger and didn't have the distinctive scar on his left cheek, but his identity was beyond doubt.

"Kelser." The word slipped effortlessly from Hellam's lips and hung before him.

Something stirred inside him that felt like an estranged cousin of anger and the sensation began to rise. But it felt odd. The emotion was mixed with something else; something that lingered in the distance. But this distant emotion was much more powerful and infinitely more unwelcome - fear.

He noticed the hand that held the photo began to shake and he consciously tried to stop – confused by his reaction. The picture slipped from his fingers and fell back into the drawer, turning over as it hit the wood. Hellam noticed there was something written on the back and he slowly read the four words: *'We're not the same.'*

"What the hell..." he said to himself and stumbled backwards, trying to comprehend what was going on.

He stopped suddenly as he felt something hard and cold touch the back of his skull, realising what it was immediately. He stopped breathing while his heart continued to thump hard behind his ribs. That once distant and unfamiliar emotion suddenly began to sprint towards him.

"What do you want Kelser?" he managed to croak, not turning, but certain of who was holding the gun to his head.

A hand from behind was pushed into his jacket pocket and it pulled out Hellam's mobile phone then handed it to him.

"Call Hal and tell him to let the girl go," came a low voice from behind, the gun remained motionless, stuck to Hellam's head.

"They won't..." Hellam began but was cut off.

"Do it."

Hellam selected Hal's number and pushed the phone to his ear.

"Hal, listen we've changed the plan. We need to let the

girl go."

"What?" Hal replied incredulously from the other end of the phone.

"Something has happened and we need to call it off."

"Are you crazy?" Hal said, the rising anger unmistakable. "We're not letting her go; we're just about to begin."

Hellam felt pressure as the gun was pushed harder against his skull. "I said let her go, that's an order."

"An order? Fuck you, you don't know what you're talking about. She's seen my face for Christ sake! She's seen *your* face! Have you lost your mind?"

Hellam covered the phone with his hand and spoke to the man behind him. "He's not going to do it. They're all ready to start."

"Convince him."

Hellam felt pressure again and slowly placed the receiver back to his ear. "The fact she's seen us won't make any difference to you. If she was to recognise anyone then it would be me. You have nothing to concern yourself about. Let her go."

There was a pause on the other end of the line and Hellam could hear breathing through his ear piece before the response finally came.

"I can't risk it. What's this all about?"

The voice from behind whispered again. "Just tell them to wait for me to arrive."

Hellam spoke into the mouthpiece again. "It doesn't matter... listen, at least wait for Kelser to arrive, he'll be there."

He heard a snort of disapproval from the other end followed by a long pause.

"He has twenty minutes then I'm finishing this mess."
The line went dead.

"He's hung up, he's only going to wait for twenty minutes," Hellam said, lowering the phone.

"Well that causes me a problem," the man behind him replied, the words spoken with apparent ambivalence.

"Kelser, what do you want? We can talk this over; there is always some kind of attainable compromise."

"The code to your safe, what is it?"

Hellam felt something cold slither along his spine, *the laptop*.

"Why do you want that?" Hellam asked, confused.

"The code."

Hellam thought for a second – why should Kelser need the laptop; what did he have planned? He contemplated giving a fake code, but at best that would only buy him a few seconds and he realised he had little to bargain with.

"8349284, why do you want..."

Hellam felt the gun pull away before something collided with the side of his head and darkness suddenly fell.

***

The two men placed full-face balaclavas over their heads and pulled them down to conceal their features as Sarah watched, terrified. The lights that shone down on her were bright and she struggled with her bound hands behind her back. But it was no use; they had been tied too securely, as had her legs, which were bound with plastic cable ties to the thick wood of the chair. She wondered briefly why the two men were hiding their features now; after all, Sarah had already seen their faces.

You fool! She thought as shards of panic pricked her skin, *they're hiding them from the camera, not you. They don't need to hide from you because you won't be around when they've finished.*

She screamed again, feeling her throat burn from the continued effort. She prayed that someone would hear, but knew that wouldn't happen. The two men weren't concerned about the noise she was making so they had obviously brought her to the middle of nowhere – to hell.

She had tried reasoning with them, but they had remained silent as they prepared the camera and re-positioned her chair, dragging her across the dusty concrete floor.

The hunched man positioned himself behind the camera and turned it towards her. Sarah watched as the other one walked slowly over to the metallic table and shuffled the objects around for a moment as if deciding on which he should use. The steel objects clinked together and grated on the metal surface of the table. She saw the hunched man look over and give a thumbs-up. A small red spot of light flashed above the lens of the camera and Sarah suddenly felt herself collapse inside as all hope dissipated. The tattooed man turned and began to walk casually towards her. He slipped a metallic object over his fingers. The object resembled four thick, steel rings all connected together. He flexed his fingers and then gripped hard around the knuckle duster to form a huge fist. He paused as he stood over her and glanced at the camera. Only his eyes were visible but Sarah could tell he was smiling as they shone in the bright lights.

The world seemed to slow down around her and she

stared up at the man before her as tears fell. There was nothing left for her now and she knew the end was inevitable. She felt a curious relief which surprised her as she watched him slowly retract his arm and stand poised, ready to release his fist. The terror she had felt just moments earlier had suddenly receded and her relief was born from knowing that soon it would all be over. But it was accompanied by something else – uncompromising sadness; sadness for her daughter who would now have to grow up having never truly known her mother. This was all she could think about as she stared at the butterfly tattoo on the huge arm. Sarah's tears fell not for herself, but for Cassie and she wished she could go back and start her life over; start it from scratch. If she could do this, she would do it so very differently, except for Cassie – Cassie would be her constant.

Suddenly there was a deafening explosion from across the barn and Sarah shrunk down into her shoulders. She saw the tattooed man turn and she watched as the hunched figure behind the camera fell backwards and crumpled to the floor. The man before her stepped backwards as he looked over to the door of the barn, shock clearly visible in his eyes through the narrow slit of the balaclava.

Sarah turned to look but before she had time there came a second explosion and the large man stumbled backwards. A scarlet stain began to form around a single hole in the man's lower chest and he shuffled his feet backwards, eyes staring in disbelief. He pulled off the balaclava and looked down at the growing red stain on his shirt before falling to the floor by the barn wall. He slumped back and dragged in long, laboured mouthfuls of air.

Sarah looked around and saw someone walking slowly towards her. She couldn't see him clearly; the huge floodlights hindered her view, but as he stepped over the cables and past her, she noticed the thick scar running the length of his left cheek. He glanced at her, his face showing no emotion as he strode past and behind the camera. He flicked it off and the red light faded then he went over to the hunched man who lay motionless on the floor. He regarded him nonchalantly for a moment and Sarah noticed a gun which was held between loose fingers in his right hand. He tightened his grip and aimed again at the body before firing another shot and the corpse lurched from the impact. Sarah turned away, stifling another scream, then looked back.

She saw the gunman casually walk over to the larger man, sitting with his back to the wall and staring in terror at the approaching threat. He crouched down beside him and gazed silently for a moment.

"Hal," the scarred man said finally and pointed the gun to the butterfly tattoo on the wounded man's arm. "It isn't a bird at all; it was a butterfly all along."

Hal kept his eyes locked on the scarred man and continued to force his lungs into movement. He coughed and blood fell from his mouth and down his chin.

The scarred man reached into his pocket, pulled out a small piece of paper and held it in front of Hal's face.

"Do you recognise her?" he asked.

Hal appeared to study the photo for a moment then shook his head violently as he looked back at the scarred man – pain and desperation twisting his face into unnatural expressions.

"Her name is Hannah Jacobs and five years ago you and a man called Jonah murdered her in her home." He tilted his head sideways. "Do you remember now?"

Hal said nothing and continued to make unpleasant choking sounds as he stared at the man before him with rapidly glazing eyes.

"I think you do remember," the scarred man said and then looked down at the wound in Hal's chest. "Your lungs are filling with blood. You're going to drown in it soon."

Hal didn't move or make any sound other than the constant rasp as air and liquid was pushed from his lungs. He coughed again and fresh blood appeared around his mouth.

Suddenly the scarred man stood up and pointed the gun at Hal's head. "The pain you're feeling now will only get worse as your lungs fill with blood. You'll be in agony soon." He glanced at Sarah then turned back to Hal and raised the photo in his other hand so Hal could see the picture of the girl. "Say her name and I'll make it quick."

Sarah's eyes bulged as she watched Hal glare at the scarred man then move slowly over to focus on her. He looked at her for a moment as if she was able to save him from what was going to happen, and for some inexplicable reason, she felt sympathy for the man who was going to kill her just a few moments earlier.

He looked back at the gun, inches from his face, and gurgled something then winced in obvious pain.

The scarred man leaned forward. "Say her name and it will all be over."

"H... H..." Hal said through forced, unpleasant breaths and his face contorted as muscles tightened from the agony. "H... Hannah," he finally managed to blurt out and looked up, his eyes filling with water.

The scarred man turned and looked at Sarah, who knew instantly what she was to do. She turned her head away and closed her eyes. The deafening crash of thunder came seconds later. The gun was fired and Hal's choking breaths were finally silenced.

Sarah tried to scream but only a croak came out. She heard the scarred man approach her, his footsteps the only sound in the silent barn. She began to tremble as she felt his presence beside her, but still refused to turn and face him.

Suddenly she heard a snap and the plastic bindings on her arms became loose. She pulled her arms round before her and felt a wave of relief in her shoulders. Finally, she looked up at the scarred man. He bent down and used a knife to cut the cable ties that restrained her ankles then stood up and helped her to her feet. She was trembling as she felt his hand touch her arm and when she looked up, she found that he was staring at her.

"Please..." she said quietly but not knowing how to finish the sentence.

He gently squeezed her arm and she remembered how he had done the same thing a few days before when he had visited her with the others.

"You don't need to worry; no one will hurt you now."

She continued to tremble as she regarded his face. He wore it like a mask and his muscles barely moved as he spoke. The thick, light pink hue of the scar was dominating the left side of his face. As she looked, and as he squeezed her arm, she noticed that his mouth opened slightly, as if he wanted to say something else, but then it slowly closed. For one fleeting moment, she saw something behind his eyes that seemed out of place and alien for some reason, as if it was no longer welcome there - warmth.

He led her out through the barn door and into the cool night. He took her to a car and opened the driver's side where he gestured for her to sit down, which she gladly did. She sat with the door open and her feet resting on the ground outside as he disappeared around the back of the car. She heard him open the boot and the car rocked as he pulled something out. She turned to see, but her line of vision was obscured. She could only listen, hearing him drag something back into the barn.

When he returned he pulled something else out of the boot then closed it and stood beside her, holding a small cardboard box under one arm. When Sarah looked up, she noticed that yet again his mouth opened slightly before slowly closing, as if thinking better of whatever he was going to say. He pulled out some keys from his pocket and handed them to her.

"Take the car... go... go to wherever… you want to go." The words came out stilted and with pauses between them, as if he had more to say.

Sarah glanced down at the keys, barely able to believe what was happening. "You're letting me go?"

"Of course."

"What about you? What..." again she couldn't think of anything to complete the thought.

"Go," the scarred man ordered and pushed her legs into the car then slammed the door shut behind her.

Sarah watched as he walked away then she turned the keys in the ignition. She drove along a dirt path towards a road, glancing back and seeing the man disappear back inside the barn, still carrying the box.

She had no idea where she was, but took a left when she hit the main road and turned on the lights. The dark countryside slipped away behind her as she approached civilisation and she began to cry. She tried not to think about how close she had come to death or about the days she had spent in the tiny cage, not knowing if it was day or night. She concentrated on her daughter's face and that alone managed to guide her to familiar roads.

By the time she reached Surrington, the salty tears had dried on her face and lethargy had overwhelmed her. She felt drained as she pulled up outside her building and lifted her body out of the car on legs made of jelly. The stairs and corridors that led to her flat seemed darker and more hostile than usual and Sarah felt a sting as fresh tears welled.

Don't lose it now, she told herself and blinked hard as she reached her door. She suddenly realised that she didn't have her keys and cursed herself for being so stupid. She had no idea where the keys could be now - probably taken by one of her abductors, but she tried the door anyway and found it was open. They had obviously left it unlocked when they had taken her. She took a deep breath and went inside the dark room.

Images flashed through her mind - the silhouette of the hunched figure in her bedroom and his awkward lunge towards her - but she pushed them away. Turning on the light, she went to her drawers and, breathing hard, pulled out the stash of money from the metallic box. She couldn't help the smile from creeping on her face as she discovered it was still there then she pushed the notes into her pocket. She looked around but saw nothing else she required and went to leave.

She paused when she reached the doorway and looked over in the direction of her bedroom. Through the open door, the room was in darkness and appeared identical to how it had a few days earlier when the man had been waiting for her. She fought against the instinct to leave and walked towards it. She glanced inside and saw her bed in disarray with the broken lamp resting on the carpet. Reaching in, she turned on the light and saw the scene fully illuminated. In the corner of the room, where the man had been waiting, she saw a plastic bottle lying on the floor but ignored it. Her attention was focused on her bedside cabinet and the object that wasn't there.

Slowly walking over, Sarah felt her breathing quicken and forced her reluctant legs to continue. They felt as if they were going to fall away from beneath her at any moment but she had to continue; there was something she wanted - something she needed. The cabinet was askew and pulled away from the wall due to the fracas days earlier and she leaned over to see the gold-rimmed frame lying by the wall.

She picked it up and stared at the tiny photograph of Cassie for a moment, studying the round, smiling face through the cracked glass. She wanted to lie on the bed and gaze at the photo for a few hours when, after a while, she would fall asleep with the picture of her daughter filling her dreams. But that wouldn't happen, sleep would never come in this place; not now, or ever.

She took the broken picture with her and left, stumbling down the stairs and back out into the street. She placed the photo frame on the passenger seat beside her and started the car, revving the engine hard as if to highlight her departure. She glanced up towards the window of her flat and slowly shook her head. She knew she would never return now; she was finished with that place - finished with that life.

As she sat behind the wheel and drove towards her mother's home, Sarah thought briefly of the scarred man and the mask he appeared to wear. He had saved her, and she was grateful to him, but would be more than happy to never lay eyes on him again. In spite of him rescuing her, there was something disturbing in that face. She didn't want to dwell on anything from the past few days and the thoughts of him were quickly lost in an ocean of others.

She drove fast all the way, unable to contain her excitement of seeing the little girl in the picture beside her, which she glanced down to every few seconds. Her life would be different now, she told herself. She had told herself the same thing hundreds of times before but for the first time in years, she believed it.

Things will be different, it'll be better! She thought silently as she pulled up outside her mother's house and turned off the engine. *Everyone can change.*

***

Kelser carried the box through to the back of the barn and placed it inside the cage that, for the past few days, had been home to the girl. He stood in the darkened room in silence and closed his eyes, trying to think of nothing. But thoughts began to creep inside, like roots from a tree breaking through tarmac and he winced as he thought of the dead bodies in the barn.

The thoughts lingered for barely a moment before he forced them into submission and regained his composure. He had become used to beating down the guilt and the nightmares and his face slowly returned to its vacant, emotionless appearance. He glanced down to his watch, suddenly realising something for the first time. The date was the 16th of August, 2013 - it was his birthday.

Chapter 21

Lewis

The calendar on the wall in Lewis's flat told him it was the 16th of August, 2008 as he picked up the handful of birthday cards that had arrived through his door that day. He placed them, unopened, on the table then walked into the bathroom. His face looked older with his hair short and a beard darkening his jaw. Darkness also circled his eyes, small wrinkles creasing the skin at the corners.

But this didn't concern Lewis as he stared at the thick scar that painted the left side of his face. It had been two months since he had killed Jonah and gained the injury, but it felt like decades. He had closed the wound using only steri-strips, refusing to risk a hospital admission, and it had not healed well. It was broad and long, stretching from his left eye and down, through the beard before thinning to a point at the bottom of his jaw.

He picked up an aerosol of shaving foam and sprayed some into his hand then spread it over the bottom half of his face, nursing it into the beard around the scar carefully. He used a fresh blade in his razor and delicately ran it down his face. Hair fell into the sink below. He took his time and was careful as he moved the blade over the tender skin around the healing wound.

When he was finished, he threw the blunted razor into the bin and scrutinised himself in the mirror. The face gazing back looked older and more tired than the one he had been used to. His pupils were dark, looking more like the black marble eyes of a shark. He ran a towel over his face and returned to the front room where he glanced at the unopened birthday cards.

He had barely spoken to another human being in the two months since he became a killer, closing himself in his cocoon as he slowly made the metamorphosis inside that had been initiated the moment he pushed the knife into Jonah's chest.

Lewis had been a nervous wreck in the first few days, panic attacks haunting him like some kind of malicious poltergeist. He was convinced the police would knock at his door and arrest him for the murder at any time and he barely ate or slept during those early days. But the police didn't call and the murder of Jonah hailed only a small article on the website of the local newspaper. Jonah was a known drug dealer and it came as little surprise to the authorities that his end arrived in such a way.

As the days past by and the threat of arrest became less of an issue, Lewis contemplated what Jonah had told him about the murder of Hannah. He pushed away the details of her death and instead concentrated on the part about the man known as Hal, and of course Joseph Hellam.

Guilt would rise and fall repetitively as the days dropped away. Some days, Lewis felt almost no regret -

Jonah deserved to die for what he had done to Hannah. But at other times, he questioned his actions and was unable to fully believe that he had killed another human being. He felt sick that he had taken such a route rather than going to the police with what he had discovered. But it was too late for that now; Lewis knew he had started along a path and he had to see it through, no matter what.

The guilt subsided slowly as he began to rationalise his actions and his thoughts changed. The thought that Jonah deserved to die gradually led him to other thoughts which could not be ignored. If Jonah deserved to die, then surely his companion in the murder and the man who ordered the death in the first place, also deserved such a fate.

Lewis contemplated the situation almost constantly during his waking hours, sometimes dreaming of various scenarios as well. He was confident that he would be able to find the man with the tattoo known as Hal, but his biggest problem would be getting to Hellam. Even if he found a way and managed to kill him in cold blood, where would that leave him? Who would he be killing? To the general public, Joseph Hellam was a kind and respected member of the community and his murder would cause outrage. Not only that, but Lewis would definitely be caught for killing such a man; a man who had given millions to charitable causes over the years. Lewis could protest and offer information to the fact that Hellam ordered the murder of Hannah, but who would believe him? He had no definitive proof that Hellam was involved and Lewis was certain he would have suitable distance between himself and any direct evidence of involvement in the murder which might exist.

As he thought about all of this, his mind continued to

fall back to George Langton, the former teacher and now, for some inexplicable reason, involved in Hellam's business in some way. He couldn't shake the feeling that Langton could somehow be his way 'in'. Perhaps provide some information in some way. But how? And why would Langton bother?

The weeks rolled by and Lewis's scar began to heal, not closing as much as he would have hoped, but the pain had subsided to the point where it was no longer a constant distraction.

As he continued to contemplate Langton, he began to ask questions about Michelle Layne, wondering about the proximity of her disappearance to where Langton lived at the time. He went back onto 192.com and paid a small fee in order to see the full address of Langton's home in Alderidge. Shocked, he then re-checked the old newspaper archives of the time and found that George Langton lived on Forest Road, the same street on which Michelle Layne lived. Lewis could barely believe this coincidence and he dwelled on it for several days, running through the available details of Langton's life.

George Langton, albeit in a hushed manner, was a man dismissed by his school for inappropriate behaviour with female pupils. He then moved to a small village in Somerset. Two years later, Michelle Layne, a thirteen-year-old girl who lived on the same street as Langton, went missing under suspicious circumstances. The police questioned Langton, but never suspected him of anything; why should they? The circumstances for his dismissal were covered up and never disclosed in order to conserve the school's reputation. George Langton was therefore never placed on the sex offenders register and by-passed all systems that would place him in the authorities radar as a possible suspect.

Lewis considered this and ran through the scenario again and again. Perhaps it would be jumping to conclusions to say that George Langton was definitely the man responsible for Michelle's disappearance. But at the same time, Lewis had to acknowledge the fact that, had the police known about his history, then he would have almost definitely been on their list of suspects. It was a long shot and Lewis knew it, but it was certainly something that he could use as possible leverage in getting information from Langton.

Lewis began to write more notes in his pad about the various people involved, and over the weeks, the pages filled with various lists and diagrams. He put a line through Jonah's page and concentrated on Hal, George Langton and Joseph Hellam.

He began to follow Hellam, who was often accompanied by Langton, and noted where he went and with whom he spoke. On one occasion, he saw him pick up a large man in his limousine. Lewis noticed the large butterfly that was tattooed on the man's arm and realised who he was immediately.

The notepad became full and was joined by several more as Lewis obsessively kept details on every insight he gleamed into Langton and Hellam's lives. He kept track of where they went, who they met, where their favourite places were to eat and drink. He slowly became an expert in the parts of their lives that he could gain from a distance.

On one occasion, Lewis followed Langton to a bar and watched him become inebriated during the course of the evening. This was a little odd and certainly out of character since Langton never usually went drinking alone. Lewis followed him as he staggered home and stumbled into his house, mumbling something to himself. It was only later that evening, while Lewis was sitting in his flat, that he noticed the date. It was the fourteenth anniversary of Michelle Layne's disappearance. Again, it could have been a coincidence, but the more Lewis discovered, the more convinced he became that Langton was the man responsible. There was nothing definitive, certainly nothing that the police could use to convict him, especially without a body, but all the small coincidences coalesced and began to gain momentum inside Lewis's mind.

As the weeks changed into months, he began to assemble a plan in order to expose Hellam as the man he really was - the criminal, the murderer. He followed him and then followed the people he met with. He became confident that Hellam was involved in a number of criminal activities involving drugs and prostitution in some way. But Lewis knew that Hellam distanced himself through several degrees of personnel and was never committed to direct involvement.

Through old newspaper articles, Lewis learned that the police had conducted a short investigation into Hellam a few years earlier but it had come to nothing; Hellam just couldn't be pinned down as being involved in anything criminal and could always claim ignorance if some of his employees *were* in some way associated with criminality - the trail ended long before it ever led to Hellam and no charges were brought against him.

Lewis slowly realised that he needed to get close to

Hellam in order to truly expose him. He would need to find a way to get hold of something - anything that could reveal who he truly was: documents, records or witnesses. Lewis remembered Hannah's letter and the 'bad films' she mentioned. It had certainly crossed her mind to go to the police and that was what had ultimately led to her death. But Lewis wondered if he could obtain these films somehow and use them as proof of Hellam's criminality.

He knew that he wouldn't be able to get as close to Hellam as Hannah had when she had found the films, but he might be able to get close enough to gain some kind of incriminating information. His thoughts also returned to his suspicions of George Langton and wondered if he could exploit that information somehow. Lewis wasn't certain of all the facts, but knew he had to gain a degree of trust from Hellam for his plan to work.

The unopened birthday cards remained in their envelopes on the table as he ran a hand across his now smooth chin. The weeks of following people and making notes were almost at an end. He picked up a photograph from the table that had been its home for the past few weeks then carried it into the kitchen. He poured himself a glass of water and began to drink, gazing at the picture between mouthfuls.

Hannah was in the centre, surrounded by her friends as Lewis stared at her with a curious smile. As he stared at Hannah's face now, he didn't feel like smiling anymore and wasn't sure if he ever would again. He no longer felt like the man in that picture; he had changed from one into another, like the rotating shapes inside the kaleidoscope.

But there was something constant between the man in the photo and the killer he now was; something that was entirely undeniable and represented by the beaming face of Hannah.

Both men did, and always would, love her.

Chapter 22

Hellam

The light pierced the narrow gap between Hellam's eyelids as they slowly opened and he winced with pain as its brightness tore into his retinas.

"What the..." he said with a thin, croaking voice.

The intense white around him billowed out like a gigantic sheet then faded and, as his pupils contracted, he began to see shapes form. He tried to move his arms but he couldn't and he felt pressure around his wrists. He attempted to stand from the chair he found himself in but, like his arms, his legs were bound and unmovable.

He raised his head, since the light no longer burned quite so much, and saw he was in the barn, the floodlights observing him menacingly from above. How had he got here? Why was he here?

The last thing he could remember was arriving at his office; he was fetching the keys to his car and... Kelser. His memory returned, regurgitating the photograph of Hannah with all those people and then he remembered how Kelser had been in the picture too. Kelser had known

Hannah, but how?

Hellam looked ahead and saw the camera pointing towards him. Beyond the camera, he saw a dark shape moving.

"Kelser? Is that you?" he croaked.

The shape sharpened into a figure which slowly stepped out into the light. Hellam saw the penetrating intensity as Kelser regarded him and walked slowly forward. He saw that in his right hand, he held a gun.

"Kelser, what the hell is going on? Where are..." he stopped himself as he noticed another shape behind the camera - this one horizontal. The body was unmistakable and belonged to Tyler, his hunched frame still visible even though he was sprawled on the floor. He looked over to his left and saw Hal sitting on the floor, his back leaning against the wall. But he was slouched to the right and had a large wound to the side of his head, with bright scarlet fluid staining the front of his shirt. "My God, what have you done?"

Kelser responded with only silence and long, drawn out scrutiny as if trying to decipher some newly discovered hieroglyph.

"Answer me you lunatic! What the hell have you done? Why am I tied to this chair?"

Kelser still said nothing but took several more steps towards Hellam, each one raising the uncomfortable unease inside the bound man.

"What was that photo about?" Hellam asked, craving any kind of verbal response. "Did you know her? The girl... Hannah?"

"Yes I knew her," Kelser finally said and Hellam breathed long and hard, glad to have gained some kind of reply and to have opened the lines of communication.

"How did you know her? Listen Kelser, you don't need to do whatever you have planned here. I didn't kill her you know... him over there," Hellam nodded towards Hal. "You've already got the bastard that killed her; it makes no sense to go after me now."

"Hannah Jacobs was my friend Joseph," Kelser said slowly, seemingly ignoring all but the first part of what Hellam had said and using his first name to address him; something that unnerved Hellam far more than it should have. "Three men killed Hannah. Hal is dead." Kelser pointed the gun in the direction of Hal's slumped body. "Jonah is dead."

Hellam suddenly remembered Jonah, a man he used to hire for specific jobs, along with Hal. Tyler had joined them later, after Jonah had been found in his house with a knife buried in his chest. Hellam's eyes widened as the realisation spread through him like a virus.

But no, it couldn't have been, he thought, *Jonah was killed five years ago*. He forced his eyes to meet Kelser's.

"You killed Jonah?"

Kelser ignored the question and continued along his own path. "That only leaves you Joseph."

"Listen to me Kelser, Listen. You've got the men who did it. I told them to just rough her up... you know, as a warning. They took it upon themselves to kill that poor girl."

"I'm not here to listen to your lies. I'm here to finish what *you* started five years ago." He stepped closer still and raised the gun. "I could have killed you a long time ago Joseph. But I wasn't interested in killing a caring member of the community; I wanted to expose you for who you truly are." He paused and glanced at the floor for a moment, as if contemplating his next move. "I didn't have a clue back then just how sick and sadistic a man you are."

Hellam forced himself into nervous laughter. "Me? You should look in the mirror Kelser. Look at what you've done here. These men are dead and you killed Richards for Christ sake, a cop! Don't tell me you didn't enjoy doing that; I saw the look in your eyes as you placed that bullet inside him. I know I saw it because I know it well. We're more similar than you realise."

Kelser tilted his head as something in his expression changed by an amount that was almost imperceptible.

Hellam grinned wildly. "You *know* I'm right Kelser. If you pull that trigger, you'll be nothing but a hypocrite. You and I, we're the same."

Kelser spoke again, but this time his voice was quieter, less confident somehow. "Perhaps you're right Joseph. There was a time that you couldn't have been further from the truth, but now..." He lowered the gun slightly and Hellam felt hope rise inside. "But now... perhaps I am closer to you than I realise. I killed these men..." he said, using the gun to point towards the two bodies, "...And felt almost nothing. Jonah was harder, I almost couldn't do it. But these..." He gazed back at Hellam, his expression altered yet again and Hellam suddenly felt the brief glimmer of hope evaporate as Kelser continued. "These two were easy."

Hellam tried not to look at the gun in Kelser's hand but found it difficult not to.

"You see Joseph," he continued. "When I tried to kill Jonah, it suddenly hit me; I can't kill a human being. But

271

then, humans have certain qualities – undeniable qualities that he didn't possess. It's difficult to think of him as human because what he did to Hannah isn't something a normal person should be able to do. And that's why it's also difficult to think of *you* as human."

Kelser took the final steps towards Hellam and stood beside him, pointing the gun at his head. "They say that when you kill someone it changes you," Kelser continued in his low monotone as his eyes appeared to glaze over. "And I can tell you Joseph, it changed me."

Hellam's heart began to pound and he felt the rush of panic flow through his veins.

"Please Kelser, I beg you. Don't do this." He felt water in his eyes and closed them, squeezing the tears free to fall down his cheek.

"I read somewhere that psychopaths like you can only truly cry for themselves. They can't empathise with anyone else and are purely driven by their own selfish desires. I don't expect you to feel remorse for what you have done; I don't even think you're capable." Kelser became silent as the air congealed with the sound of Hellam's unpleasant sobs. "I'm not going to kill you Joseph."

Hellam opened his eyes again and looked up in disbelief.

"But I want everyone to know just *who* you are; I want this disguise you wear to be lifted and the *real* evil exposed. The police will be arriving in a few minutes and they'll soon have in their possession thousands of documents which prove who you are."

Hellam's face contorted at this, thoughts of death lost, and suddenly outraged. "You're bluffing, even if you were crazy enough to call the police, you don't have anything on me."

"You have Langton to thank for the documents finding their way into my hands," Kelser replied slowly.

Hellam sniggered, the tears and panic forgotten, "I've known George for a long time Kelser; he would *never* betray me."

"You've known me for five years and... well, here we are."

Hellam shook his head. "No, not George, he would never..."

Kelser reached into his jacket and threw some papers onto his lap. "Here's a sample for you."

Hellam looked down and studied the photocopied pages on his thighs, recognising the bank account numbers and the large quantities of money shown in the columns. Another page displayed a hand drawn diagram of various people in Hellam's criminal organisations - names of people that he shouldn't know; people who could be used against him.

"No, not George. How the hell did you get these?"

"Langton doesn't have many secrets Joseph, but those he does are very, very big." Kelser gestured to the pieces of paper. "But laundering money from drugs and prostitution doesn't quite get to just how fucked up you really are does it?"

Hellam struggled with his wrists and legs and the pages fell to the floor.

"I was half expecting you to have given me a fake code to your safe. But now I have the last thing you would want me to possess - your laptop. Hannah found the snuff films on your computer all those years ago didn't she? So you had to protect it. Has anyone other than me even seen the films on there?"

Hellam felt perspiration roll down his forehead.

Kelser continued. "These films are what really reveal you to be the sick bastard you are."

"You're no better than me, we've both killed Kelser," Hellam rasped.

Kelser nodded slowly. "Yes, we've both killed but I'm not here to make excuses. The police will be getting the documents and the laptop very soon. You'll be arrested and the investigation will be very long and very public. Your life is over Joseph."

"You think they'll let you just walk free? You're a killer. If I go down, you won't be far behind; especially when they learn about Richards. And I'll make sure they get all the grisly details of everything you've done for me over the years you righteous fuck."

Kelser stared at him, his expression showing nothing again; vacant, unmoving. "No, I don't think they'll let me walk free," he said as he lowered the gun and walked around the back of Hellam's chair, pulling something out of his jacket.

Hellam felt pressure around his wrists and then there was a sudden relief as they separated. He noticed that Kelser put something under his chair before he began cutting the ties that bound his legs.

"The police will be here soon Joseph. You can run if you choose but they'll catch you. You can't control this situation anymore. You'll be spending the rest of your life in prison. But there's a gift for you under the chair - a gift from Hannah. You can have it when I'm gone."

Hellam remained seated as Kelser stood up and

pointed the gun at him again. He wanted to lunge at Kelser; bury his fingers into his eyes and rip his face apart. But he knew that if he attempted that he would gain nothing but a bullet in the head.

He watched as Kelser retreated, the gun remaining fixed on him. Kelser moved around the back of the camera and opened a slot on the side of the plastic casing. He removed something that looked to be a memory card from the camera and placed it into his pocket then stepped past Tyler's lifeless body, and towards the door. Hellam did nothing but stare as the man he had known and trusted for the past five years disappeared into the darkness.

"You stupid little bastard," Hellam spat and leaned forward to look under the chair, half expecting some kind of bomb to be resting there. His eyes sparkled as he saw a gun lying on the floor below him. "You're a dead man."

He crouched down and picked up the gun then stood as he checked it. The gun was loaded with a few rounds and Hellam felt a rush of adrenalin surge through him. He made for the barn door, swinging the gun in his hand. He felt some kind of strange abandon purge all other emotions inside him, and at that exact moment, he wanted nothing more than to end the life of the man he called Sebastian Kelser.

He reached the barn door and glanced outside, the cool air wrapping his cheek as he glared into the night. He saw no one and stepped out. He turned his head, scanning both directions. He saw Tyler and Hal's cars, but no others. He wasn't sure where Kelser's own car was, but he hadn't heard an engine start. He moved forward and squinted as his eyes adjusted from the brightness inside to almost total darkness, and gazed into the trees behind the barn. Had he gone that way? There didn't seem to be any other direction he could have disappeared and Hellam was about to give chase when he suddenly heard a sound.

He gripped the gun tightly as he looked up the dirt path, towards the main road and saw three sets of headlamps speeding towards the barn. Confused, Hellam stood paralysed as they rounded the bend and pulled up next to the farm house.

It was only then that his swirling mind remembered what Kelser had said a few moments earlier - *the police will be arriving*. He thought about running, but there would be little point; he wouldn't get far into the trees before they caught him, and that was if he didn't run across Kelser first.

Hellam held the gun by his side and stared at the three cars as several doors opened and officers stepped out.

"Drop your weapon then turn and face the barn."

Hellam heard the fuzzy words, spoken through a megaphone by one of the men, as if they were thousands of miles away. He recognised the words but couldn't fully comprehend what they meant. He tightened his grip on the gun as a sudden thought hit him like a gust of wind, forcing a sharp intake of breath. He glanced down at the gun that Kelser had left for him then slowly turned his head. He looked through the open barn door and could see the two crumpled bodies lying motionless beyond. He looked back at the gun, realising that he would bet his life on the fact that the gun he was now holding, once held the bullets that were now residing inside Hal and Tyler.

Hellam could think of nothing else to do, so sniggered softly to himself as he contemplated that for a moment.

Bet your life would you? he thought quietly. Several more prompts from the man holding the megaphone washed over him and he gently raised his head to look back at the cars. A thin, bitter smile formed on his face as he saw someone he recognised step out from one of the cars. He should have been surprised to see the man, but the truth was, he wasn't - not in the least. He glanced back into the barn for one final look at the two dead men before turning his head and focusing his gaze on the man he knew only as Carl Richards. Richards was standing next to the officer with the megaphone, a look of subtle contempt shaping his expression.

"Put the weapon down!" shouted the distorted voice again.

Bet your life?

Hellam raised the gun, considered shooting at the police before thinking better of it - he had already made his decision. He thought fleetingly about the man he had come to know over the past five years; someone he had grown to trust implicitly, with whom he had shared his darkest secrets. But he didn't allow the thought to linger since it left a bitter taste at the back of his throat.

Hellam's thin smile slowly expanded as he placed the barrel of the object which Kelser had said was a gift from Hannah, in his mouth. After only the briefest spark of hesitation, he pulled the trigger.

***

Carl Mayhew watched as the back of Joseph Hellam's skull exploded and his body collapsed the dirt below.

There were shouts around him while several of his colleagues rushed towards the corpse, and the man holding the megaphone beside him picked up his mobile phone and began to call an ambulance. Carl didn't rush forward like the others however; he had known what Hellam was going to do as soon as he had seen him standing outside the barn with the gun in his hand - probably before Hellam knew himself.

He walked away from the cars and up towards the barn, shuffling uncomfortably as the healing bruise on his chest, left by the bullet which had been absorbed by the Kevlar vest a week earlier, sent a vibration of pain through his body. Several officers were gathered around the corpse of Joseph Hellam but Carl didn't even glance at them as he passed by. He stepped through the open door of the barn, walking slowly forwards as he took in the sight.

Three huge floodlights illuminated the space with their intense beams and Carl saw the camera pointing at a wooden chair between them. He walked around the back of the lights, carefully stepping over the cables and noticed the metallic table, grimacing at the objects of torture that lay on the surface.

He stopped when he reached the body that lay in a crumpled heap behind the camera; two gunshot wounds in the man's head released surprisingly little blood. Carl looked up and around the barn to a second body over by the wall, apparently shot twice; once in the chest and again in the head.

Where the hell is Kelser? Carl thought silently. *Why would he leave Hellam with a gun?*

He scanned his surroundings and saw another doorway

on the far side of the barn so walked over. It led into a small partition that was poorly lit and he had to pull out an LED torch from his pocket to see clearly. He moved the tiny beam around the room until it fell on a cage, barely waste height and with thick steel bars. He walked over, studying it carefully. Inside the cage was sitting a small box with writing on the top. Carl moved the torch over the handwritten message.

'For Carl Richards, whoever you really are.

And sorry.

Sebastian Kelser.'

Carl Mayhew was glad that he would never have to use his Richards identity again as he opened the door to the cage and lifted the box out then carried it back into the barn for further inspection.

As he tore off the tape and opened the lid, the first thing he saw was a laptop sitting on the top of several brown documents. A small note was taped to the top of the laptop which read: *'Hellam's laptop. Details of films containing actual murders, sourced from a contact in Sweden, can be found on the hard drive of this laptop (decryption by experts will be required).'*

He placed the laptop on the floor beside him and looked at the first document. This one was the largest by far and contained a thick pile of papers in a brown cover. Like the laptop, there was a small post-it note stuck to the front: *'Bank records of accounts used for laundering money from several drug and prostitution rackets by Joseph Hellam, 2009-2013.'*

Carl flicked through the first few papers and found photocopies of bank statements for accounts based in the Caribbean and Switzerland. He turned and looked towards the barn door at the frenzy of activity outside. Several officers had now made there way inside the barn, one of them taking photos of the crime scene. He looked back at the document and frowned.

What good is this to me now? He killed himself for Christ sake, Carl thought, still flicking through the documents. *Why did you leave him with a gun?*

But Carl already knew the answer to that question. Kelser had *wanted* Hellam to kill himself; he *wanted* him dead and everything he had done during the past five years had led to that moment.

Carl looked at the next document, reading the note on the front first: *'Evidence regarding the murder of Michelle Layne by George Langton in 1995.'*

Carl's eyes widened as he opened the brown cover to reveal two pages of a typed document. It outlined a short history of Langton's life and as Carl scanned its contents, his shock only increased. He could barely believe what he was reading as he learned about Langton's dismissal from teaching and his subsequent move to the village of Alderidge. He read some sections twice but was still unable to work out how Kelser had discovered Langton was responsible for the murder. There was very little in the way of hard evidence, but the last line, handwritten in blue ink, rectified this with a simple and undeniable fact: *'The body of Michelle Layne can be found under the garden shed of George Langton's former residence on Forest Road, Alderidge.'*

Carl stared at the page for a few minutes, attempting to absorb this revelation. *George Langton?* Disbelief wrinkled his forehead. *Langton killed Michelle Layne all those years ago?* If what Kelser was claiming was correct, Carl had no doubt that the truth would soon be known. He called over one of the officers behind him and handed him the file on Langton.

"Get this checked out. We need to begin verifying the facts in this document immediately." Carl wondered where George Langton was at that precise moment but knew that they would be speaking very shortly.

He turned and looked back into the box. There was one document left which he lifted out, noticing that there was no note stuck to the front of this one. He opened it and saw a single piece of paper with a title in bold letters printed on the top: *'The confession of Lewis Foster.'*

Carl already knew the name well. He had never directly asked Kelser for his real name, but Carl had used his time during the past week to find out a little about the man he was relying on so much. After all, up until a week ago Carl had only known Kelser as a violent thug with unquestionable loyalty to Hellam. It was only when Kelser had pulled him aside after the Deacon job and revealed his past that he realised there was far more to the man. Carl had looked into the details of Hannah Jacobs' murder and gone to interview her former flatmate, Kelly Newham. Carl had asked her about Hannah's male friends and Lewis Foster was the first name she mentioned. She said that she hadn't seen or heard from him for a very long time.

Carl read the confession which outlined Lewis's involvement in Hellam's business and some of the terrible things he had forced himself to do in order to get close to the person who murdered Hannah. Around half way down the page, Carl noticed a name that he didn't recognise - Jonah.

He read on and discovered that this Jonah, together

with one of the men now lying a few feet away with a bullet in their head, carried out the murder of Hannah Jacobs in her flat. Lewis confessed to killing Jonah in his home, giving the address and said that this was the person who originally informed him that Joseph Hellam had ordered Hannah's murder.

Carl shook his head, unable to take in every piece of information he was reading. He placed the documents back in the box, together with the laptop and sighed, slow and long; he was going to have his hands full during the next few weeks.

He picked up the box and carried it back to his car as the forensics team began to place small, numbered squares of plastic next to the various objects in the barn and the flash from cameras exploded around him. As he passed by, he glanced again towards the metallic table, and the instruments it held. He had known Hellam was a violent person, but could scarcely believe that even he was capable of an operation like this. Snuff films were thought to be nothing more than rumours; the stuff of urban legend, but here he was, in a place where they were going to film someone being tortured and killed.

When Carl received the call from Kelser earlier that evening, and he told him about what Hellam had planned at the farm, he felt sick. Surely even Hellam wouldn't have anything to do with making actual snuff movies; killing people for the viewing pleasure of rich sadists around the world seemed like madness.

Kelser should have been waiting with Hellam, having agreed that when it was all over he would gladly hand himself in. Carl knew that sentencing would not necessarily have been light for Kelser; he had killed after all. But Carl would have made a personal plea on Kelser's behalf, citing the emotional distress he suffered after Hannah's death for his unique and extreme actions in exacting revenge on the men responsible. Not that Carl was under any illusions about how much sway his plea would have. He had allowed Kelser finish something the man had started five years earlier and by doing so, he was going against almost every basic rule in the book. There would be meetings in the weeks ahead regarding his questionable actions, and he would be extremely surprised if he came out of it with any future in the police force at all.

He looked again at the two dead men in the barn. He knew that Kelser had been the one who had killed them, but that wasn't what everyone else would see. Carl suspected that the gun Hellam killed himself with was the same that had been used to shoot them, but he wondered if he would ever share that piece of information.

He stepped out of the barn, this time glancing at Hellam's corpse as he walked by, all the time thinking of Sebastian Kelser; or Lewis Foster as he now knew him. Whatever the man wanted to be called, by fleeing the scene he went against the agreement he had made with Carl. The death of Hellam and the two dead bodies in the barn were a direct result of his actions and, while bitter, Carl found it very difficult to truly blame the man.

'Don't take this away from me.' That was what Kelser had pleaded in the car just a week before and Carl could remember the expression on Kelser's face with such clarity; desperation and pain colliding behind hollow pupils.

And I didn't, did I, Carl thought to himself as he gazed

at Hellam's fragmented skull. *Death was too good for you Joseph Hellam*. The words repeated inside as he wished more than anything that Kelser hadn't left the gun.

Chapter 23

Lewis – 20th September, 2008

Lewis opened the door to Jannson's bar and stepped inside, pulling the collar up on his jacket. After only three months of living with the wound, he was still self conscious about the scar on the side of his face and didn't like the thought of people staring. He knew that he would need to get over that fear pretty damn quickly if he was going to get anywhere. The character that he had created over the past couple of months simply wouldn't care about something like that.

Lewis had moved to a different flat a few miles away from where he used to live and rented it under his new identity. He was able to pay cash monthly so the owner only required a couple of carefully altered bank statements, which bore the new name, for their records.

He severed all ties with his family and friends, telling them he was going away on another trip for a while. No one he had known in his previous life had seen him since he gained the scar and even to his own eyes, as he stared at his reflection, he appeared different regardless of the new addition. Something had changed in the way he looked and felt; even in the way he viewed at the world. He no longer felt like Lewis Foster and if anyone he knew was to give him a fleeting glance, he doubted they would recognise him. If they stared for a few seconds, then perhaps, but he would be careful and was confident that he wouldn't run in to anyone from his past. He couldn't afford for that to occur because he was no longer that man.

He strode up to the bar with confident nonchalance and ordered a glass of water, ignoring the disapproving glance of the bar staff. Having been playing the character of Kelser for over a month, and apart from the stares, Lewis had grown comfortable in his new skin. It had been easier than expected to make the transition to this ruthless thug, but whenever he felt doubt, he imagined himself back in Jonah's flat, pushing the blade between the dying man's ribs. That wasn't something Lewis Foster could ever do - but to Sebastian Kelser, it was second nature.

Lewis turned and scanned the room. The place was ornate, decorative, very expensive, and filled with thirsty patrons. He sipped his water and watched the door as someone entered. Like him, they seemed strangely out of place, surrounded by customers in expensive suits and dresses that were drinking vulgarly overpriced beverages. The man was large, obviously spending several hours a week lifting weights, and he wore a stretched, red t-shirt. He stumbled through the doors, laughing at something which eluded everyone else, and staggered towards the bar.

Lewis continued to sip his water and watched as the man approached, stumbling and laughing several times while making his way over. When he got to the bar, he hit it with his fist.

"Hey, over here," he said through wide lips.

The barman grimaced as he walked over. "Yes sir?"

"Lager please," the man replied, pulling out several twenties.

Lewis looked at the money, knowing exactly how much the man was holding and then turned back to the door.

He waited for fifteen minutes while the large man drank his beer, noticing he took only three sips during that time, before he saw Joseph Hellam glide through the entrance with a tall, red haired woman on his arm. Somebody came from behind the bar and rushed over to greet him then led them both to a small booth on the far side of the room.

Lewis glanced at the red-shirted man beside him and noticed that he was also looking at Joseph Hellam. After a few minutes, the man placed his almost full glass of lager on the bar and glanced at Lewis with an almost imperceptible nod then began to walk over to the booth.

Lewis watched, leaning casually against the bar as the man flexed the muscles that were scarcely being retained by his shirt and fell into Hellam's table. There were raised voices after that and heads began to turn, which gave Lewis his cue.

On his walk over to Hellam's table, and his first instance of being in close proximity to the man who ordered Hannah to be killed, nerves never made a single appearance. Lewis felt confident and... something else that he couldn't quite place; almost as if he no longer had emotions at all - a ruthlessness that gave him a sense of power. But he knew that this was because he was no longer Lewis at all - he was Kelser.

He heard the argument as he got closer and was pleased with the man that he had only met a couple of hours earlier; he was putting on quite a show. They had met in another pub a few streets away. Choosing him was easy because Lewis wanted someone who was sober and physically intimidating. The man had accepted the task of causing trouble for Hellam surprisingly quickly once the £300 fee was mentioned and downed his orange juice as Lewis went over the details.

After following Hellam for so long, Lewis knew where he frequented and he would always make an appearance at Jannson's at some point on a Friday night; the location was perfect.

As he got closer to the table, Lewis saw a glimmer of fear in Hellam's eyes as he was confronted by the huge, throbbing veins on the large man's arms. Lewis savoured that fear, pleased that the sociopath could feel the emotion in all its glory.

Lewis put an arm around the man's thick neck and pulled backwards, pushing his knee behind the back of his leg until he dropped. The large man grunted as he fell to one knee and Lewis grabbed his arm which he then proceeded to twist at unnatural angles.

'For three hundred, be as rough as you like. I'll make it clear when you can stop.' The man had told Lewis in the previous bar, so he took him at his word. He lifted him up, guiding him by his restrained arm and neck towards the exit. They fell through the door and onto the pavement outside. Lewis released the man then forced the remaining £200 into his hand before pushing him away.

The man walked away a few steps then turned towards

Lewis and grinned. "Good enough?" he asked as he walked away.

Lewis allowed the shadow of a smile crack his skin and formed a ring with his thumb and index finger - *perfect*. He went back through the doors and walked towards the bar where he continued to sip his water, holding his breath and trying to resist the temptation of looking over in Hellam's direction.

When, a few moments later, one of the bar staff informed him that Hellam wanted to thank him personally, Lewis allowed himself to breathe again. He walked back over to the table and, as he approached, he saw the casual smile painted on Hellam's face; a smile that he would grow to loath.

You killed her, he thought as he made the final steps from one life to another; washing clean every micron of Lewis that remained.

"Thank you for that, can I buy you a drink?" Hellam said, smiling condescendingly.

"Just a water, thank you," Lewis replied.

"Take a seat, what's your name friend?"

Lewis studied the man sitting before him in the booth then glanced at the beautiful woman with huge, sparkling eyes beside him. As he sat down, feeling strangely at home in his new guise, Lewis wondered if, not so long ago, Hellam had been sitting in this very same booth with another woman - a woman who now would never open her eyes again. He felt something twist in his stomach as he thought of this but fought it back - he wouldn't let anger get the better of him anymore. He turned to Hellam and considered the question for barely a second before answering.

"Sebastian Kelser."

Chapter 24

August, 2013

Article in the Surrington Post on 18th August, 2013:

'Local Philanthropist shot as Police Arrive'

On Friday night, a local philanthropist was shot when police arrived at one of his properties, following a tip off regarding his alleged involvement with organised crime.

A spokesperson for the police confirmed yesterday that the man in question was Joseph Hellam, 39, chief executive of H.K Communications and the founder of The Hellam Foundation. His death is being considered a suicide.

Donating over £2,000,000 to local charities in his lifetime, Mr Hellam was a well respected member of the community. His impeccable reputation was tarnished when he was investigated in 2006, although no formal charges were apparently brought.

Two further bodies were also reportedly found at the scene, and both men are believed to have died from gunshot wounds. Police refused to comment when asked if Joseph Hellam was suspected of their murder. Although it has been confirmed that they are not searching for anyone else in connection with these deaths.

***

Extract from an article in The Somerset Mail on 27th August, 2013:

'Body found under Patio in Michelle Layne Investigation'

A body has been discovered by police investigating the disappearance of Michelle Layne at the former home of lead suspect, George Langton, 61.

Michelle Layne went missing while walking home from a friend's house in the Somerset village of Alderidge. In spite of an extensive police search and wide media coverage at the time, Michelle was not found.

Mr Langton, recently discharged from hospital following an attempted suicide, is in Police custody, pending a hearing.

***

Extract from an article in The Surrington Post on 29th August, 2013:

'*Philanthropist linked to murder tapes*'

Deceased local philanthropist, Joseph Hellam has been linked to the production of murder films in both the UK and abroad.

Joseph Hellam committed suicide on Friday 16th August after allegedly murdering two unnamed men at his farm.

It is believed that he was making a real-life 'snuff movie' when police arrived at the property on following a tip off by one of his employees.

He has also been linked to a number of other 'murder' films, produced in Sweden over the course of eight years by a man known to Swedish authorities.

Trevor Chamberlain, Chief

Superintendent for the Surrington police, spoke to this newspaper:

"It is now beyond doubt that Mr Hellam kept a great number of things concealed from the general public. In my twenty two years on the force, I have never come across a case like this and I believe Joseph Hellam was responsible for unprecedented levels of criminality which involved drugs, prostitution and sadistic acts of murder."

Police continue their investigation into Joseph Hellam as more people come forward with new information…'

Chapter 25

Kelser – 17th August, 2013

The rain had begun to fall while Kelser was riding in the back of the taxi and he noticed the splashes hit the windscreen with increasing rapidity as he neared his destination.

"You don't want to stay here long," the driver had said as Kelser got out. "It isn't forecast to improve."

"I won't be here long," Kelser had replied.

Now, as he watched the car drive away, the rain lashed against his face. He turned and began to walk up the narrow gravel path from the car park with the smell of the sea circling around him. The wind swept sheets of water sideways and he pushed his hands into his pockets, wrapping his right fist around the gun and clutching the soft leather of the object in his left.

The path slowly died away and soon he was walking on short grass that covered the incline which led to the top of the cliff. His legs were aching when he reached the top. Not just his legs but his entire body; he felt so tired and wanted nothing more than to sleep.

He hadn't been to the cliff for a long time and as he reached the top, he looked at the spot where he and Hannah had sat all those years before. The rain fell as the sun rose in the distance and he remembered that beautiful summer's day, sitting on the blanket as they both gazed out at the vast quilt of water before them.

But then he remembered; that hadn't been him at all, it was an illusion. It was someone who looked a lot like him, even had some of his mannerisms; but no, it wasn't him.

The mask he had worn over the past five years had buried deep into his skin, absorbing and digesting the man who once existed - a good man. But Kelser wasn't good anymore - he was a killer, a monster. He remembered what Hellam had told him on several occasions; words that tore into him like the knife he had placed in Jonah:

You and I, we're the same.

Kelser didn't truly believe that; deep inside, he knew that they were worlds apart, but that held little comfort when he considered some of the things he had done over the past five years - things that could be ignored until they came to visit him when he slept.

He looked out at the sea, the waves rising and falling in pyramids of water as they were bombarded by rain. He walked towards the edge of the cliff, carefully stepping over the small, mesh fence and through some taller grass. A gust of wind threw more rain sideways and he narrowed his eyes, still gazing out.

He pulled the gun from his pocket and studied it for a moment. It looked very similar to the gun he had taken with him when he called on Jonah, but it wasn't the same one. That gun had long since departed but to Kelser both guns represented the same thing. Violence and death had surrounded almost every second of his waking thoughts during the past few years and he knew he wouldn't be able to escape them now. He was a man who had gone too far over to the other side.

He took a step closer to the edge of the cliff, able to see the rocks below now then held the gun out in front of him and let go. He watched as it fell, colliding with the cliff face a couple of times before hitting the rocks below and disappearing into the frothing water.

He caressed the leather cover of the diary in his pocket and watched the sea crash beneath him. He was scared. It was an emotion he hadn't felt in such a long time and he had forgotten how fear could truly consume.

He thought about Carl Richards, knowing that by now he would be in possession of the laptop and the files. For some reason, he trusted Richards even though he didn't really know the man at all. But Richards had given him the opportunity to finish what he had started. And where had that trust got the man? Kelser imagined Richards cursing him for running and allowing Hellam to kill himself. Kelser allowed the guilt to roll over him, since the truth was, he had become desensitised to that emotion - he had to be.

Hellam had to die, he thought to himself. *I couldn't allow him live.*

But of course, he *had* allowed him live. He had allowed Hellam to make the choice; Kelser had only provided the means. But he had always known what Hellam would do because, when you know someone the way he knew Hellam, it is all too easy to read them.

Hellam was addicted to violence and torture but more than that, he was addicted to *control*. Once he had discovered what Kelser had done - who he really was - then all control was lost. For Hellam there was only ever going to be one way out and the thought of prison would never have been entertained.

He took another step towards the edge of the cliff, his feet hanging over the soft, grassy verge, and wondered why he allowed Hellam to pull the trigger himself. Kelser had already killed three people, why not the man who had ultimately been responsible?

He considered this briefly as the rain ran down his face. It was a good question; he had nothing to lose by shooting Hellam. But it had actually been Hellam's own words that prevented Kelser from finishing him.

'You and I, we're the same.'

By pointing the gun at the back of Hellam's skull and pulling the trigger, it would have validated that statement in some bizarre way. It made little sense since, a few moments earlier, he had killed Tyler and Hal in cold blood. Nevertheless, that was the way he rationalised his decision in his own mind.

Kelser thought as the rain whipped his scar. *They were all murderers.* He felt sick as he thought about this and the slow realisation dawned on him of who he had truly become.

"But now you're a murderer too." The wind carried the words away as it slammed into his arm, pushing him sideways and he moved his right leg to keep from falling. His foot slipped on the wet grass and he stumbled before regaining his balance. He stared down at the glistening rocks below.

He pulled Hannah's small, leather bound diary from his pocket and began to flick through the pages, allowing the rain to soak into the paper. He read occasional sections but absorbed none of the content; he had read those pages so many times over the years. He had taken in and contemplated Hannah's most personal thoughts in those pages - something that only added to the tormenting guilt he tried to suppress. But he couldn't resist her words.

Time is supposed to heal all wounds but it didn't feel that way to Kelser. He had missed her a little more with each passing day and the only thing that could prevent the pain from reaching beyond its already unbearable agony, was to wrap himself in her thoughts.

He skimmed through the pages until they had all passed and only the back cover of the diary remained. Droplets of water fell onto the brown leather and gathered then ran down, falling to the grass below. He shuffled his feet on the edge of the cliff and a strange sensation of hopelessness moved through him like a visiting ghost.

His eyes moved slowly over the leather cover and suddenly noticed a small, white triangle protruding from inside the leather pocket. He stared at it for a moment then used his finger nail to pull the piece of paper out and slowly began to unfold it. It was a letter and Kelser recognised Hannah's handwriting immediately as he read the date: *20th April 2001*. He looked down and read the first line that simply read, *Dear Lewis*.

He began to read the letter slowly as water soaked into the dried ink. When he was finished he read it again, unable to believe the message it held. He checked the date again then scanned down the page, reading the last sentence over and over.

The sun climbed the distant pale blue of the morning

sky as water continued to fall from retreating grey clouds. Kelser wondered why the letter had never been sent, but the mere question seemed insignificant somehow. He glanced behind him to a small patch of grass and remembered the memory that belonged to another man, but savoured it nonetheless. The past five years had consumed who he had previously been but the letter had suddenly allowed something to flicker and reignite inside; something that brought him a little closer to home. But even then, he was still light years away.

Sebastian Kelser held the soaking letter between wrinkled fingers and gently leaned forward. As he fell, Lewis Foster allowed the three words that had been written by Hannah, twelve years earlier, to carry him down.

'I love you.'

Epilogue

The Comet, 1986

We'll see it together...

As the breath left Lewis's mouth, the cool, gentle breeze lifted it towards the sky. He could see the sparkle of stars reflecting in Hannah's eyes as she gazed up and wondered which sparkle she was staring at. But of course, he already knew that the sparkle which captivated her wasn't a star at all - it was a comet.

I can't miss it, I can't...

They separated their gloved hands after a while and Lewis suddenly felt the cold air surround him.

"It's freezing," he said, turning to Hannah.

Her nose was red and her lips were beginning to turn a pale blue. "You're right," she said. "Let's go back inside the tent."

They hurried over and opened the zip. As they stepped inside, they saw Ben stir and shuffle in his sleeping bag, but he didn't wake. Lewis turned and closed the zip behind him then got into his own sleeping bag, not daring to take off his coat. He watched as Hannah did the same, pulling the draw string on the bag tight around her shoulders and sealing in the warmth. As they shuffled around and got into a comfortable position, the tent frame moved and the small torch, hanging from a hook above their heads, swayed gently before gradually coming to rest.

"Have you seen my book?" Hannah whispered, suddenly sitting up and squinting through the dimming light of the failing torch.

Lewis turned his head and saw it lying beside his pillow. "Here it is."

He picked up Hannah's book, scanning the cover. He was unable to read all the words but attempted to anyway.

"Exploring the Universe by Sebian Kes... Kel..."

"Sebastian Kelser," Hannah corrected with a smile as she loosened her sleeping bag and lifted the book from Lewis's hand.

Lewis lay back on his pillow while Hannah flicked through the pages for a few moments. Then the torchlight dimmed a little more so she closed the book and lay down. Lewis glanced over to Ben who was still fast asleep and noticed a small object resting next to his pillow. It was an object that Lewis was already familiar with - Ben was rarely seen without it.

"He loves that thing," Hannah said.

Lewis looked at her and realised that she was staring at the kaleidoscope as well.

They both lay in silence for a long time, the lumbering breeze outside occasionally knocking into the fabric of the tent and forcing the familiar low, flapping noise. The torch finally gave up and the last photon of light left its bulb. The tent was in almost total darkness; only the moon outside managed to penetrate the dark blue fabric. Lewis could hear Hannah breathing and realised it wasn't the slow, drawn out breath that accompanied sleep - she was still awake.

"I wonder..." she suddenly whispered and Lewis turned to look at her silhouette on the other side of the tent.".....I wonder if we'll ever find something to love as much as Ben loves that toy?"

Lewis didn't say anything and, after a few more minutes, they were both drifting away into sleep. As his eyes closed and his breathing slowed, Lewis's thoughts meandered back and forth between Ben's toy and Hannah's question. He half pictured himself looking through the kaleidoscope and imagined the colours and shapes intertwining and distorting from one manifestation into another. The light would sparkle through the different shades, illuminating, but also obscuring with its brightness. And the shapes would change - they would all change – he remembered that especially.

Then Lewis thought fleetingly about Hannah's question. Although his young mind didn't yet know the answer, and it wouldn't for many years, he felt that he didn't need to worry too much.

He finally floated away on a blanket of sleep as he realised something that would leave him as swiftly as his dreams upon waking the following morning. He thought of Hannah's smiling face, and knew that he had already found his kaleidoscope.

THE END

Printed in Great Britain
by Amazon.co.uk, Ltd.,
Marston Gate.